Wednesday, 19 April 1995.

The bomb went off just after r
called: "Tess, we need you."

She'd been watching an Oklahoma City channel's feed via CNN since nine-thirty and had already packed. The dogs were watching, too: the big shepherd in his favorite spot on the battered sofa; the black collie mix on the floor at her feet, their eyes and ears focused on the set as if they understood what was being said, as if they knew as well as she did that the phone would ring.

"The Air Force has routed a C-5 out of Edwards to pick us up," Dave Branson explained. "Can you be at McClellan by noon?"

"I can be there in fifteen minutes," she replied. "I'm already packed."

"The dogs?"

The dogs had shifted their attention to her, their dark eyes intense, sadly eager. "They're ready," Tessa answered. Cody, the shepherd, whined and put his head on his paws. Blackie had the pink tip of his tongue stuck between his front teeth, an idiotic expression which she knew he only wore when he was concentrating.

They knew.

"How bad is it, Dave?"

"Bad," he replied hesitantly. "There may have been nine hundred people in that building."

ISBN 978-1-63789-840-6

For information address Crossroad Press at 141 Brayden Dr., Hertford, NC 27944
A Macabre Ink Production -Macabre Ink is an imprint of Crossroad Press.
www.crossroadpress.com

20th Anniversary Edition

THESE I KNOW BY HEART

20TH ANNIVERSARY EDITION

BY BRIAN A. HOPKINS

ACKNOWLEDGMENTS

"A Thousand Doors" first appeared as a tri-fold broadside from Lone Wolf Publications (1995)

"Ten Days in July" first appeared in *The Beekeeper* (1994)

"Five Days in April" first appeared in Chiaroscuro: Treatments of Light and Shade in Words (1999)

"Roses in December" first appeared in *Millennium Science Fiction and Fantasy* (1998)

"Scarecrow's Dream" first appeared in The Best of the Midwest's Science Fiction, Fantasy, and Horror: Volume 2 (1993)

"Shrovetide" first appeared in *The Midnight Zoo* (1993)

"And Though a Million Stars Were Shining" first appeared in *After Hours* (1994)

"The Scissor Man" first appeared in *Terminal Fright* (1996)

"The Woodshed" first appeared in *Sleuthhound* (1999)

"These are the Moments I Live For" appears here for the first time

"The Grotto of Massabielle" first appeared in *Lost Ages Chronicle* (1999)

"All Colors Bleed to Red" first appeared in *Pulp Eternity* (1997)

"The Endless Masquerade" first appeared in The Endless Masquerade and Other Vignettes of the Fantastique (1996)

"To Walk Among the Living" first appeared in *The Midnight Zoo* (1992)

"Dead Art" first appeared in *Bones of the Children* (1996)

"The Trouble with the Truth" first appeared in *Unnatural Selection* (2000)

"Out the Back Door" first appeared in *Pirate Writings* (1997)

How frail the human heart must be—
a mirrored pool of thought.

—Sylvia Plath, "I Thought I Could Not Be Hurt"

"In the depths of every heart, there is a tomb and a dungeon, though the lights, the music, and revelry above may cause us to forget their existence, and the buried ones, or prisoners whom they hide. But sometimes, and oftenest at midnight, those dark receptacles are flung wide open. In an hour like this, when the mind has a passive sensibility, but no active strength; when the imagination is a mirror, imparting vividness to all ideas, without the power of selecting or controlling them; then pray that your griefs may slumber, and the brotherhood of remorse not break their chain."

—Nathaniel Hawthorne, "The Haunted Mind"

CONTENTS

This One I Know by Heart
An Introduction By David Niall Wilson xi

A Thousand Doors 1
Ten Days in July 4
Five Days in April 15
Roses in December 42
Scarecrow's Dream 45
Shrovetide 57
And Though a Million Stars Were Shining 81
The Scissor Man 89
The Woodshed 113
These are the Moments I Live For 117
The Grotto of Massabielle 133
All Colors Bleed to Red 149
The Endless Masquerade 172
To Walk Among the Living 178
Dead Art 198
The Trouble with the Truth 206
Out the Back Door 227

Brian Hopkins and "The Great & Terrible Good"
An Appreciationi by John Puerto Wiske 230

A Writer, A Reader, a Friend, and the Passing of Time
An Appreciation by Mark Lancaster 236

This one's for *true* storytellers everywhere–brave souls whose explorations take them deep into the wilderness of the human heart.

THIS ONE I KNOW BY HEART

AN INTRODUCTION BY DAVID NIALL WILSON

I started Early – Took my Dog –
And visited the Sea –
The Mermaids in the Basement
Came out to look at me –
– Emily Dickinson

Back in 1991, I used to attend a bi-monthly writers group. Among the luminaries present were author John B. Rosenman, and author and, at the time, editor, Richard Rowand. I was writing, and also editing my own magazine, *The Tome.* Richard was the editor of a science-fiction magazine called *Starshore.* I won't bore you with the details of any of that, but it serves to set the scene for an introduction that has turned into a life-long friendship, collaboration, and mutual artistic respect.

Starshore was primarily a science-fiction magazine, though they did occasionally print some speculative stories, like my own "A Candle Lit in Sunlight." One night I got a call from Richard. He had a story that he really liked, but he couldn't use it. He thought, maybe, that the story would be a better fit for *The Tome.* That story was "Of a Darker Kind," and the author was, as you've likely guessed, Brian A. Hopkins.

"Now she stood, toes hanging over the dark precipice, faced with her lifelong enemy. Below, the water whispered a mocking invitation, silent to all ears but her own."

I made some suggestions on the story, after reading it, and sent a letter off to Brian. "Of a Darker Kind" was published in *The* Tome, and that was the beginning. That was thirty years ago. We subsequently published Brian's story "The Night was Kind to Loretta," oddly, once again in a project involving Richard Rowand, where Richard wrote a letter to the editor to *The Tome* praising, title by title, an issue that had never been published. Then, we commissioned the stories and published it after the fact. It was fun, and Richard's own contributions, "Waterspout Down," and "A Great Day for Monkfish," were among the best things I published in my tenure as editor.

Brian's story, though, revealed the next level. Some of us research for our writing. Some of us are even scrupulous about it, digging for hidden gems of forgotten knowledge. Brian takes that all to different levels. In The Night Was Kind to Loretta he told a harrowing tale, while gifting the reader with a wealth of information on decomposition of bodies in peat bogs.

"You never heard of Lindow man 'cause you probably can't even fuckin' read. Sumbitch died in a peat bog in England two thousand years ago. Couple a' fellas stumbled across him in 1984. He looked like he'd died yesterday, Sweetpiece." He started working off the lid of the bucket. "No oxygen. Acidity in the peat. A body will last a long time under the right conditions."

When an anthology opened up looking for superhero stories, I suggested that his character from "Of a Darker Kind" might work, in a sort of dark, anti-hero way. She kills serial killers and very bad people. We ended up writing that story together, "La Belle Dame, Sans Merci," and though it did not get finished in time for the anthology, it was published for a decent payment, and followed later on by "La Belle Dame Sans Regret," a series of stories about a one-eyed cowboy named Jack and many others.

One of the reasons I've always been drawn to Brian's writing is that he is one of those that I believe "gets" it. Just telling a fun story is great entertainment. There are hundreds of thousands of books where you can read, enjoy, and never think about the words again. To me, that's never been what writing is really about, and possibly to a greater degree, the same is true of Brian. There is always a reason for the story. There is always something to learn, or some point. There is often a lot of tragedy and pain. If you don't believe that, read "Five Days in April" and come back to talk with me. Or "Diving the Coolidge," from a different collection.

In 2020 I asked Brian for a story. I knew he'd not been writing, and I missed the words. That anthology, *Voices in the Darkness*, contains not only a new story, but a short novel, where his love of setting and history and detail is at its finest. It is the best part of that book, but the best part of the *story* is that Brian is writing again. The world will thank me for that one day.

This introduction won't be about this particular volume if that is what you are looking for. It will be about why I am proud to publish it (the twentieth anniversary edition, anyway), and why you should read and cherish it.

When I write with Brian, the stories are beyond what I could conceive on my own. Hopefully he feels the same. We've written about a runner whose endorphins gave him short glimpses into the future. I would not have researched the "smart pills" as he did, lending that hint of "this could really happen" to an otherwise fantastical story born of my own experiences with "runner's high."

We had no idea how close we were coming to a pandemic future when we wrote "Virtue's Mask," about a world where actual physical contact during sexual encounters did not exist. People met and "touched' on opposite sides of clear sanitized curtains, and one man was struggling to be free.

"And your lips are covered with poison, running through my brain…"
– Alice Cooper

When the world was concerned about the Millennium shutting down major computer systems, we wrote what is one of my favorite pieces ever, though I'm uncertain Brian likes it as much, "A Poem of Adrian, Gray." It was about a programmer fighting against time to prevent that disaster, who meets a poet. She "writes" him, though she does not want to. As things progress, spillage on the napkin where she wrote it, words fall way, and he starts to slip, as if parts of him are disappearing as well—like the Portrait.

dangling carrot perfection
slides easily through
timorous groping talons of
self-imposed
inadequacy
chemical bandaged mind
driving drained and broken frame
buying time/love/nothing
until the 2000th time
a day is born
and truth and reality
merge-reform-destroy
and twist in endless spirals
ending

There are a lot of reasons you should know Brian's work. He's an author and a poet, and one of the best friends I've ever had. We send him things now and then, addressed to Gator Dawg, care of "Man Who Pees in Yard," all the way to Road's End, home of dogs and chickens, kids, grandkids, "big head" cows and snakes. Home of a couple who have been in love since they were sixteen. Home of one of America's brightest talents.

Go, read this book, and then come back and read this part again. You won't be sorry. Take this with you—it's a poem he wrote a very long time ago that I've never forgotten, and my addition to this new edition of *These I Know by Heart:*

Flesh Wounds

With each stroke,
he dips his pen.
And between the space
of one gasp and the next,
he writes.
Sometimes a word.
Sometimes three.
Sometimes a complete thought.
The red letters
stare back at him,
indecipherable rosettes,
as the muse strikes again.
He shudders,
dips the pen,
tries to record the pain
before…

But there it is again,
the stroke of the muse,
and that last thought is lost
before it could be written.
Every wound tells a story.
Some of them scream.
Some of them whisper.
All of them hurt.
And when the pages
of the book are full,
he gives it away
and begins the next,
this gift of the muse called Life.

A THOUSAND DOORS

Dreamed I saw a building with a thousand floors,
A thousand windows and a thousand doors;
Not one of them was ours, my dear, not one of them was ours.
—W. H. Auden

Tall ones and short ones, pink ones and green, wire-meshed windows with views in between; mahogany and oak, brass knockers and glass, "Please do not enter" and "Thou shalt not trespass!" exits to Summer and a trap door to Fall, views of Valhalla and the Policemen's Ball; morning's mauve splendor and a three-moonlet night doorway to romance, heartache, and fright…

Pacing the gray-green hall, Cameron created the litany. Because the absolute silence of the endless corridor forbade him to speak aloud, the litany played over and over in his mind like an obstinate commercial jingle.

Interminable hallways. Door after door. Randomly placed stairwells leading up and down to more of the same. Cautious at first, he checked every third or fourth door, hoping each time for something familiar, but all he found was new lines for his growing litany.

He remembered bits and pieces of who he had been, what he had done, how he ended up. He knew his name, and he thought he remembered his twenty-ninth birthday. If he concentrated hard enough, he could remember faces, but as he focused on each individual face in an attempt to recall a name or the sound of a voice, the visage dissolved forever. Thus, in that first hour, he reduced his makeshift companions to one soft-eyed, grey lady who he decided to call Mom.

Mom and he opened a dozen more doors without finding anything that looked like home. He was assuming, of course, that he would know home when he saw it, an assumption for which he had absolutely no basis save Faith.

Cameron was looking on a barren landscape baked red by a larger than normal sun when a new face leaned in over his shoulder and said, "Mars. Yes, definitely Mars."

She was blonde and, though plain, not what one might call unattractive. His age. Perhaps even his type. He noticed right off that she was taller than he and maybe, since she'd recognized the Martian landscape, smarter. "Are you sure?" he asked.

"Absolutely. That canyon's the Vallis Marineris. And there's Phobos on the horizon."

Definitely smarter, thought Cameron.

She extended a delicate hand, "Summer."

Third door down on the left, he almost told her, then realized it was her name. "I'm... Cameron."

"Are you sure?" teased Summer.

"No."

While she pondered his honesty, he closed the door on Mars and proceeded down the hall. He was reaching to open the next door when she caught up with him.

"Don't open that one."

"Why?"

"Because I asked you not to."

Together they strode off down the hall.

"This one?" he asked.

"No. That one."

He opened the door, and they looked out over a turquoise sea.

"I think," he told her as they moved on down the hall, "that Cameron might have been the name of a boy I knew in the third grade. His family was very wealthy. Even his name sounded high and mighty to me then. I used to wish I had a name like Cameron."

"Now you do."

"What about you?"

"I've always loved Summer."

She picked another door, and he opened it.

"Bombay," she said. "The towers with the vultures are where they put their dead."

Cameron shuddered and closed the door.

The next one opened on an empty room. The one after that, an Andean summit. Then, in rapid succession: a desert, the Galapagos Islands, pitch blackness, and Hiroshima just after the bomb. Somewhere in between, he realized he'd forgotten Mom's face.

"Do you remember how you got here?" he asked.

She walked out ahead of him where he couldn't see her face. Several minutes and two doors went by before she said, "I'd rather not talk about it."

"I think I was in an auto accident," he explained, wanting to alleviate her fears. "I hope no one else got hurt."

They thought they saw someone in the distance, but when they got there, weak-kneed and out of breath, they found a mirrored door. Reflected side by side, Cameron realized she wasn't taller. Not by much anyway.

"You can't be sure we're dead," she told him sometime later.

And he, later still: "Do you think we knew each other before?"

She stopped and studied him for a minute. A slow smile came over her face and she took his hand. He thought then that she was almost beautiful, that he'd probably been down these halls with her more than once.

"Pick a door, Cameron."

He did. Brought so close, the moon's craters were breathtakingly beautiful.

"This could take forever," he sighed as he let the door close.

She laughed. "I think we have at least that long."

Hand in hand they continued down the hall.

TEN DAYS IN JULY

Wednesday, July 1, 1992.

This morning I accompanied George Lott to Fort Worth's Tarrant County Courthouse. Around ten a.m. he pulled a Glock nine millimeter from a blue bag and with calm precision emptied all seventeen rounds from the weapon, gunning down Appellate Judges Ashworth and Hill and Assistant County District Attorney Chris Marshall. Lott reloaded, fired a few more rounds, then fled. In the stairwell he shot another man, Dallas Attorney John Edwards. Edwards and Marshall died on the scene. The others will survive, but any self-patronizing sense of security they once possessed will be impossible to recover.

I followed Lott as he left the building. At 4:15 p.m. he entered WFAA-TV in Dallas and asked to speak to the news anchorman. The young station employee who hassled Lott had no idea how close he came to being Lott's next victim, but Lott finally relinquished his weapons, two guns and a knife, and was allowed to give his confession to the anchorman. In a divorce trial several years ago, a Fort Worth jury awarded Lott's wife custody of their son. Lott is presently up on charges in Illinois, where his wife resides, for sexually assaulting the boy. None of Lott's victims had any connection to either of these cases; they were just in the wrong place at the wrong time.

"It is a horrible, horrible thing I did today, "Lott told the anchorman. "I sinned. I am certainly wrong. But you have to do a horrible, horrible thing to catch people's attention."

Thursday, July 2, 1992.

Crossmaglen, Northern Ireland: I was there for a press release wherein the Irish Republican Army admitted responsibility for the murders of three alleged informers whose naked, battered bodies were left beside a road in Armagh. The Roman Catholic community of Armagh, known as a safe haven for the IRA, is sickened by the brutal killings, but they haven't withdrawn their support or come forth to identify suspects.

Meanwhile, in Tokyo, Dr. Masahito Tokunaga was charged with murder. A 58-year-old cancer patient at Tokai University Hospital in Isehara had for some time begged the good doctor to put him out of his misery. Tokunaga finally relented and administered a lethal injection to the patient in April. He wasn't formally charged until today. If found guilty, Tokunaga will spend the rest of his life in prison or be put to death... while the IRA salute one another and publicize their killings.

Friday, July 3, 1992.

Time and all that I have witnessed press at me this morning, relentless, suffocating, like the weight of the Pacific on its deepest trenches. Screw the Timekeepers; I couldn't go out and do my job.

Still, I read the *Los Angeles Times* when it was delivered. Front page news:

The Defense Department has evidence indicating that several dozen United States soldiers who disappeared during the Korean War were captured and sent to China where they were submitted to psychological and medical experiments designed to determine how differences between blacks and whites affect their ability to withstand torture and interrogation. The ultimate fate of the captives is unclear, but the Defense Intelligence Agency concludes that those prisoners who did not die during the experiments were probably executed.

Around eleven p.m. I knew I had to do something or the next

day would find me bedridden again. I plunged into the Atlantic just off Daytona Beach, sank to the bottom and scrubbed with coral until I bled. Scientists are still trying to determine what caused the 15-foot wave that hit 27 miles of Florida coastline. Hours later, I returned to the surface no cleaner in body or spirit.

Saturday, July 4, 1992.

Fairmont City, Illinois: Determined to make up for the day before, I arrived early. Another 100 railroad cars filled with New York City trash had arrived in the night. That brings the total to 22,000 tons of garbage which the good people of Illinois have taken off New York's hands—for a price, of course. Another 20,000 tons of trash awaiting transfer to Illinois landfills is sitting on train cars in Sauget. As they wait—within 400 feet of a residential area—viscous poison sludge leaks from the railcars, slipping silent and deadly into the earth beneath the tracks, working deeper and deeper, looking for the water table. The EPA should be concerned, but it is, after all, the Fourth of July.

As the garbage in Fairmont simmered in the summer sun, several cars burst into flames, burning in pretty yellows and blues, belching noxious black smoke. The smoke drove a cloud of moths from the sky. They swarmed about me, a maelstrom of black, red, and white lighting in my hair, on my shoulders, down the bow of my bare arms. As I left for Oklahoma, dozens of them accompanied me.

Shawnee, Oklahoma: I arrived in a flurry of tiny, talcum-dusted wings to find the man I sought wasn't home. Watching the workmen loading furniture, I overheard that the house on North Beard Street no longer belonged to Dr. Sidney Laughlin. Bankruptcy. Perhaps there is some small measure of justice in the world after all.

"No one lives there anymore," said a small voice behind me. I turned to find a little girl, no more than six. She was staring at me with impossibly big brown eyes. Children, like moths, have a way of sometimes seeing what adults cannot. "Mama says that's good, 'cause he was a *bad* man," the little girl added.

"They found dead babies in his trash. I hope he rots in... in Hell!" She backed up a step as if I might chastise her for her language.

I smiled and dropped to one knee, "There is no Hell, little one."

"Mama says there is!"

"It's up to people like your mama to make *this* world right, not count on gods or devils or an afterlife to straighten it all out."

Her sun-speckled face scrunched up, and for a moment she was ready to argue, but then she pointed to the colorful moths that still clung to me. "What are those?"

"*Hyalophora cecropia*. A moth named after an ancient king." I took one of the delicate insects on a fingertip and extended it to her.

She shook her head. "Mama says I can't take things from strangers."

The moth suddenly took to the air, apparently a signal to them all, for suddenly they abandoned me. The child and I watched as the swarm circled the house where Laughlin had performed illegal, late-term abortions, and then they were gone, a swarthy haze lost against the sun. "I have to go now," I told the child. "Remember what I told you."

"About the moth?"

"About making this world right." I brushed the back of my hand against her cheek, felt warmth and youth and vitality glow like the promise of a new day.

And then I jumped to...

Paris, France: Beneath a moonless sky dominated by Saturn in the southeast and Jupiter in the northwest—two gods whose vigils have run far longer than mine—the French truck drivers set up their blockades, reclined with their wine and their music, and settled in for a quiet night of passive protest. But the music that night was the scream of tortured metal, the tinkle of shattered glass as it danced across asphalt, the stale hiss of blood on hot manifolds, and the soft sigh of last breaths. The truckers were protesting new driver's license regulations. In the dark, dozens of motorists ran into the heavy rigs left blocking the highways. Three died. I sat with one of them into the quiet hours of the morning. In his last moments, he was perfectly aware of my presence.

"Are you Death?" he asked.

"No. I am only Cecrops."

"Can you help me?"

"I cannot even help myself."

"But my children—" He gasped. And he died. I looked up at the ambivalent faces of Saturn and Jupiter, wondered that they could not see the tears on my face.

Sunday, July 5, 1992.

I awoke to reports of Independence Day accidents: a half-acre fire in L.A.; seven people hurt in Bel Air, Maryland, where debris from unexploded pyrotechnics fell on spectators; more spectators burned in New Ulm, Minnesota; a seven-year-old girl shot in the neck while attending a fireworks display in downtown Fort Worth... the list went on and on. Fireworks manufacturers don't expect the accidents to affect next year's sales.

After breakfast, Ireland again: Belfast's North Howard Street, often called the "peace line" because it links the Catholic Falls and Protestant Shankhill districts. I watched Protestants with spiked wooden staves club a Roman Catholic to death. Religion is such a wonderful thing.

Then, Sarajevo in the former Yugoslavian republic of Bosnia-Herzegovina. I toured the streets of Dobrinja, a Muslim suburb pounded incessantly with mortar, artillery, and Serbian sniper fire since fighting began in February. I walked the dangerous downtown neighborhoods surrounding the Maria Square District where tracer bullets haunt the night sky. And I visited the Koshevo Hospital where the innocent are brought to heal—or to die.

Monday, July 6, 1992.

Morning. Peru… with the sun slipping pretentious shafts of gold through the Andean summits to light the remote highland village of Huamamquiquia. A dog barked somewhere, but otherwise the village was quiet. The gunfire—and the screams—ended just moments before I arrived. Death carpeted the streets of Huamamquiquia that morning, a red carpet walked by resolute beams of light as the sun climbed the sky. As the sun struck each corpse I whispered the peasant's name that it might not be forgotten.

Death's entourage numbered eighteen. Men, women, and children. The Maoist Shining Path guerrillas who slaughtered these eighteen peasants are gone now, no closer to the objective of their insane 12-year war.

Northern Iraq: The attempted murder of French President Francois Mitterand's wife. The bomb which missed Danielle Mitterand injured nineteen people and killed four. The dead included three Iraqis in the last vehicle of the motorcade—Kurdish guerrillas sent to guard Mitterand—and a 10-year-old boy standing nearby. The boy died in my arms asking what he'd done.

"Nothing," I assured him, "You've done absolutely nothing. They'll just never learn."

"Who are you?" he whispered.

"Cecrops, once King of Attica. A long time ago I founded the city of Athens—Did you know they named it after me? Cecropia it was originally called. A beautiful city. I taught the Greeks marriage, respect for the dead, and—"

The boy's eyes fluttered and he was gone.

"—and I made them understand that blood sacrifices were no longer necessary."

No one claimed responsibility for the bombing, but I saw who did it. I added their names to my list.

Tuesday, July 7, 1992.

Busy day. And a day, it seemed, for children. I spent the morning in Gulfport, Mississippi, with Shannon and Melissa Garrison, ages 17 and 15. With the help of Melissa's boyfriend, Allen Goul, also age 15, they jumped their mother in bed where they proceeded to stab, strangle, and smother the woman to death.

I did not try to stop them.

At an arson fire in Baltimore, I watched four children die horribly. Though they could hear me, they couldn't see me in all the smoke. I don't know what the Timekeepers would do if they had caught me calling out to the children.

I saw who set the fire.

Visalia, California: Asian gangs clashed over territory, killing one and wounding another. I didn't try to reason with them.

I finished off the day by running with rioters in the Washington Heights area of New York City.

As I retired that evening, I heard that Sauget, Illinois, had issued an ultimatum concerning the 20,000 tons of NYC garbage sitting in their rail yard: the Oklahoma-based trash hauler responsible for the mess was given thirteen days to move the railcars. There was no mention of the garbage sitting in Fairmont; presumably it was *properly* placed in an Illinois landfill.

Wednesday, July 8, 1992.

The Garrison sisters came forth and confessed today. They'll be charged as adults. Their mother's winking out there somewhere, beyond Saturn and Jupiter, silently watching with the billions of others who've been sacrificed.

Today the Japanese slaughtered another minke whale in the name of research. Norway, having announced several weeks ago that they will no longer abide by the international ban on commercial whaling, shipped equipment to its Arctic processing plant in preparation for the slaughter of thousands more. Should I have expected the sacrifices to be confined to man?

The refuse in Sauget was moved to landfills in Litchfield and Staunton. Case closed. Unless you happen to live in Litchfield or Staunton.

I spent most of the day with Leo Wells, a drug addict in Norman, Oklahoma. Leo is HIV-positive, but refuses to refrain from unprotected sex. He's popular at the local night clubs.

That evening I hopped from one city to the next. Eight murders in three hours. There may be a record there somewhere.

I'm not sure how much more of this I can take.

Thursday, July 9, 1992.

Topeka, Kansas. Connie Hayes walked out her front door just short of midnight. She was in her nightgown, having already been in bed when she remembered her errand. Connie's an average woman, not particularly beautiful or smart, but a good mother and wife. A woman with a kind heart. Practical. Responsible. Her neighbors have always been able to rely on Connie when they leave town. There are the fish to feed, the plants to water…

As she crossed the suburban street, I saw in Connie Hayes everything stable about the human race. There was a certain beauty in her deliberate strides, a supple grace to the way she carried the extra pounds acquired bearing three children. Though the moon drew silver from her auburn tresses, Connie's husband still thought her the most beautiful thing on Earth.

The star-studded sky was a bespattered drop clothe, Saturn watching from the southeast, Pegasus dominating the eastern skyline. Draco the Dragon was curled about the sky's nexus, his diamond-shaped head almost directly overhead. Using Draco's tail I found Ursa Major and, with Dubhe and Merak, the outermost stars in the dipper, I located Polaris, the North Star, at the tip of the Little Dipper.

Polaris. The *truest* of all. Always there, never setting. Eternal, yet apathetic, vigilance.

Polaris would have watched. They'd *all* have watched insouciantly as Connie Hayes walked up her neighbor's driveway and into the house to feed the fish. The burglar there would have grabbed her and dragged her into a back room to sodomize and rape her, quickly, brutally, for he'd realize he hadn't much time before Connie's husband would wonder what was taking her so long. When the burglar finished, he would have cut her throat.

It had already been written, in essence it had already happened, a probability which the Timekeepers had calculated to the thousandth decimal place. I had my schedule to keep. Occasional lapses—like the Friday before—were barely tolerated. I could fail to do my job, fail to watch, but it would still happen.

Connie Hayes would die.

I'd take down the murderer's name for my own useless records—records I'd vainly shown the Timekeepers a hundred times—but the Tenth of July would dawn like any other day. Except Connie Hayes wouldn't be in it.

But there's always that element of uncertainty. That last thousandth of a percentage point that says the Timekeepers can't be right *every* time. Thus, watchers like me. Watch and record. When nothing goes as planned, when the threads of time and reality fray and unravel, then the Timekeepers will step in.

As she crossed the street and started up the drive, her pink bedroom slippers going *swish-swish* on the cement, something in me screamed that enough was enough. I darted in front of her, called her name, did my best to block her way. She passed right through me.

"Connie!"

Halfway up the driveway. Shadows cast by streetlights and moon fought one another for her attention. I screamed and waved, jumping about like a mad man. For a second it seemed I'd caught her attention. She paused and seemed to listen, but for her the street was silent save for the buzzing of streetlights and insects. She couldn't hear me.

Her momentary apoplexy passed, and she started back up the drive.

Ten feet to the door.

I could have run to her house, awakened her children… They would have heard me. But there wasn't time.

Five feet.

A cloud of moths circled the pale light over the drive.

Three.

The Cecropia Moth!

One.

She slipped the key into the lock and turned it, grasped the doorknob in her other hand, but the moths suddenly swarmed about her, a dark cloud that forced her back from the door. She let out a startled yell, not quite a scream, and swatted at the bright insects, stumbling back as if the door was the focus of their attention. The moths followed her.

She saw me.

The moths swirled up like a black tornado, climbing above our heads, lifting with such force that her hair floated on a muted breeze. Their circle widened and then, just as suddenly, plunged down to encapsulate us in a dark maelstrom of powdered heartbeats.

"Don't go in the house," I told her.

"I don't believe this," she muttered, meaning the moths. I'm not even sure she heard my warning.

"There is a man in the house who will kill you if you go in." I left out the things he would do *before* he killed her, but I'd tell her if I had to. Anything to keep her from going in.

"How do you know this?" Understandably, she didn't trust me. I doubted she'd trust anything that night. There was magic in the air and the only magic she knew was what she'd created herself with sweat and blood.

"Go home, Connie Hayes." The moths rose at a point closest to her home, forming an insane, dented hula-hoop that spun off-kilter like the wheel on a battered bicycle. "Go home to your husband and children. Live a long life."

"I don't… Who are you?"

"Nobody. Just go home."

Midnight. Most of the moths had chased off after the moon. A score or so remained, silent company perched on my shoulders and in my hair, waiting with me, knowing the Timekeepers would come.

My job was to record, but I'd tampered. Connie would wake beside her husband, find one of her three children in bed with them, rise and fix breakfast before her husband went to work.

I thought about the excuse I'd give the Timekeepers when they showed up. All that came to mind were George Lott's words. The cynicism of those words, applied here, amused the dark places in my heart.

It is a horrible, horrible thing I did today.

I saved a woman's life, aborted a murder, stopped another senseless sacrifice... sent ripples through the lake of time that might have dire repercussions.

But you have to do a horrible, horrible thing to catch people's attention.

Even the attention of gods.

Today, July 10, 1992.

From this distance, out beyond massive Saturn and Jupiter, beyond even Pegasus, the world spins quietly, effortlessly. I can no longer see the violence, the daily oblation, the endless drama of lives traded for whimsy.

Beyond me, others wink into existence with irrational regularity, an eternity blossoming against the heavens. We wait. We watch over the shoulders of Draco and Hercules, Perseus and Cassiopeia. We can't see a lot from here.

But the Timekeepers have their watchers below. Perhaps one day mankind will be ready.

And we can all move on together.

FIVE DAYS IN APRIL

Wednesday, 19 April 1995.

The bomb went off just after nine a.m. At ten fifteen, they called: "Tess, we need you."

She'd been watching an Oklahoma City channel's feed via CNN since nine-thirty and had already packed. The dogs were watching, too: the big shepherd in his favorite spot on the battered sofa; the black collie mix on the floor at her feet, their eyes and ears focused on the set as if they understood what was being said, as if they knew as well as she did that the phone would ring.

"The Air Force has routed a C-5 out of Edwards to pick us up," Dave Branson explained. "Can you be at McClellan by noon?"

"I can be there in fifteen minutes," she replied. "I'm already packed."

"The dogs?"

The dogs had shifted their attention to her, their dark eyes intense, sadly eager. "They're ready," Tessa answered. Cody, the shepherd, whined and put his head on his paws. Blackie had the pink tip of his tongue stuck between his front teeth, an idiotic expression which she knew he only wore when he was concentrating.

They knew.

"How bad is it, Dave?"

"Bad," he replied hesitantly. "There may have been nine hundred people in that building."

In the immediate aftermath, Dubbiel prowled the rubble, struggling through the dust and billowing smoke, buffeted by the fleeing masses of bleeding downtown employees who failed to see him. He followed brave men and women into the depths of the carnage and watched as they assisted, carried, and dragged free those who were too injured to move. Many of the rescuers were themselves injured, blood flowing in copious streamers from cuts on their desperate faces. Most had come from surrounding buildings, their wounds from broken glass. Windows for a nine block radius had been blown out by the force of the explosion that had destroyed the federal building.

Dubbiel watched people out on the street loading complete strangers into the backs of their pickup trucks to rush them to a nearby hospital. He watched workers who had just escaped the building going back in to scream for their coworkers and friends. He watched as horribly injured Oklahomans waved off assistance. "I'm okay," they cried, motioning toward those still trapped within the crumbling building, "help someone else."

One man stopped three times to perform CPR on his friend as he tried to drag him out of the building. Another stumbled out with his secretary draped over his shoulders. Her feet were bare and most of her clothing was gone, having been blasted off by the bomb. A police officer shoved out past Dubbiel with an infant cradled in his arms. The policeman didn't realize that the child was already dead. Perhaps it wouldn't matter if he had. Dubbiel knew that to the policeman the atrocity merely doubled with any thought of leaving the tiny corpse inside the rubble.

A nurse rushed into the building only to be struck by falling concrete. A man in a blood-soaked shirt and tie took the nurse under the arms and dragged her limp body toward the smoke-filtered sunlight and out into the street. The man would later wonder at the ease with which he had escaped the building. A second before the explosion, he had been standing on the fifth floor. That floor, like those beneath it, was now collapsed and pancaked at ground level with the living, the dead, and the dying trapped between. As for the nurse, Dubbiel knows that she will die, but she will still save the lives of others. Her courage began, not on this day when she rushed into a crumbling building, but on the day she signed an organ donor card.

Dubbiel knelt amid the scattered bodies of the children who'd been at the day care center on the second floor. Soberly, he touched each tiny, crushed form, cataloging each wasted soul. There were more, he knew, buried in the rubble beneath his feet. To view those, he would have to wait on the firemen and rescue squads.

He flowed with the turmoil for nearly an hour, allowing both carnage and bravery to sweep him from one side of the destruction to the other, alone only when the rescuers were driven away by police who claimed to have located a second explosive. No one could see him. Not the living. Not the dead. Not even, for once, the dying. It was as if the sensory epiphanies typically granted in those final seconds of life had been rendered numb by the explosion.

While the rescuers waited on the bomb squad, Dubbiel was left alone with the dead and the dying, unable to comfort them or offer aid. He listened to the terrible sounds of shifting concrete and settling debris: the eerie squeal of hanging iron rebar stressed by Oklahoma winds; the water surging from broken pipes; the crackling of severed electric wires; the fire alarms; the tires and gas tanks exploding outside where the cars in the parking lot were still burning; and the moans of the injured and trapped. He listened to the sound of blood raining down through the collapsed layers of cement and beams. He looked up through the holes in the wreckage at the bodies and limbs hanging above him. He could smell the bomb, smell the blood, smell the overwhelming aroma of death.

He wept.

The C-5's Loadmaster met her at the base of the ramp. Because the big jet's engines were already running, she had to shout to be heard. "Tessa McEvoy, Urban Search and Rescue." She showed him the Sacramento USAR patch on the shoulder of her jumpsuit, hoping she wouldn't have to dig for identification.

He ticked off her name on his clipboard. "Welcome aboard,

Miss McEvoy. If you'll wait here, I'll send someone for your dog pens and get them loaded immediately."

She shook her head. "My dogs don't travel in pens, Sergeant. They'll fly topside with me."

"Ma'am, the gangway up to the passenger compartment is kinda' hard to maneuver."

"Sergeant, you weren't there in Kobe or you'd know these dogs can climb, tunnel, and damn near walk a tightrope—"

"Space is rather limited."

"They'll lay in the aisles, Sergeant." Shouldering her overnight bag, she pushed past him and up the ramp before he could think of another excuse. Cody and Blackie ran ahead, their nails ringing off the cargo plane's aluminum floor as they wove through the pallets of equipment and supplies. The two dogs took the tricky spiral ladder up to the passenger compartment like old pros.

On final approach for Tinker Air Force Base, Sacramento's USAR team crowded the C-5's windows, hoping for a glimpse of the bomb site.

"There," said Pete, pointing.

"Doesn't look bad from here," Keith ventured tentatively. He was playing with his electronics, trying to snake the 16mm crevice camera up Tessa's pants leg. Cody kept snapping at it—playfully though; he knew it was all a game. In addition to the seventy inch, serpent-like optical unit, Keith had infrared sensors capable of detecting temperature variances as small as two degrees Fahrenheit and delicate listening devices capable of hearing the beating of a human heart through several feet of concrete.

The Air Force captain assigned as their liaison leaned around Tessa and looked down at the city's skyline. "Can't tell much from here," he said, "the bomb went off on the north side." He keyed an intercom and asked if the pilot could get permission to circle once.

"Cancel that," Branson growled, just emerging from the bathroom where he'd probably been throwing up again. "Important thing now is to get us on the ground. We'll see it soon enough."

"Important thing now," Keith chided, "is for *Branson* to get on the ground before he's sicker 'an a dog." This was followed with a sheepish glance at Tessa and the two dogs. "Uh, no offense intended, guys."

"None taken," Tessa replied. "You just remember to bring your shovel this time." It was common knowledge that her dogs sniffed out more in an hour than his sophisticated electronics could in a day. The stock joke was that Keith should always bring a shovel since all he was good for was digging. The levity was forced, however, and brought only polite laughter from the six other team members. These were jokes that worked best several days afterward, when it was all said and done, when all the survivors and the dead had been recovered, and the team was between calls. Lately, though, it seemed like there were fewer and fewer *in-betweens*.

The C-5 banked to the south, hit an air pocket, and lurched several feet. Branson turned a greyer shade of sick. "Excuse me," he mumbled and turned back toward the bathroom. Tessa fought the urge to go after him. Dave Branson had made it very clear that their relationship was over.

From the base, they were taken downtown in a van. Branson fumed at the delay, insisting that a helicopter be brought in. Their latest liaison, a nervous man who'd given his title only as "a city official," apologized, but insisted that the scene was still too chaotic. Branson knew this was true, but he was steeling himself the only way he knew how, letting his rampant impatience temper him for what lay ahead. He could be almost cruel at times; Tessa knew this better than any of them.

It was one-thirty by the time they reached the bomb-blasted building, fifteen minutes later before someone tracked down the Oklahoma City Fire Chief and obtained permission for them to enter the site. They waited on the far side of the thirty-foot crater, looking up at the gaping nine stories above them—all except Branson, who paced the crater's rim, hating the delay, but knowing if he charged his team forward without clearance it would bend someone's nose out of shape. An ATF agent hollered at him for kicking a chunk of cement from the rim. A reporter—the police were still working to clear them all back—asked if they were from Atlanta. Branson growled at him.

By two-fifteen they were in, and by three Cody had located his first survivor while Blackie whined on a leash in the staging area. Tessa set her mind on her job, trying to remain clinically detached, but reminding herself that the mangled carcasses they climbed over were still human and deserved their utmost respect, even though all they could do was set them aside for now. Bodies that were too hopelessly buried, they left in place, marking their location with orange spray paint. Later, they'd be extracted by crews who'd measure success in their ability to remove the corpse intact. The priority now, and throughout the next crucial 72 hour window, was to locate the living. The dead could wait.

At a quarter to five, Cody found a hole he liked in what the rescuers were already calling the Cave. Because the building had been built on a split level, access from the streets on the north and south sides had created a debris-choked pocket in the center, just behind ground zero and extending down into the basement. This pocket was fast becoming a catacomb of mines as rescuers tunneled into the wreckage and construction workers shored up the resulting tunnels with timber and pipe. The wreckage itself determined the path these tunnels took, as rescuers worked around immovable objects and unstable areas. Above the Cave hung what had been dubbed the Mother Slab, a massive section of the ninth floor suspended high and deep in the center of the building, dangling by nothing more than rebar. The structural engineers were still debating whether the Mother Slab would fall. Some said it would at any moment. Others argued that it would have already come down if it was going to. Because all the engineers agreed that the Mother Slab couldn't be safely removed, construction workers were working carefully to secure it in place.

From Cody's frantic barking, Tessa knew he had a live one. Both dogs could tell the difference between a survivor and a corpse. Listening to them, so could she. Tessa called out, but there was no answer. Procedure was for Keith and his electronics to give a second opinion before they pulled diggers from other locations.

Cody wanted to go down into the crevice, but Tessa held him back. She radioed for Keith and his snake. Branson came back on the radio to tell her that Keith was on the eighth floor where a reporter claimed to have spotted a woman waving near the jagged precipice. Though it appeared to be a mistake—they'd already swept the entire eighth floor once—they wanted to be certain. It would take at least ten minutes for the crane operator to bring Keith down in the basket they were using to reach the upper floors.

Tessa crawled down into the mouth of the crevice and shone her light into the darkness.

"Help me," whimpered a barely audible female voice.

"You're going to be all right," Tessa assured her. She spoke in the calming voice she'd practiced, the one she'd used even in Kobe and Mexico where some of the victims hadn't even understood English. "We'll get you out of there." The crevice narrowed ahead and turned to the right so that Tessa couldn't see the woman. "Can you see my light?

"Yes. Please help me."

"Help is on its way. You're going to be just fine. What's your name?"

"Tammy. Help me. I can't feel my legs." Sobs. Desperation and pain. "Oh, God, why me? What did I do? What happened?"

"You didn't do anything, Tammy. It's not your fault. It was a bomb. Just hold on, and we'll get you out." Cody added his own encouragement by barking.

"Is that a dog?"

"That's Cody. He found you."

"Thank you, Cody."

Tessa scrambled back out of the hole where she could speak without the woman hearing her. Keying her radio, she asked, "Where the hell are you guys?"

"Coming down from the eighth now," Branson responded. "False alarm. Keith will be with you in five."

"I don't need Keith anymore; I need diggers."

"Roger that. We're on our way, Tess."

The woman was crying when Tessa crawled back down into the hole.

"Please, could you hold my hand or something?" There was such terror in her voice, the fear of being abandoned, the fear of being buried alive, the fear of not being able to feel parts of her body... Tessa almost scrambled down after her. But she'd never fit around the bend. "I can't move my legs. I'm scared. I think there's a dead man pinned under me. I can feel him, but he's not breathing."

"Calm down, Tammy."

"Please, God, don't let me die down here."

Cody whined and strained at his leash.

"Do you like dogs, Tammy?"

"Dogs? I love dogs."

Tessa unhooked the leash. "Cody's coming down to wait with you."

Dubbiel watched from the shadows, careful not to let the injured woman see him. Somehow her shock and delirium and the specter of death looming ever closer had allowed her to see what the others had missed. As they'd worked to free her, she'd asked the firemen if they'd seen the angel.

"I didn't see him, ma'am, but you can bet if there are angels anywhere on Earth today, they're here," one fireman replied.

"She's in shock," whispered another.

"He's here somewhere," Tammy insisted. "I saw him moving through the smoke and the rubble, touching the dead, showing them the way to Heaven."

None of the firemen pointed out that she'd been buried beneath a ton of concrete and office furniture until just moments ago, and there was no way she could have seen anyone, even an angel, walking around in the building. But Dubbiel knew that she had seen him, had watched him with some inner clairvoyance that impending death had granted her in the darkness of her tomb. She'd seen him. And so had the reporter who claimed to have seen a woman waving from the eighth floor.

During the extraction, Tessa McEvoy had continued searching with her second dog, leaving the German shepherd to comfort Tammy. She returned now to collect Cody. As the firemen were maneuvering Tammy into the basket to take her down, Tessa leaned out and squeezed her hand.

"Thank you," Tammy whispered, "thank you for sending down the dog. If it wasn't for that dog and the angel..."

"Angel?" Tessa asked.

But they were already moving the basket away from the edge. Tessa was left standing there with her dogs as the basket swung out over the rubble piled against the building's gaping north side. Keith was marking the spot where the woman had been so that later they could extract the dead man still buried there. Branson was arguing with a FEMA Director who wanted to pull them out and send in the Atlanta team that had just arrived. Dubbiel remained in the shadows, content to wait until the USAR team moved on, knowing there was nothing for him to do until later that evening when the last of the survivors would be located and brought out. For days after, they would search, but Dubbiel already knew that after tonight there were none but the dead. The schedules provided by his masters were always accurate.

The dogs saw him.

They howled and pulled at their leashes. There was nothing Tessa could do but let them go.

"Do you have something?" Branson called, eager for an excuse to keep his team in the building.

"Maybe," she answered. "I'm not sure. I've never seen them act this way before."

Dubbiel stroked their dusty fur and calmed them down, letting them smell his hands and lick his face, while Tessa studied the dark corner in bewilderment. "Quiet," he whispered, brushing their ears back against their heads.

"Tess?" Branson yelled in frustration.

"No," she called back. "There's nothing here. I don't know what's gotten into them, but there's nothing here. You want me to start another sweep from the east end?"

"Negative," Branson growled. "We're to stand down for now and pick up a six hour shift at midnight. Lawson's crew is coming in."

Thursday, 20 April 1995.

The sun came up, obscured by bloated red clouds and a crimson haze. The Oklahoma wind struggled to replace the smell of death with ozone and impending rain, but all it did was stir up the dust of broken concrete. Tessa waited with Blackie near the precipice on the fifth floor. A recovered flag hung above her on the ninth. She could hear it flapping defiantly in the breeze. She'd been told that the crane would be back for her and Blackie in about five minutes. A crew from the Mid-Western Elevator Company was working on one of the passenger elevators and hoped to have it running before the end of the day, but for now they were stuck with the basket. Branson and the others had already gone down.

The Atlanta team had returned early, but rather than relieve the exhausted Sacramento USAR team ahead of schedule, they'd opted for some media coverage. From where she waited, Tessa could see them mingling with reporters, leaning into microphones, posing for video and stills. The Atlanta dog handler was getting a lot of attention. People were always intrigued by the search and rescue dogs. Lawson, the Atlanta chief, was pontificating before a gaggle of reporters. Behind him sat a CNN van that looked like something out of *Star Wars,* bristling with antennae and satellite dishes. Branson and Lawson had exchanged words last night, none of them pleasant. Branson believed the job of USAR was to slip in and out unnoticed, with little or no fanfare, devoting their full attention to the task at hand. The important thing was saving lives; everything else be damned. Lawson believed the only way to ensure funding for future USAR programs was for them all to play hero for the media. You saved more lives by having more USAR teams. You got more USAR teams by getting more money.

Both of them were probably right.

While contending with a cold drizzle, the Atlanta team had extracted one survivor at 9:15 p.m. Just one. But they'd done better than Sacramento on the midnight to six shift. Branson and company had spent all night locating pockets of dead. Neither the dogs nor Keith's sophisticated equipment had been much help. Sixteen times they'd drilled bore holes into air pockets in the ruins, dropping in Keith's audio and video equipment. Each time they'd come up empty-handed. Their window of opportunity was narrowing.

From her vantage point, Tessa could see all three cranes, two of which were supporting parts of the building: great slabs of concrete dangling by nothing more than a few strands of rebar. Crews had been working all night to get these dangerous pieces removed before they broke loose and fell on the rescue workers below. Directly beneath her feet was the crater, eight feet deep they said, thirty feet in diameter, partially buried beneath the Pancake, a thirty-foot-high pile of rubble that had once been the north face of the building. The Pit, the Pancake, and the Cave.

The FBI was already saying it had been a Ryder rental truck loaded to the gills with fertilizer and diesel fuel, parked before the building just a few minutes before nine. Parts of the truck had been located up and down the street. Its rear axle had landed on a parked car a block and a half away. One of its tires had landed on the roof of a 24-story apartment complex. Rumor was that the FBI had even located the VIN off the truck's dashboard. The search for the perpetrators was every bit as intense as the search for survivors.

Beyond the crater, amid a tableau of mangled, blackened automobiles in the parking lot on 5th, was a small village of tents: triage and first aid; the command center; supplies, bunks, and a cafeteria for those who'd flown in to help. Beyond that, emergency vehicles, the police barricades, a crowd of onlookers, and the media. Across the street was a completely destroyed restaurant and several other buildings that had taken severe damage. To the northeast was the YMCA where the terrorist act had reached yet another day care center. To the northwest, the scarred face of the post office and the apartment complex where the truck's tire had been found. The windows were gone from all the surrounding buildings, and they looked to have been sprayed with gunfire.

Tessa had spent her off shift pacing the front of the building, hurt by the lecture she'd gotten from Branson for allowing Cody down into the hole. The dog, he'd explained, was more valuable than any one victim. If the hole had collapsed, they would have lost the dog and all those whom the dog might have saved. It was a lecture she'd endured before. Sometimes it was the dogs she risked. Sometimes it was herself. She'd heard the same lecture a half dozen times at least... but it still rankled. She'd seen him violate his own rules countless times. Once she'd even made the mistake of pointing that out to him. Only once, though. Dave Branson's bite was every bit as bad as his bark.

While she had paced, she'd watched Oklahomans come to pay their respects on the other side of the chain link barricades. Most of them left something behind. A ribbon on the chain. Cards and letters. Stuffed animals and dolls. Prayers. There was a handwritten sign on the fence now that read:

We're here and we're committed.
We are steadfast and strong in our combined strengths.
We're Oklahomans.
And we're not leaving until this job is done.

Blackie turned and stared back into the interior of building. He whined.

"What is it, boy?"

The dog shook his head. He licked her face. Then he returned his attention to the devastated interior of the building, staring back toward the elevator shafts on the south side. She listened for the elevator crew, thinking maybe Blackie heard them, but last she'd heard they were in the basement trying to get power restored.

"Pickup's on its way, Tess," squawked Branson over the radio.

She keyed her radio. "Copy that."

Blackie whined.

She had a couple minutes yet. Time enough to let Blackie investigate the area around the elevators. It would mean another lecture from Branson. She wasn't supposed to reenter the building alone. She could easily fall. Or something could fall on her. Branson expected her to remain where she was, in sight. As soon as she disappeared from view, she knew he'd call.

Tessa switched off her radio and took out her flashlight. "Come on, Blackie. Let's see what's bugging you."

Huge spotlights had been rigged to shine on the north face of the building, but they barely penetrated the interior. The further south she walked, the darker it became. Her flashlight cast macabre shadows among the wreckage, lending an extra layer of depth that shifted and moved as if the building was collapsing around her. The dangling light fixtures and shredded conduit were a jungle from some apocalyptic nightmare. The floor felt less stable than it had in daylight or under the large spots that her crew carried. Debris crunched beneath her boots, brittle sounds that were suddenly much too loud in the tomb-like stillness. The wind waved a dangling ceiling tile to her left—movement which she caught from the corner of her eye—and she spun the light in that direction, startled. Her heart was racing. Her teeth were clenched. The smell of death was thick.

Blackie tugged against his leash. *This way,* he implored. His attention remained focused on the elevators. The hair on his back was up, but his tail was wagging. It was an unusual expression for him. *Okay, I know you're friendly and won't hurt me—but, dammit, I'm still scared.* Tessa had only seen it once before: last night as the crane was lowering Tammy to the ground, when both dogs had created a ruckus.

There was a body near the elevators, an older gentleman who'd been thrown back from the blast and crushed in a tide of filing cabinets. He'd been found and marked in the first few hours after the explosion. His body would probably be removed today. Tessa studied Blackie. It wasn't the body that held the dog's attention.

She probed the darkness to the right of the elevators, beyond the body and the filing cabinets. Dust motes swirled in the beam of her flashlight.

Blackie barked.

The dust motes paused. Shimmered. Seemed for a second to adhere to a shape.

"Who's there?" Tessa croaked.

Nothing.

Except…

The dust motes. A tall, transparent form. Eyes.

For a moment, she saw it—or thought she did. The flashlight shook in her hand. Blackie strained against his leash.

"Tessa!"

She jumped and very nearly dropped the flashlight, waving the light erratically across the south wall and over a skeletal framework that had once supported the ceiling. When she got the light focused again, the shape that she thought she had seen was gone. Had she really seen it?

Branson bellowed for her again from the north side of the building.

"Here!" she shouted.

"Get out here!"

Carefully, she worked her way back toward the blasted edge of the building. It wouldn't do to rush and be careless. That would only anger him further.

"What the hell were you doing?" he demanded.

"I thought I heard something."

He glared at her. "You're smarter than that, Tess." Whether he meant smart enough to invent a better excuse or smart enough not to go off on her own, she couldn't say. "What about your radio? You don't know how to call for someone? You don't know how to answer me when I call?"

"I never heard you call. Batteries must be going out," she lied.

"Bullshit, Tess. That's just bullshit." For a moment she thought he was going to ask to see her radio. His eyes were red. He looked exhausted, too exhausted to chew her out the way in which she really deserved to be chewed out. He pointed toward the crane. "Get your ass in the basket before I throw you over the side."

And on the way down: "The dogs, Tessa… you're lucky you're the one with the dogs. Otherwise I'd put your ass on a plane for Sacramento right now. Don't think for one moment that I wouldn't."

She stared at her feet, stroking Blackie's head. She kept her mouth shut. She didn't tell him about the angel.

Keith brought her a cup of coffee. "You should have gotten some sleep."

"Couldn't," Tessa said.

"Yeah, me either," Keith admitted. "Did you see your bunk, though? There were candy and letters on my pillow. Gifts from nearby school kids."

"Mine, too. I had a little stuffed giraffe."

Keith sipped his coffee and watched her watching the television. The station was replaying video shot earlier. Approved video. Nothing live had gone out since the police had gained control of the area. Firemen in yellow suits were scrambling up the side of the Pancake.

"And they say our money's no good in Oklahoma. Anything we need, we're just to ask. The local firemen told me the only problem is that anything they ask for, they get ten times more than they can use," Keith told her. "As soon as word gets out that something's needed, people just go to the store, buy the stuff, and bring it out to one of the drop-off points. And the food! I think every restaurant in town has come out to feed us. I've never seen anything like this, Tess."

She nodded. "I know." But she was feeling a sense of failure. The rescue operation was beginning to feel like a retrieval operation. The medical workers standing by for a second wave of casualties had been left with nothing to do. No one had been recovered alive all day. Other USAR teams were arriving: Phoenix, New York, Menlo Park. But they were only finding more dead. It seemed there was no end to the bodies. She refused to give up hope, though. In the Mexico City earthquake, there were babies found alive in a nursery nearly a week later. In California, survivors had been located three and four days after the quake.

"Branson chew on you pretty good?"

She shrugged. "No more than usual. No more than I deserved."

Keith looked away. "I always used to think he was harder on you 'cause the two of you were dating. He didn't want the rest of us to think he was playing favorites. Several times I wanted to take him out and beat the crap out of him for you."

She smiled and touched his sleeve. "That's sweet of you, Keith. I can take care of myself, though."

"Good thing," he chuckled, "'cause wanting to do something and doing it are two separate things. Branson would have kicked my ass."

She laughed with him, maintaining the facade that it was all a joke, that she didn't know that Keith had had a thing for her for several years. The job made sure that the team saw more of each other than they did friends or family, husbands or wives or lovers. It was impossible not to develop special bonds between team members. The death that they were constantly subjected to left them with a fierce need to hold someone warm at night and celebrate what life they had left. But she'd seen it too often to think it would ever work out. She'd had her best run at it with Branson and that had fallen apart. Eventually, it just hurt too much to see your pain in your partner's eyes. People should hurt in different ways, she thought. That way they can comfort each other. Who do you cry your sorrow to at night, when your lover has witnessed the same horror?

On the television, several of the firemen had taped the word HOPE in big letters on the back of their coats, on the sides of their helmets.

"Locals," said Keith. "Why do they do that? Does it help them continue?"

"No. It's for them." She hooked a thumb at the back wall of the tent, in the direction of the media and the spectators. "It's a message to them. The firemen know the cameras are focused on them, focused on their backs, focused on that one word. If you have friends or loved ones who are missing, don't give up. We're looking. Don't give up hope."

Friday, 21 April 1995.

Dubbiel watched Tessa and the German shepherd.

They were trying to reach the day care center, but progress was hampered by an unstable floor and debris. Once already she'd nearly lost Cody in a crevice. The construction crew was trying to shore up the floor and remove some of the obstacles, but Tessa was impatient. Against Branson's orders, she'd taken Cody and pressed on, digging wherever the dog became most agitated.

Dubbiel knew that Tessa had seen him yesterday. He couldn't say why or how. Some empathy with her dogs perhaps—tuned into their senses, to interpreting the things they saw and smelled. Or perhaps here, with the air so thick with death, barriers were crumbling. This world and the next were but a heartbeat away. After all, that reporter had seen him, too.

He caught her looking for him now, watching the dog for a clue. But Cody had become accustomed to Dubbiel's presence. He was focused on his work. Clearly, though, the things the dog smelled here upset him. He whined and paced as Tessa dug through the rubble, retrieving in turn a child's shoe, a post-it-note with several phone numbers and a doodled heart, a family photo in a broken frame, and a Matchbox car. Tessa set these things aside for safekeeping in case they were later needed to help identify a body. Dubbiel watched as Cody returned with a battered rag doll in its mouth, laid it at Tessa's feet, and cried.

Tessa knelt and took Cody's head in her hands. "I know, boy. I know." Wiping tears from her eyes, she kissed his dusty black nose. "It's killing me, too. What kind of monster would do this to babies? I don't understand it. Perhaps there is no understanding it. Just keep looking, Cody. We have to keep looking."

The dog's eyes shifted, gazing over her shoulder at Dubbiel.

Tessa stiffened, but didn't turn around. Dubbiel saw her red-rimmed eyes mirrored in the eyes of the dog. He knew that she was looking at his own reflection there.

"Are you an angel?" she asked.

"I am Dubbiel," he whispered, his voice so soft that she might think she'd heard nothing but the wind, "one of the *bene-ha-Elohim*. A *Grigori*."

"Do you know why this happened?"

He didn't answer. Though he knew the answer, he didn't know how to explain it to her. It didn't make sense, not even to him.

"Do you know who did it?"

"The man who set the bomb has already been arrested. The police will realize this later today."

"What about survivors? Do you know where I should be looking?"

"There are no more survivors," he said, unable to keep his voice from breaking.

Tessa turned at the sound of such pain and anguish, but he fled.

They brought in counselors for rescue workers who were having difficulty dealing with the things they'd seen inside the Murrah Building. Another tent was set up and partitioned for privacy. Appointments were made. Schedules were adjusted.

One of the counselors was a Catholic priest.

"Please have a seat," he told Tessa. "How are you holding up?"

"Do you believe in angels, Father?"

"Angels?"

"The heavenly host. Wings. Haloes. 'Holy, holy, holy,' and all that. Do you believe in them?"

"I think it's more important that we establish what *you* believe. Perhaps you should sit down so we can talk." He motioned her to a chair.

Tessa sat. "I think I saw an angel."

The priest nodded knowingly. "Perhaps you saw what you needed to see. Perhaps God believed that you needed an angel to help you through this difficult time."

"God sent me an angel?"

He couldn't help but hear the cynicism in her voice. He smiled and folded his hands on the table between them. His brows were monstrous and grey. They came down over his eyes as he studied his hands. "Angels are usually messengers. Perhaps God was sending you a message. What did the angel tell you?"

"He said they were dead. All of them. He said the police already have one of the men who did this."

"We don't know that there aren't any more survivors," the priest replied, ignoring the second half of her statement. He still hadn't looked back up at her. "We must maintain hope. We must keep looking."

"I know that. And we are looking. But I believe the angel is right."

"Why would an angel tell you to give up hope?"

She didn't answer.

"God asks for our faith every day," said the priest. "We must have faith in him now. This tragedy serves some higher purpose. Those whom God has chosen to be with him in—"

"The angel said his name was Dubbiel."

The priest looked up.

Tessa leaned forward. "You recognize the name?"

The priest waved it off, pushed back in his chair and tried to compose his face. "You must understand that there are really only three angels mentioned by name in the Old Testament—only two if we exclude the Catholic Book of Tobit." He reminded her of a teacher she'd once had who would always go into a lecture when caught off guard. "Virtually all the popular information on angels comes from apocryphal texts and—"

"You recognized the name," she insisted.

The priest pursed his lips. "If I'm not mistaken, Dubbiel is mentioned in the Chronicles of Enoch, declared apocryphal by St. Jerome in the Fourth Century."

"What do you mean, apocryphal?"

A bead of sweat broke from the priest's sideburn and ran down his neck. His forehead and upper lip glistened. It was hot in the tent, but Tessa could tell that he was also uncomfortable with their conversation.

"The material which comprises the Old Testament was originally gathered over a period lasting about a millennium. These Hebrew scriptures were translated into Greek to form the Old Testament in the Second Century B.C., but the Church Fathers rejected some texts from the canon. The excluded works are known as the *Apocrypha,* the hidden books."

"They were rejected because they were deemed untrue?"

The priest frowned. "No, that would have made them *pseudegrapha*... false writing... texts which were *never* part of the original canon."

"You're telling me that this Book of Enoch was part of the Bible, but then someone decided it should be thrown out?"

He nodded uneasily. "Most *Apocrypha* was excluded because of inconsistencies with more accepted doctrine. Enoch described a journey to a Heaven in which some angels were set aside in a penal colony and punished. Because this vision was inconsistent with the doctrine of a separate Heaven and Hell, Enoch's work was disputed." He shrugged apologetically. "Enoch's writing, however, was remarkably free of the usual religious extravaganzas. Some of his work found its way into the New Testament. His writing has been something of a hobby for me—a scholarly pursuit that was frowned upon in my youth, but the Church embraces a broader scope of studies these days."

"And what about Dubbiel? Who was he?"

"Guardian angel of Persia," replied the priest. "Legend has it that he even stood in for Gabriel once when that angel was in temporary disgrace. Dubbiel was a member of the Ninth Choir of Heaven. As angels go, the Ninth Choir is the closest to humankind. These were the messengers, the *mal'akh* in Hebrew, which becomes the Persian *angaros,* meaning courier, and appears in Greek as *angelos.*"

"And what became of him?"

The priest swallowed. "Dubbiel identified too closely with his human charges and fell from grace with God."

"Fell?"

"With Satan."

Outside, there was a sudden commotion. They exchanged looks, each thinking that perhaps a survivor had been found. A Red Cross volunteer stuck her head in the tent. "They've arrested one of them," she said. "One of the bombers. It's on the news. He was actually arrested right after the bombing, but they just now realized who they had in custody. Can you believe that?" She didn't wait for an answer.

Dubbiel's words came back to Tessa. The man who set the bomb has already been arrested.

She got to her feet, avoiding the puzzled look on the priest's face. He was wondering how she could have known. From the look on his face, there was only one conclusion to be drawn.

"Wait," said the priest.

She shook her head violently. "I need to go. My team is already in the building and the dogs don't work as well with Pete."

But she couldn't help but remember the angel's other statement. *There are no more survivors.* And something else... She paused at the door.

"The angel said he was a *bene-ha* something or other."

"*Bene-ha-Elohim.* A son of God," the priest translated.

"And he used another word. *Grigori.*"

"Those who never sleep," said the priest. "A watcher."

Saturday, 22 April 1995.

Saturday's dawn was lost in bitter wind and freezing rain that persisted throughout the day. It was a slow, quiet rain. Miserably solemn. No lightning to be seen. The only hint of thunder just the occasional weak, distant rumbling. It seemed as if all passion had been consumed by grief.

That afternoon, Tess sat in the children's playground on the south side of the building, hunkered down under a donated parka, where she could be alone with her thoughts.

Her dogs were exhausted. Their feet were ravaged and torn. When word spread on the news, locals came forward with rubber dog booties, but the footwear didn't work. The booties made the dogs uncomfortable. They needed their claws to scramble through the rubble. A slip could mean injury or death. Tessa had seen it before. She was using a sealing glue to affect a temporary repair on the pads of their feet, but the glue was no match for the millions of glass shards in the building or the ragged edge of broken concrete. Their time left in the building was running out. With more than half a dozen FEMA USAR teams now on site, it was only a matter of time before the Sacramento team was pulled out and sent home.

Oklahomans had been more than kind to them. The gifts and encouragement, the mints and stuffed animals left on her pillow at night. Clothing and food and essentials. Anything. Anything at all. Less than an hour after she'd expressed a need for food for the dogs, a mountain of dog food had grown beside the chain link fence—more food than her dogs, and all the other dogs working the disaster, could eat in a year's time. When the handler from Atlanta mentioned the need to bathe his dogs, someone bought plastic swimming pools from a local department store and delivered them.

But Tessa felt that she'd failed them. Each time she went in, she wanted so badly to leave the building with more than the location of yet another corpse. The dogs felt it, too. They were every bit as despondent. Late last night, when the risk of being misunderstood by spectators and journalists was minimal, she'd recruited an off-shift fireman she didn't know and was certain the dogs wouldn't recognize. She'd had him hide in the building in civilian clothes, buried in the rubble. Then, one at a time, she'd let the dogs find him. Seeing how the dogs reacted, their sheer joy at having finally located what they took to be a survivor, the fireman's partners had joined in and carried the fake victim out on a back board, further substantiating the facade for the dogs. Canine morale skyrocketed. They were still exhausted. Their feet were still bleeding. But nothing could keep them from going back into the building and searching for more victims.

If only the same could be done for the human half of the equation.

Oklahomans dealt with it as best they could, with a certain nobility and grace she'd seen at no other disaster. There was a constant and genuine concern for the safety and well-being of the rescue workers, even from those who had the greatest need for the rescue to proceed swiftly, the family members of those still missing. "Are *you* all right?" she was constantly asked. "How are you holding up?

Is there anything you need?" She'd never seen anything like it.

Symbols of determination and hope were everywhere. The yellow roses. The ribbons. The headlights which wouldn't be turned off until every victim had been retrieved. The shrine along the fence. Just that morning a local sculptor had delivered a beautiful stone angel to the site. It was a childlike miniature, nothing like Dubbiel, but Tessa couldn't bear to look at it. It reminded her of the children whom they still hadn't reached.

The rain hampered their efforts, made treacherous surfaces completely impassable. One of the damaged buildings across the street collapsed. The structural engineers swore the Mother Slab was going to go, taking the rest of the building with it. The Regency Towers apartment building was evacuated for fear of further structural damage in the rain.

Saturday was proving to be their worst day yet.

Assistant Oklahoma City Fire Chief Jon Hansen finally went before the media. In his hands he carried a broken red fire truck that one of his firefighters had retrieved from the day care center. "This broken toy," he told reporters, "is a symbol of our broken hearts..."

"You did all you could," whispered Dubbiel at her shoulder.

She didn't turn. The building was behind her. She chose not to see it. Wasn't sure she wanted to see him either. Grim a reminder as it was, the sight of the small playground was preferable.

"You don't know that there aren't still survivors," she threw back over her shoulder.

"My masters' schedules are very precise."

"And what masters do you serve, *fallen* angel? Is it Satan that brought this building down on so many lives?"

"Forget all you've been told of God and Satan... of angels and Heaven and Hell. Most of it is myth. What little your churches have gotten right has been misconstrued, misunderstood, and manipulated for someone's gain. Like all *Grigori,* I serve the Time Keepers. I watch their prophesies unfold. I record the lives that are wasted."

"Then it's your Time Keepers I should blame?"

"It's man that you should blame, Tessa McEvoy. Mankind's own wickedness has brought you to this day."

"Not all men are wicked," she protested.

"No. Not all men."

"For every man who played a part in this atrocity, there are thousands who have come forward to help set it right."

"It's not enough."

She did turn then. He didn't really look like an angel. Not in the rain. Not with that tortured look on his face. "Not enough for what?"

"Not enough to prove my masters wrong."

She shook her head. "You don't know anything."

"True."

"And your masters don't know *everything*."

"How I wish that were so." He shuddered, releasing a tide of rain from his sodden hair and shoulders. "Tomorrow I will leave this place. My masters are sending me to Rwanda. Nearly two thousand people will die there tomorrow, murdered by Rwandan soldiers who will bury their victims in a mass grave about twelve miles south of a little village called Gikongoro. Because of the coverage the bombing is still getting, your newspapers will barely mention it, but it's my job to record that it happens... exactly as my masters have predicted."

She reached out as if to touch him, but hesitated just before contact was made. What if she *couldn't* touch him? What if he wasn't real? "You don't have to go. You don't have to... watch."

"If I don't watch, someone else will. It won't change anything." He waved his arm as if to encompass the dark sky. "If I fail in my duties, the Time Keepers will retire me and send me out there to wait." He looked away, his face pale with fear. "I'm afraid the waiting might be worse than the watching. An eternity is a long time to go without human contact."

"I don't understand. Where would they send you?"

He nodded again toward the heavens. "There. Each star that is born is another soul set to wait for a time that my masters fear will never come. A time when your kind is ready for... for whatever comes next." He shrugged awkwardly. "Some of us watch for the signs. Others wait." He looked down the bombed-out shell of the Murrah Building. Through the open windows on the south side, they could see the clouds and the rain on the north. It was as if the building were some false facade in a Hollywood set.

"They're out there," he said. "Those who were lost to the bomb. They're waiting with all the others. New stars is what they are now, so distant that you can't even see them from Earth...

but they're there... an eternity blooming in the heavens." The rain painted his cheeks. She couldn't tell where his tears began and the rain left off.

"I won't see you again?"

"No."

She got to her feet and paced the distance between the swings and the merry-go-round. "How do you expect me to believe all this?" She looked up at him, tears in her eyes. "How do I know I'm not losing my mind?"

The angel gathered his robes about him. He seemed to retreat, not into the rain and the gathering gloom, but into himself. He looked small and hopeless there in the pouring rain.

"Dubbiel, give me something I can believe in. Give me something to prove you're real."

"I've already gone too far, risked too much. I've nothing to give you. And there's nothing to believe in so long as man rules the earth."

"Then I'll leave here and forget you," she said. "I won't even believe you existed."

She saw his eyes then, saw his fear of being forgotten, of being ignored. What torture it must be to watch, to suffer, and not to be able to tell.

"You're not real," she told him, hating herself when he flinched.

"The building across the street," he whispered, his voice near lost in the rain. "Search there."

"Which building?" she demanded. "We've searched all the buildings."

"The Water Resources Management Building. Search it again."

And then he was gone.

Dubbiel watched her from among the spectators that had gathered, same as every other day, despite the rain. If she saw him at all in the poor light and the downpour, he was confident she would lose him against the crowd. The mass of humanity huddled beneath their umbrellas, slickers, and plastic sheets took no notice of him.

She took Cody, led him limping across the street, his tail down and his hide soaking wet. Branson followed, demanding to know what she thought she was doing, insisting that it was time for them to make another sweep of the federal building. If they were slow to respond, Branson insisted, they'd be pulled out and another USAR team assigned their shift. Tessa brushed past him without answering. She helped Cody through a broken window and into the building. Fuming, Branson followed.

Twenty minutes later, Branson emerged to summon an extraction team. Cody had located two bodies in a collapsed rear section of the building.

While Tessa sat on the curb in the rain and watched, the bodies were uncovered, bagged, and removed. Dubbiel watched her back, saw her shoulders shaking, with tears or with cold, he couldn't say. He wanted to hold her, but didn't know how.

When the bodies had been taken away, the FEMA Director thanked Dave Branson and even made a show of hugging the dog. But then he delivered the news.

Branson's team was to stand down and return to Sacramento at their earliest convenience.

Sunday, 23 April 1995.

There was a memorial service that morning. Sacramento USAR was there. Even the dogs. Much was said about the heroes who had come to Oklahoma City to rescue those buried in the Murrah Building.

Afterward, they rushed to catch a military flight leaving from the Air Force base. For once, the Loadmaster of the cargo plane said nothing about where the dogs should ride.

Tessa stood on the ramp as long as she could, waiting. She'd almost given up when he breathed on her shoulder.

"I was worried you wouldn't come," she said, conscious of the airmen nearby, but determined to tell Dubbiel a few things, even if it meant bystanders thought she'd gone crazy. "You said you had an appointment."

"I'm on my way now," said the angel. "There's no hurry. Travel for a Watcher is almost instantaneous. And I know the moment of each and every death there. I will arrive in time." He smiled bitterly. "Why have you waited for me, Tessa McEvoy?"

"To tell you that you're wrong."

He cocked his head.

"You're wrong to think we can't change. You're wrong to think mankind is lost."

"Am I?"

"Hope is all we have," she told him. "Our faith will see us through."

"Faith? In what?"

"In ourselves. In the good in all of us. What happened here might have tested it, but it certainly didn't erase it. Even you can't have been blind to the courage and honor and dignity shown time and again this week." She reached out and caught his shoulder, squeezed with all her might. "Hope is all we have. If you've lost yours, Dubbiel, if you can't hope for the salvation of the human race, then you're the one who has truly lost. That's your hell… living without hope.

"That's how far you've truly fallen."

Then she turned and walked up the ramp and into the plane. The big engines howled and the ramp slowly ascended behind her. She didn't look back.

She found a seat near Keith. The dogs made themselves comfortable in the aisles. Keith smiled and tenderly touched one of the tears on Tessa's cheeks. Without a word she put her head on his shoulder and let his arm gather her close.

ROSES IN DECEMBER

God gave us memories so that we
might have roses in December.
—James M. Barrie

The new nurse found the missing old man in the garden, head back and moonlight in his eyes, howling like a wolf. He'd ripped open his pale blue pajama tops, the ones with the Wintercrest Nursing Home logo on the right breast pocket. His hairy chest gleamed silver. Discarded buttons littered the snow like pocket change. He was barefoot. He was howling. He must be, thought the nurse, a total loon.

"Mr. Holstead?" She leaned in close enough to turn and read the plastic band on his wrist. "Barry?"

"*Arrrrrrrrrroooooooooooo*!" howled the old man, a bitter breeze tossing his long grey hair.

The name was familiar—something she had been told by one of the day nurses. Holstead… Yes, that was it. The poor man's wife had died just last week. Compassion displaced her irritation at being outside in fifteen-degree weather. She touched his arm. "You're going to catch a cold out here, sir."

Another melancholy howl. From somewhere beyond the grounds a neighborhood dog answered. She looked in its direction, but could see little for the security wall. A rooftop just the other side twinkled with Christmas lights.

She took him firmly by the arm and tugged him toward the home. "Come on, Mr. Holstead. We're going inside." The old man was stronger than he looked. She pulled, but he didn't budge.

"Do you smell it?" he asked unexpectedly.

"Smell what?"

A long, deep shuddering breath. Head back. Eyes closed. Moonlight in his beard. "Yesterday," he whispered. "As clear and sweet as a rose. Yesterday."

"I don't know what you mean."

He smiled at her gently. "Christmas Eve, 1944. Glenn Miller caught a plane to Paris and was never heard from again. I was in the Philippines, having just taken Guam with Admiral Halsey. I was on R & R, mourning Miller's death with too many beers and howls that sent the local girls to work the other side of the room, when this U.S.O. dancer put on *Moonlight Serenade*."

She smiled at him indulgently, shivering now. "We can continue this story inside, Mr. Holstead."

"Sweet, sweet Betty. The first time I saw her, I knew this day would come." He leaned back against the nurse's arm, opened his mouth, emitted another of his eerie howls. It seemed to go on forever, the nurse pulling unsuccessfully on his arm, the hound on the other side of the wall adding its own sad harmony, and the ambivalent full moon dominating the sky.

"Betty? Was she your wife?" the nurse asked when the howl had finally died.

"Yes."

"I'm sorry for your loss, Mr. Holstead." It sounded condescending to her. Insincere and contrite. She struggled for a better response, but before she could say anything else, he spoke again.

"I loved her," was all he said, softly, wistfully.

"I'm sure you miss her terribly," added the nurse.

He nodded. "Her and all the others."

"Others?"

"Deborah and Julie. Delice and Dina and lovely Paula Jean. I miss them all. And each time," he said, staring now into her eyes with an intensity that made her step back, "I tell myself I won't fall in love with another.

"But I always do."

He howled.

Pity, she thought, that such a nice old man should be so

delusional. But enough of this; it was time to get him back inside. "If you don't come in with me now," she said, breaking into the middle of the wolf's call, "I'll have to go in and get security. They'll bring you in by force, Mr. Holstead. You don't want that, do you?"

He smiled at her, snorted a small careless laugh. "No. I suppose not. Someone might be hurt." Then he seemed to notice her shivering. Wrapping an arm around her shoulders, he steered her toward the door.

Moments later, they were back in the Spartan room where he'd spent the last seven years watching his wife deteriorate. The nurse tucked him into bed and, on impulse, planted a single brief kiss on his cheek. "You buzz for me if you need anything, Mr. Holstead."

"Thank you." His eyes twinkled in the light from the window. She had the impression that he was laughing at some secret joke.

"Goodnight." At the door she smiled back at him. "And Merry Christmas, Mr. Holstead."

"Merry Christmas to you, too."

Closing the door behind her, she stopped in the hall and stood there for a long minute, hand on the knob. *Moonlight Serenade* by Glenn Miller—could she get it on compact disk or would she have to find an old album at an auction? It would have been nice to have given it to the old man tomorrow for Christmas. Obviously no one else had remembered him.

A cold breeze kissed her ankles. Drafty old place, she thought, just before she realized that the chill was coming from under the old man's door. She turned and pushed it open. Swept her eyes around the empty room, across the deserted bed, to the curtains blowing back from the open window. The old man's pajamas lay on the floor. She ran to the window and looked out, but there was only the wind and the cold and the moonlight.

And a set of tracks leading out across the snow toward the security wall.

Wolf tracks.

From somewhere beyond the wall came an echoing howl…

SCARECROW'S DREAM

On cold, unyielding nails red with rust I hang in tattered silence, dreaming of summers and springs, make-believe-things... and replacement.

My weathered cross bends in the wind that cuts unchallenged across the barren fields. The weight of accumulated ice sheaths me in a diaphanous cloak, failing even to hide the hollow places Time has plundered. My life lies pooled like blood about my feet: strands of unclotted splendor, all but lost against the blinding white.

A bevy of dark veterans pass, their mocking calls so keen as to crack the ice on my face. There's nothing for them here—save the taunting. Their somber wings dip in spurious salute as they wrestle the wind and soar away. I close my eyes to their freedom, flex strands of harnessed muscle, and dream...

Carey Singer was fleeing the latest in a series of bad relationships. She swore, not for the first time, that this would be the last selfish bastard with whom she'd fall helplessly in love. At thirty-eight, wasn't it about time she realized Mister Right was a fantasy? The specifics of this breakup aren't important; suffice to say she was driving entirely too fast on a Kansas back road with which she was completely unfamiliar.

Highway 25 was covered in a thin layer of ice, compliments of the sleet that continued to fall, hissing like sand across the roof of her rusted Plymouth Duster. The Duster's defroster was doing a poor job on the windshield, and she had to keep switching the air to the floorboard so her feet wouldn't freeze. What with the swirling sleet and snow, the ice coating her windshield, and the tears in her eyes, visibility was poor.

Russell Springs had just slipped past in the night—without it's single blinking yellow traffic light she would have missed it. The road took a sharp turn to the west here, a dangerous curve that Carey might have seen, and slowed down for, if not for the aforementioned conditions and a pickup truck that had gone off the road… taking out the yellow warning sign.

The rear end of the Duster slid to the left. Carey never had learned which way to cut the wheel—was it into or away from the skid? She turned the wheel to the right and suddenly she was in a spin. She felt the tires leave the road and watched, in more amazement than fear, as a winterized oak swept past the passenger side of the car, missing by less than a foot. A snow drift slapped like a wet sponge against her door, slowing the careening auto, but by no means arresting its flight across the snow-shrouded cornfield. Something that might have been a fence, but offered too little resistance to have been functional, crunched under the front bumper. Then, as the car slewed around tail first, her gaze swept across the rearview mirror, and she caught a brief glimpse of a tall man with arms raised in terror.

Carey had time to gasp, one sharp intake of breath, preface to a scream, then the figure went down beneath the Duster with a sickening *thump!* The car slid another four or five feet and came to a halt.

"Oh God. No. Please. Let him be all right." She fumbled the door open and sprawled out into the deep snow, the numbers nine-one-one racing round her head like a gerbil in its wheel. She looked around for help, but the only building in sight was a dilapidated farmhouse, one end of which had collapsed in blackened ruin some time ago.

The poor man was literally crushed into the loose snow, his limbs twisted in awkward directions. The first thing she saw was a ragged edge of broken bone standing up from one of those contorted limbs. Her stomach turned and her eyes almost rolled back in her head. She'd never been able to cope with the sight of blood. Simple lacerations left her faint. Shattered bones transcended anything she'd ever had to face before. But she moaned and forced herself forward, fighting her fear as she struggled against the wind and blowing snow.

A derelict, she thought when she was close enough to see the condition of his clothing. A second later she realized there was no blood. Then she saw the straw.

Carey fell in the snow, incapable of choosing between laughter or tears, finally settling on a combination of the two. A scarecrow. She'd run over a scarecrow. What she'd taken for a broken bone was an old broom handle that'd been used to support its arms. And of course it looked like a bum. Who dressed a scarecrow in anything but rags? She took one final look at its head, a carefully painted gourd now broken in two. Someone with real talent had painted the face. It was no wonder she'd mistaken it for a man.

She struggled back to the Duster, wincing on feet that had gone numb. Sliding into the frigid vinyl seat, she discovered the car had stalled during its wild flight across the field. "Please start," she begged. Her words hung like cotton in the cold air and left a thin fog on the inside of the quickly chilling windshield. The engine turned over easily enough, coughing to life with a burst of white fumes that spun away in ghost-like tatters. She sighed and patted the dash. Ugly and old as it was, the Duster was still reliable. She dropped it into gear and gave it some gas.

The tires whined softly in the snow and the Duster's rear end slid an inch or two to one side. Carey gave it more gas, but the Duster sat in place, the tires finding no purchase as they hissed in the deep snow.

"No," Carey groaned, reopening the car door. She got out, leaving the engine running and the transmission in gear. She went around the car and looked with some dismay at the rear tires spinning lethargically, submerged to the wheel-wells in powder. She put her shoulder against the trunk and pushed with all the energy her 115 pounds could muster, but the Duster didn't budge. She was leaning against the trunk, panting white fumes of frustration, when the engine died again.

Her options were few. She could walk back to Russell Springs. It was only three or four miles, but in this weather that'd be a major hike. Ice was already forming in her hair. Her ears had quit stinging in the cold wind—*not* a good sign.

She could wait in the car and hope someone driving past would see her. How much traffic did this road get? Who in their right mind would be out driving in this weather? Would they even notice the Duster? Blowing snow was already piling against its windward side—as Fate would have it, the same side that faced the road. A few more minutes and the car would look like every other snow drift. Not to mention it'd be dark soon.

That left the farmhouse and the abandoned pickup. Surely the pickup's driver wouldn't have left it behind if it was serviceable. Still, it was worth the few minutes it would take to be certain.

Decision reached, she wasted no more time with the Duster save to shut off the key, grab her purse, and slam the door. She gave the scarecrow an apologetic shrug, then struggled through the drifts toward the truck.

The pickup had taken a rougher course than she, plowing through the yellow warning sign that might have kept her on the road, careening off a scrub oak, and dropping into a shallow ditch that the Duster had somehow skimmed across. All that remained of the driver was his keys, a notebook on the floorboard, and dried blood where his head had cracked the windshield. There was no clue as to what had become of him.

Carey didn't bother checking to see if the truck would start. There was no way the front end was going to climb out of that ditch. Shivering, on legs that were trembling with fatigue, she started back across the field to the farmhouse.

The porch steps creaked and groaned and threatened to collapse beneath her. She walked the edge where her weight was over the supports and thus made it to the porch without mishap. The deck seemed stable enough. The same could not be said of the roof overhead. One end hung as if it had been dealt a great blow, clinging to the remainder of the roof by a few rusted nails and sheer tenacity. Snow drifting down through a myriad of blackened holes had left the deck littered with foot-high stalagmites. She felt as if she were walking through a forest of tiny white fir trees.

The deck was scored black with the fire that had devoured the back half and upper story of the building. Looking at the gaping doorway and the shattered glass of the two front windows, she wondered if the farmhouse was any better shelter than her Duster. But there was a cord or better of firewood stacked on the porch, and the chimney, though charred like everything else, appeared to be intact. If she could start a fire, she'd be all right till morning.

She stepped across the threshold and into the house to find the shattered remains of a stairway that had once led up to a second floor. To the left was a kitchen that had been virtually untouched by the fire; to the right, a devastated family room populated with the charcoaled remains of furniture. The fire had obviously been arrested as it crossed the family room, for the far corner was untouched. In that corner was the biggest fireplace Carey had ever seen. There was already a neat stack of wood in the fireplace, sheathed in a fine mist of snow that had drifted down from the open damper. Kindling and additional logs were stacked nearby. With a soft squeal of delight, Carey started across the room. A soft moan brought her to an abrupt halt.

There was a man curled against the remains of the sofa.

Startled, she retreated a step, fear accelerating her heart, tightening her throat. He moved, a feeble attempt to raise his head, and she saw blood on his face and sprinkled where he lay. She remembered the truck with its bespattered windshield. Seeing his blood, bright and fresh where it dotted the snow, she felt ill. She thought she could smell it, like death in the frigid air. Though she told her feet to move, they remained fixed, refusing to take her to his side.

"Are you all right?" she asked lamely.

He moaned a single syllable that might have been "help." It was all she needed to free her traitor feet. Four quick strides carried her across the room and to his side.

His face was the waxy shade of raw fish. His lips were blue. The cut above his brow didn't seem serious until she wiped at the crust of dried blood with her glove and found that it was a good two inches long. Fresh blood welled up, trickling around his matted eyebrow and down the bridge of his nose. There was a travel pack of tissues in her purse. She pressed them against the wound, holding his head in her lap.

"You'll be okay," she promised, thinking that they'd both likely freeze to death if she didn't get a fire going.

"Who...?"

"Carey Singer," she answered. "My car went off the road." She took his hand in hers. His hands were bare and she could feel the chill of him even through her driving gloves. She put his hand against the tissue pad. "I've got to start a fire. I'm going to lay your head back down, and you've got to hold this compress against the wound. Understand?"

"Not sure... I can."

"You can," she encouraged. He whimpered when she moved away from him. "I'm right here," she called from the fireplace. It took a few minutes to get the snow swept away from the wood. She gathered fresh kindling from the pile against the wall and snapped it into small pieces which she packed under and around the cast iron fireplace grating. Because she had no intention of letting the fire go out, she used all the kindling, reasoning that it would start faster that way. Her lighter and half a pack of Virginia Slims were still in her purse. It took the lighter but a second to start the splintered kindling.

The injured man was sitting up against the sofa when she returned to his side. Beneath the angry red tissues, his eyes seemed clearer than they had been several minutes ago.

She pulled his hand away from the wound. "Let me take a look." As she pulled away the tissues, his eyes locked with hers. In their blue depths, there was only trust: the look a faithful hound has while you pluck cockleburs from its feet. The wound was still gaping—only stitches would take care of that—but the bleeding had stopped. When the fire was going good she was going to have to find some way to melt some snow so she could clean the wound. That would start the bleeding again, and she'd need to find something to bandage it with. Maybe he had a t-shirt she could shred.

"Who are you?" he asked.

She cocked her head at him. "You asked that one already." She held up her hand. "How many fingers do you see?"

He caught her hand in his own, pulled it down and held it tight. "You a nurse or something?"

"No," she laughed. "Just a piss poor driver like you."

He seemed to concentrate for a second. "Carey. You said your name was Carey."

"Right. What's yours?"

The concentration intensified. His eyes reflected pain. Finally, he took a deep breath, let it out with a shudder that reeked of fear. "Good question."

"You don't remember?"

He frowned at her and dug in his jacket pockets. They were empty. His pants pockets produced nothing but a small black comb. "Whoever I am," he commented, "you'd think I'd carry a wallet."

"There was a notebook in your truck," she offered.

They could both hear the wind howling outside. The light in the room now came solely from the fire she'd built. Neither said anything about going outside.

"We should move you closer to the fire," Carey suggested. "Then I'll scout around and see if there's anything here we can use."

Her hands are supple and warm, smelling faintly of glove leather and expensive perfume. She dips water from a pot beside the fire and wipes the blood from my face with a dish towel, both items found in her foray to the kitchen. In another pot, soup is warming. Its aroma permeates the ruins, chasing off the acrid fumes of burnt memories.

I ache to touch her, but fear it's too soon for such intrepid behavior. For now, I relax, content with the gentle contact of her hands on my face, the smell of her hair as she leans close, the taste of her in the air we share.

I feign fatigue and she feeds me, her eyes as concerned as a mother's. Having never seen anything so seductive, I'm in awe of her pouting lips. The smell of her envelopes me. I cannot breath without taking some part of her in, each molecule coming to rest at a nexus just behind my heart, building like an adrenaline rush.

I have never wanted anything so much as I want to hold her now.

With towels scavenged from the kitchen, Carey had made him a spartan pillow. Warmed by the fire, he had drifted off to sleep while she was bringing in more firewood. She sat now, studying the rough contours of his face, the fine blond hair that spilled over the strip of towel she'd used to bandage his head, the line of his jaw… Why did he look so damned familiar?

Tentatively, she touched his lips. She told herself she just wanted to verify they were no longer cold, but when he didn't stir at her touch, she traced their complete circle. Not once, but twice. She brought those same fingertips to her own lips then.

Did she know this man?

She got up and paced the room, casting wavering, elongated Carey-shadows across the walls. Shadows within shadows. Hers blacker than the charred commissures of the room.

"Carey?"

"I'm here," she whispered and returned to his side.

He smiled at her. "Sorry. I was worried you'd left me."

"Don't be silly. I wouldn't just up and leave you here."

He sat up and his hand came to rest on hers. "I know this sounds absurd, but I think you've left me before."

"You're right." She drew back her hand, felt the warm spot where his had briefly lain go cold. "It sounds absurd."

"I don't know who I am," he muttered, turning to look into the flames.

She studied his back, saying nothing.

"But… I know you."

"I've never met you," she countered, wondering if she lied.

"Do you believe in reincarnation?"

She didn't answer. Reincarnation. *Deja vu.* They were experiences upon which she feared to speculate.

He turned back to face her, reached out and traced her lips with his fingertips. She blushed; he hadn't been sleeping after all. She reached up to take his hand away from her face and a knot exploded in the fire, erupting behind him like a solar flare. Startled, he jumped away from the fire, toward her, winding up against her, his chest pressed against hers, his breath warm on her face.

He kissed her then. Her lips parted and his tongue, salty from the soup, passed across her teeth, probed to find her own tongue. His right hand slipped beneath her hair and rested on the back of her neck. His left cupped her breast, impossibly warm through her jacket and sweater.

"Wait," she cried, pushing away. "We've only just met." It sounded trite. She expected him to laugh, but he pulled away, his eyes downcast and despondent. It was only when his hands left her body that she realized she was trembling. There was a quivering need warming the inside of her thighs, spreading across her belly, and knotting her nipples. Her heart was racing. Her lungs refused to take air except in short pants. She was at a loss to explain her sudden desire for him.

"I'm sorry—" he started, but she interrupted him with a finger on his lips.

"Don't be," she whispered.

"It's just—" He made a fist, grappling some intangible thought. "See, if life is a continuous cycle of trial and error… and each time through we strive to reach some impossible goal… *sometimes,* while we're fighting those insurmountable odds, we find love—"

"You're crazy," she said, but there was no malice in her voice.

"If we're very, very lucky, we find that same love again and again." He touched her, his hand lightly stroking her cheek, brushing her ear, teasing the dark strands of her thick hair. "It's never perfect. Never is there a time when *both* of us remember all those other times. Sometimes one of us won't have anything to do with the other. The rejected one has no choice but to struggle on alone, certain of utter failure—for only together will we ever succeed. And sometimes… sometimes the rejected one suicides."

Carey's heart caught in her throat and suddenly she was twenty again, her first attempt through college, facing the only man who'd ever thrown himself at *her* feet. She had turned him aside for another—someone with a fast car, better looks, more money… it didn't matter why. What mattered was how he'd taken the rejection. What had his suicide note said?

Next time.

His hand trailed over her shoulder and across her breasts where it found the zipper of her coat. She laid back as the coat fell from her shoulders, felt the weight of him as he settled over her. Her other clothing slipped away as if by magic. His lips were warm on her flesh. His hands knew her curves, her recesses. This was not the first time he had loved her.

"And sometimes," he whispered, "we find a few moments in between."

Her hands brushed his bandage and it fell away. His forehead was unmarked.

She's every woman I've ever loved—the ONLY woman I've ever loved. Sought through all eternity. Lost to me as often as not.

The whisper of our bodies making contact is like an ocean breeze over warm sand, a sigh of satisfaction that ripples in tactile shivers across her flesh. The air about us whirls in winter wraiths, spectral voyeurs animated with our heat. Her nails leave chillbumps down my back, across my buttocks.

My tongue explores the supple curves of her body, counting her finely sculpted ribs, the slender bumps along her spine, tracing the scalloped blades of her shoulders. In every juncture of her body there waits a different flavor, a different smell. The hollows of her taste of salt and sweat and fine hair that tickles my tongue. I bury my face between her thighs, breath deep the musk of small animals, taste the dew that lies warm in the last rays of moonlight.

Her belly tastes of summer's promise, warm sunshine, cocoa butter, and younger days. The snow outside has left an aftertaste on her neck and behind her ears, a chill that I take on my tongue and trail down her cleavage. In the lambent orange of the fire, her breasts are alive with copper freckles, an erotic connect-the-dot game that leaves me breathless, dry mouthed, and fascinated by the firmness of her nipples.

Her legs are long and lazy, smooth as velvet as she draws them up around my waist. Her body quivers beneath me, rising to press against me with warm need. When I enter her, the world comes into a focus I've craved my entire existence…

The blare of a horn awoke her. She sat up, wincing as muscles and joints protested the long night on the hard floor. The fire was a pile of glowing embers and a chill was fast reclaiming the room. She'd have to bring in more wood—

Wait! Where was he?

Again there came the blare of a car horn. Carey scrambled to her feet and ran to the door. From the porch she leaped out into the snow rather than trust the steps. She was brushing snow from her legs, blinking in the bright light of a clear day, when she heard a voice call out.

"You okay, lady?"

There was a wrecker on the shoulder of the road, lined up with the abandoned pickup. Tow chains in his hands, a fat man in a checkered parka stood between the two vehicles. A younger man climbed from the cab of the wrecker and started toward her. For a moment, in the blinding glare of the sun off the snow, she thought it was *him*. But then he spoke: "Told you there was prob'ly somebody holed up in the house, Pa."

"Well, see if she's okay whilst I get us hooked up. Ask her if she wants a tow. We can come back after we haul in the pickup truck."

The young man struggling through the snow toward her couldn't have been more than eighteen. "You all right, Ma'am?"

"Fine," she answered. "The driver of that truck. Where is he?"

The boy shrugged. "I reckon he's still at the Days Inn, Ma'am. He walked into Russell Springs just after lunch yesterday, drunker'n a skunk. Asked us to come out after his truck, but Pa wouldn't come out till the blizzard blew itself out."

"Yesterday? Just after lunch?"

"Yes, Ma'am."

"Describe him."

"Well, he weren't quite as big as Pa, but real close. Bald, with a grey beard."

She sat down in the snow.

"You okay?" he asked again.

"Just give me a minute."

"She ain't faintin', is she boy?" bellowed the man at the wrecker.

"Don't think so, Pa."

Had last night been a dream?

Her Duster waited in the yard, rear tires entrenched in the snow. She got up and went to lean against its trunk. The scarecrow was where it had fallen. She knelt and brushed snow from its face. She studied the pale blue eyes, the cornsilk hair, the lips carefully painted in a half-smile that she recognized.

His name was Barry Holstead. He'd committed suicide eighteen years ago.

But she'd made love to him last night. Hadn't she?

"Pa's almost finished, Ma'am. You want that ride into town? You could get some breakfast whilst Pa and I come back out after your car."

She couldn't have dreamed it. Her body was sore—and not just from sleeping on the floor. This was a pleasant soreness, from the lovemaking. She suddenly remembered falling asleep in his arms. Later, waking up to find him staring at her in the warm glow of the fire.

He'd whispered that he loved her. And something else.

"Next time," he'd said, eyes near pleading. "Remember..."

The winds have died. Warm sun glistens off the fresh blanket of unbroken snow, promising an early thaw.

One of the crows, an errant scout, returns and perches boldly on my shoulder. From this vantage, he has a commanding view of the entire field, but he chooses to study my face. He cocks his head and seems to ask a question.

What am I doing here?

"Waiting," I answer, but he cannot hear me.

I wait. And, perchance, I dream.

SHROVETIDE

Shrove Sunday.

Bill Morgan found the Trans Am on his way to the cemetery. The car sat amid a host of wrecks at a body shop on Lorraine Road. Its paint had languished in the sun: no longer bright red, more the scabrous color of rust. With her decorator's eye, Kim might have described the color as burnt claret or brown garnet, but to Bill it looked like ancient blood. The Trans Am jogged memories he'd purposely forgotten, interrupting all thoughts of his destination. His foot came up off the accelerator. He pulled off the road and got out to peer through the chain-link fence.

A featureless grey lay like scar tissue across the hood, marking where the eagle decal had peeled away. Faded lettering on the scoop bragged of the 6.6-liter V-8 caged beneath the hood, an engine the likes of which hadn't been seen outside of racing circuits since America surrendered her horsepower to Japanese imports. The left rear quarter panel had that primer grey, recently-replaced look, lacking the dings and gouges prevalent on the rest of the car. The windshield was cracked, the fiberglass aircam was pulverized, and the trunk was tied shut with wire.

But it was definitely Martin Culpepper's old Trans Am. Bill couldn't say how he knew, but he knew.

"Hep ya wit something?"

Bill jumped. He hadn't seen the man stooped under the hood of a nearby Lincoln. "Just looking."

The man wiped his hands on already greasy coveralls.

"Didn't mean to startle ya." Grease smeared below one eye lent him the profile of a football player.

"I wasn't expecting anyone on Sunday."

"I'm Charlie Saucier, da owner. I come out here in my spare time and work on my collection." He made a sweeping gesture that encompassed the line of wrecks. "One day all dese babies'll look like new." When Bill made no comment, Saucier pointed at Bill's eye. "Nice shiner."

Bill scowled at mention of the black eye, but didn't answer. For a moment they stood in silence: Saucier sizing up his unexpected visitor; Bill subdued by the enigmatic appearance of the car.

"Where'd you get it?" Bill finally asked.

"Get what?"

"The T.A."

"Salvage yard," Saucier replied. His southern drawl made *salvage* sound like *savage*. "Why?"

Bill shrugged. "Just partial to Trans Ams."

"Ya ain't from aroun' here, are ya?"

"Sorta. I've lived in Chicago the last ten years, but I grew up here in Gulfport. Graduated from Harrison Central in '79."

The man relaxed, as if mentioning the high school indicated Bill could be trusted. "Trans Am's a '79."

"I know," Bill all but whispered.

Saucier didn't seem to notice. "My boy went to Harrison Central. Graduated in '84. He works up to Hattiesburg in some chemical plant." He dug a wad of keys out of his coveralls. "Ya wanta hear da car turn over? I know she ain't much to look at yet, but I got 'er engine runnin' better'un new." Saucier opened the door and slid in behind the wheel. Bill caught a brief glimpse of tattered black vinyl before the big man filled the seat.

"I really need to be going."

"Hang on a sec. I gen'ally start 'em every other day or so anyway. Worst thin' for a car is to let 'er sit idle alla time." The big engine growled and came to life like a bear at winter's end.

Bill felt the deep-throated rumble through the soles of his feet. His knees quivered with sudden memories: the puissance of the engine echoing up through the floorboards, inertia like a giant's fist shoving him deep into the clammy vinyl seat... impact.

Saucier revved the engine a few times, a boyish smile pasted on his greasy face. "I put dem new tires on 'er last weekend and ran 'er up to Wiggins—kids wanted to go swimmin' at Flint Creek, ya know. Man, can dis car fly!"

Martin had said something very similar that night on the interstate coming back from Pontchartrain Beach.

"You okay?" Saucier had shut off the motor and was staring at Bill through the cracked windshield.

"Uh, yeah. Fine. Just fine. Listen, thanks a lot. I really didn't mean to take up so much of your time."

Saucier said something else, but Bill wasn't listening. He slid back into the cramped little rental car and drove off.

He'd forgotten how mild southern winters could be. Sitting in the cemetery, wearing the windbreaker he'd borrowed from his dad, it was hard to believe that it was mid-February. Sunshine and new grass like this equated to May in Chicago, and even then the incessant wind would have carried a chill.

The sun had desiccated the fresh-turned earth over Kimber's grave and warmed the callous face of her tombstone. When he rested his hand atop the stone, he found the backside cold beneath his fingertips. It struck him as paradoxical that the two sides of the stone should disagree—a situation as abstruse as his sitting here and her being buried. Ten years of marriage and three of high school dating added up to thirteen years in which Kimber had been an integral part of his life. Where was he to go from here?

"Mom talked me into going to the reunion last night," Bill told the somber stone. He looked around nervously, but the other visitors were distantly involved with their own dead.

He and Kimber had originally decided to skip their ten year reunion. Kimber said she had no desire to destroy her memories by seeing how everyone *really* turned out. Besides, winter was the busiest season for interior decorators. Bill had also been glad to skip the reunion. He felt he'd left that part of his life behind. But the world, she does turn—evil, convoluted, twisting turns that are as apt to tear out your throat as show you something you never even knew you wanted to see. Bill had attended the reunion after all.

Funny that his first trip home in several years and his first attempt at reuniting with high school friends came as a result of Kimber's death.

He'd only come home to bury her.

"You were right about staying away, Kim. They're all a bunch of overweight assholes. Rhonda the Beauty Queen, she's got three kids and looks like a sow."

Absently, he touched the darkening bruise beneath his left eye. "I still don't like Mike Ford.

"The McCormick twins are still sickeningly cute; they have a furniture store out on Pass Road. One of them told me that Bruce Varnado's gay. Chris Flynn's acting career never paid off; he's selling used cars up in Jackson. You remember Sheri Thrasher, the girl that slept with damn near every senior our junior year? She's a model now and evidently doing pretty good. But God, Kim, she looks so... used."

Bill sighed deeply and wondered if he looked as world-weary as Sheri—"Rabbit," the seniors had dubbed her. She'd laughed at the nickname, too dumb to make the connection.

"Nobody seems to know what happened to Martin Culpepper. After school, things went bad for him. He was drinking quite a bit and lost his job. If I'd been here maybe I could have helped him, but—well, you remember the falling out we had." He dropped his eyes. "And you never did like him."

The years lay like crestfallen snow on his shoulders, impossibly heavy with burdens untold. He suddenly regretted all the things he'd never shared with her, things that would have allowed her to understand. "I never told you about the night he and I went to Pontchartrain Beach..." For a moment, the breeze seemed to carry the growl of Saucier's (Martin's?) Trans Am. He shivered, told himself he was just cold, but the sun was warm on his back. "Hell, no sense telling you now."

He dug a hand into the intervening dirt. It came up in hard-packed, unfeeling clods. "Nothing's the same, Kim. Gulfport's a different place. I don't even recognize our old friends. You were right, there's no coming home. Home doesn't exist.

"But I can't go back to Chicago. That'd kill me for sure." He wiped his eyes again, leaving streaks of dirt across his cheeks, and tried to erase the unbidden image of holes in a white wall leaking a fine mist of plaster, blood on a beige carpet, sirens... the smell of gunpowder. "If I could take it all back—make things the way they were... I'm so sorry, Kim...."

Saucier was still working beneath the hood of the Lincoln when Bill returned.

"Mr. Saucier, I want to buy that Trans Am."

The big man tossed his wrench on the Lincoln's breather cap and swung out from under the hood. "She ain't for sale."

"It means a lot to me."

"Means a lot to me too. I got 'er pretty cheap out da salvage yard, but I done put nearly a thousand bucks into 'er engine and drive-train, plus them there new tires. 'Nother thousand in body work and I'll have 'er lookin' pretty sharp."

"I'll give you five thousand dollars."

Saucier's head came up. "Five thousand? Hell, son, that car ain't worth no damn five thousand dollars. When I'm done, she might fetch three, three anna half, but—"

"I said it means a lot to me."

Saucier studied Bill's face for a minute, noting the dark streaks of dirt, the red eyes and unshaven jawline. Finally he sighed, "I reckon it does at that, son."

Shrove Monday.

Where a radio should have been, where Martin Culpepper had once installed a hundred watt Pioneer AM/FM cassette, there was only a gaping wound in the dash. No more Pink Floyd chanting "We don't need no ed-u-cation" as they cruised through the high school parking lot. No more Van Halen, Boston, Steve Miller or Peter Frampton blaring from the T.A.'s four triacs.

Without a radio, Bill found himself hypnotized by the hum of Interstate 10 passing beneath the wide tires. It wasn't until the

Long Beach exit whipped past him and the Wolf River bridge was coming up fast that he realized he'd driven nearly seven miles in a daze. As the bridge loomed nearer, Bill's foot came up off the pedal and the car began to coast.

"New Orleans!" his father had exclaimed that morning. "What the hell are you gonna do in New Orleans?"

Bill didn't have an answer he thought his father would understand. Eugene Morgan asked three more times before he switched from trying to learn why to trying to talk his son out of it. That continued until Betty Morgan glared over her needlepoint and whispered at him to stop. "He needs some time alone, Gene. Time to put this behind him."

"But New Orleans? What's he gonna do, go to the Mardi Gras?"

"He and Kim spent their honeymoon there; you know that. And remember all the fun they used to have at the amusement park at Pontchartrain Beach?"

"Hell, they closed that place years ago."

"That ain't the point, Gene, and you know it. Now leave the boy alone."

Eugene said nothing more until Bill asked if he'd follow to Hertz to dump the rental car, then drive him out on Lorraine Road to pick up the Trans Am. He asked quite a few questions about that, but Bill had no explanation for the intuition fueling his actions.

Gravel crunched like the hollow bones of dead birds beneath the tires as the T.A. rolled to a halt on the shoulder of the interstate. Bill shut off the engine and got out, his eyes scanning the tea-colored ribbon of Wolf River where it meandered through the tall pines.

There was a chain stretched across the dirt road that lead down to the river. The chain was locked to squat concrete buttresses that sat sentry-like on either side of the road. A sign on the chain swung silently in the breeze, its red block letters warning that SWIMMING, DIVING, and FISHING were PROHIBITED.

The chain hadn't been there ten years ago. Wolf River had served as swimming and fishing hole for Gulf Coast teenagers as far back as Bill could remember. He'd spent his Senior Skip Day here, drunk with Martin and a host of others. Memories of that day, his last visit to Wolf River, flooded back now, born on the soft breeze and the plaintive calls of the cicadas in the pines.

Senior Skip Day was a long-standing tradition at H.C.H.S. Every year a day was chosen. Bill had no idea how, or for that matter *who* decided, but the word would spread: "Hey, Friday's Senior Skip Day!" Most of the senior class met at some prearranged spot: the beach, Flint Creek Water Park, the Wolf River bridge. It'd been going on for so many years that Harrison Central took it in stride.

Bill spent Senior Skip Day with Martin Culpepper, cruising in Martin's brand new T.A., racing every sports car they could find, drinking till he puked his guts out over the side of the bridge, and generally making an ass out of himself, which is all Senior Skip Day was ever really about. One final romp before graduation forced them out on the world as adults.

Kim had driven up to Hattiesburg that day to look around the University of Southern Mississippi where she hoped to start college in the fall. Bill was having a good time without her, though later it would be nice to have a female body to curl up with around a fire on the river bank. No matter, if they wanted girls, Martin's new car attracted all they needed.

Funny thing about Martin. The *cool* guys, the "in-crowd," the prissy prom queen and cheerleader types had never paid any attention to him. Until he got the Trans Am. Before then, he'd always been plain old Martin, somewhat clumsy, a bit slower than the average student and not the type to catch the eyes of even the homelier Gulf Coast debutantes. But the flashy red Trans Am got their attention.

Bill and Martin had met in the third grade where they became immediate friends, a kinship born of common love for the practical joke and the good time. Martin was the first—probably the *only*—kid Bill had ever known who truly did not fear authority. Fun was fun, and no authority figure was going to stand between Martin Culpepper and a good time. Without

Martin, Bill might have grown up with his father's apathetic outlook on life. Life for Eugene Morgan meant getting from point A to point B with as little hassle—and subsequently, enjoyment—as possible in between. Martin showed Bill how to enjoy every minute. Through elementary, middle, and finally high school, Martin and Bill had been inseparable.

Theirs was an odd relationship. Martin knew Bill had an image to maintain—an image that benefited them both. Bill was the scholarly, well-behaved type, good home, good parents, church on Sunday and all that. Martin was the infamous troublemaker. They each played their roles well. It was Bill who aced every exam while Martin barely passed (and what answers he did get right, he'd copied from Bill). Whenever there was trouble, Martin took the rap; he had nothing to lose.

Bill got Martin through school; Martin got Bill through life.

Senior Skip Day '79 had been Bill's last trip to Wolf River. Before leaving Gulfport for Chicago, he would only cross I-10's Wolf River Bridge twice more. That would be a Friday evening, three weeks after Senior Skip Day, a week before graduation, to and from Pontchartrain Beach with Martin.

Bill walked out on the bridge. There was a narrow shoulder, more a curb than anything else, just wide enough that a person hiking the interstate could cross the bridge without getting run down.

From the middle of the bridge, his view of the river was unobstructed. Looking down, he shuddered to think that he and hundreds of others had once leaped from here. In drier summers, the river would sometimes drop to four feet deep at its center.

Younger days, he thought. Days of callow bravado and Devil-take-the-high-road. He'd lost all that somewhere. With a start he realized that he'd lost it right here… on this very bridge.

Open her up, Martin. Let's see just exactly what this bitch can do!"

The t-tops were off. The warm southern air whipped Martin's hair into a frenzy. He tossed it out of his face and howled at the perfect pale moon in the black sky above. "Hang onto your nuts, Billy boy! I'm gonna show you what she can do!"

The engine roared as Martin stomped the pedal. Though they were already doing at least sixty, the front end of the T.A. did a little hop. Acceleration thrust the boys deep into their seats and the little red needle on the dash fell swiftly past vertical.

"You need a radar detector, man. Highway patrol's gonna nail your ass."

Martin laughed. "They ain't gonna radar what they can't see!" He killed the headlights.

It wasn't as dangerous as it might have been. After the first few seconds of absolute darkness, it wasn't hard to see the lines down the center of the interstate.

There were cars coming and Bill didn't feel safe on the bridge. He walked back to the car and leaned against the hot hood, fighting the rush of memories.

He ran his fingertips along the crack in the windshield. It seemed a perfect match. "There was a full moon, Martin. And stars like I've never seen since. Why didn't we see her?"

The T.A. was doing at least 140 when they went across the bridge, maybe more. It was hard to tell because the needle in Martin's after-market speedometer was jittering. The T.A. was shaking like it was going to fall apart.

That night there were teenagers jumping from the bridge. Looking down the stretch of interstate, the kids would have seen nothing but darkness, no headlights, no cars coming. One girl must have changed her mind. She climbed down from the railing and stepped back into the road.

Martin hit her.

She came up over the hood, legs crushed on impact, pelvis and ribs destroyed. Her face hit the windshield on the passenger side, right in front of Bill. For an immeasurable fragment of time that clung in his vision like a retina scar, she sprawled there across the hood, blood, teeth, and brains deliquescing across the spider-webbed safety glass. The scream of the tires locking up as Martin belatedly hit the brakes seemed to emanate from her gaping mouth. The T.A. slewed sideways on the bridge, came up on two wheels and nearly rolled before Martin got it back under control.

The shattered corpse flipped over the roof, spraying blood across the boy's aghast faces. As she went by, her hand seemed to claw at Bill's shoulder. Then she was gone, slipping across the trunk like a discarded fast food sack, tumbling across the highway, all shattered bones and torn flesh, lit briefly in the T.A.'s brake lights.

Martin's eyes went to the rearview mirror, aslant and coated with fine droplets of blood. Hand shaking, he adjusted it. He let off the brake and floored the accelerator, fighting the car till it was straight on the highway.

"Stop the car, Martin!"

Martin shook his head vehemently, his jaw set, and his eyes locked on the rearview.

Her name was Roxanne Ladner. She'd just turned thirteen.

Martin held the peddle down, his face set like someone who'd just tasted sour milk, while the Ladner girl's blood streamed across the windshield, following the jagged lines writ in the glass. Bill could remember curling into a shuddering ball on the floorboard for the remainder of the ride to Gulfport, all the while the T.A.'s motor purring like some sated predator. Martin never said a word till he hit the Gulfport exit, and then it was only to curse when he almost lost control of the car on the cloverleaf ramp. He switched on the headlights when they pulled out on Highway 49 heading north towards Bill's home in Orange Grove. Five minutes later Bill was home, shuddering on the porch swing, afraid to go in the house for fear his parents would ask how his evening had been.

Later in school, Martin bragged about getting a cousin to fix the car. "Told him I hit a deer and didn't want Mom and Dad to know about it." Bill had never spoken to him again.

Though downtown New Orleans had undoubtedly changed in the years since, to Bill it seemed she wore the same tawdry face that had fascinated him as an adolescent. Like a high-priced whore promised a better life, she waited for him after all these years. She'd been in the business too long, but knew no other way of life. Her beauty lay all but invisible beneath time's footprints and scars, beneath the lipstick of cruel lovers and the bruises of those who'd used her to vent their hatred. Driving through town, Bill still felt something. Maybe nothing more than the lingering warmth from memories of time spent here with Kim, but something all the same.

He followed Esplanade towards the river, the rust-colored Trans Am winking back at him from shop fronts and plate glass windows. The streets were lined with Mardi Gras crazies in costumes and colors: billowing pantaloons, sequined gowns, gaudy masks. They carried drinks in one hand, beads, doubloons, plastic swords, and assorted parade-offal in the other. Their necks were adorned with great halters of cheap plastic beads, glittering beneath the street lamps like diamonds and pearls. Those without costumes were dressed with a drunken immunity to the cold wind that came in off the Mississippi River and wound ghost-like through the streets.

Normally, it'd be a simple matter to spot the local prostitutes, but not tonight. Tonight they *all* looked like hookers in their dark hose and short skirts, their cut-offs and tube tops, their unfettered breasts bobbing beneath shirts wet with liquor, their legs long and their heels high. Strangers cruised the boulevard, hanging from car windows and shouting, "Show me your tits!" From his own days cruising these streets, Bill knew that at least a fourth of the women would. For beads, for doubloons, for candy they wouldn't even eat the next day, they'd quickly yank up their blouses to prove they had as much as the next gal.

He tried to turn down Bourbon Street, but a cop waved him off. The street was choked with drunkards, tank-topped muscle men, painted women, and fags. He took Decatur to Saint Peters and Saint Peters to the *Vieux Carre* Riverview where he found a spot to ditch the car along the railroad tracks. He doubted anybody would be out giving tickets tonight. And with a gaping hole where a stereo should be, it was equally unlikely that anyone would break in.

He walked back to Bourbon Street and lost himself in the

crowds. Elbows jostled him. Women rubbed hips and breasts against him. A stranger put a plastic cup full of beer in his empty hand. His shoes stuck to the pavement as he walked, the result of a thousand spilled drinks. Each step he took was accompanied by a desperate little squelch, the struggles of a cockroach trapped in a roach motel. There were cops everywhere, some on horseback, the eyes of their mounts wild in the sodium lights. Between the crowded bars and strip joints slunk dark alleys, un-traveled corridors in a haunted house. From these fetid recesses trickled streams of foul urine. The stench rose like steam and mixed with the heady odor of alcohol.

A parade was making its way down Canal Street. Even here, six blocks away, he could hear the shouts of "Throw me sumthin', Mistuh!" He thought he heard the sound of doubloons tinkling on the pavement, but it was only a drunk dropping his change.

He came across a dark-eyed beauty too busy holding up a lamp post to go for a drink. He gave her his beer and ducked into the first bar he came to. There wasn't an open seat in the house, but he found a dark corner that suited him. It wasn't until a waitress approached that he wondered where he was.

"Where am I?" he asked, putting his lips to her ear. She smelled of cigarettes and impromptu, back-alley sex.

"Hurricane, babe. That's what everyone's having."

She left with a swirl of skirt and tanned thighs. He realized that she'd thought he'd asked about a drink.

His overloaded ears were assaulted with a hundred conversations laced with belches and calls for more beer. The room was filled with smoke: cigarette and the sweeter aroma of Mary Jane. Beneath the smoke hovered the stench of stale bodies and beer farts, whores working their third or fourth trick of the night, and vomit. Bill's head spun and his stomach did a quick roll that left him leaning against the greasy walls in the corner. Seeking a focus, he fixated on the conversation nearest him.

"Man, I heard sum fuckin' niggah mugged Clarence last night when he was takin' a piss inna alley offa Iberville."

"I wisht some niggah'd try it wit me, by God! I'd shure like to kick me sum—"

"The niggah hadda gun, Henry. What da fuck you gonna do?"

"Shit. Need to pass a law that don' allow dem niggahs to have guns, das for shure!"

"Can't make a law jus' for niggahs. Dey'd hafta take white folks guns too, Henry."

"An' who says dat's all bad? Hell, jus' last week sum dumb sumbitch upta Chicago blew his wife away cause he thought she was a fuckin' burg'lar. Tell me sumbody shouldn'ta took dat sumbitch's gun away!"

Bill pushed away from the corner and ran. The waitress yelled at him as he hit the exit door. She was waving a drink in a tall glass shaped like an old fashioned hurricane lamp.

Recklessly, he shoved his way through the crowds. Women slapped at him. Men cursed. More than one shook his fist—Bourbon Street and Mardi Gras are famous for street brawls, hence the multitude of cops—but Bill kept moving. His head hurt and his mouth was dry. His stomach was twisted in knots. He bumped into one particularly large fellow in a Mötley Crüe t-shirt who shoved him back against a wall. Bill's head smacked sharply against the dingy bricks, and it was then he spotted Martin.

He saw him only briefly, through a momentary break in the crowd, on the other side of the street.

"What's your hurry, asshole?"

Bill pushed past the man. He caught another glimpse of the back of Martin's head. The big man caught Bill's wind breaker and pulled him up short. Bill spun, twisted free of the jacket and darted into the crowd.

He tripped on the curb on the other side of the street. He nearly went down, but a smiling drunk in pirate hat and eye-patch caught him. Without thanking him, Bill pushed on up Bourbon Street. He saw him again, yelled. Martin paused and looked back. Just before the crowd blocked him from sight, Bill saw his eyes. They were glazed. Unfocused. Lost.

"Get out of the way!" Bill pleaded, pushing at the milling crowd. A fist clipped his jaw, a punch that would have surely dropped him had it connected. He caught one more glimpse of Martin, thought he saw who Martin was following, then someone tripped him. By the time he got back up to resume the chase, Martin was gone.

Desperately, Bill searched up and down Bourbon Street, looking for that one particular mop of dark hair for more than two hours.

He couldn't find him.

The more he looked, the more he doubted what he'd seen. It'd been ten years since he'd last seen Martin Culpepper. He could have been mistaken.

He didn't even want to think about the girl he thought he'd seen Martin following.

The car was where he'd left it, untouched.

He got in and locked the door, dropped the front seat back and closed his eyes. His head still pounded and there seemed to be a black hole where his heart should be. The hole was eating him from the inside out. He could feel it painlessly absorbing, a dark maelstrom that left an empty, lost kind of numbness behind.

Tell me sumbody shouldn'ta took dat sumbitch's gun away!

Bill curled up against the tattered vinyl and wept.

Shrove Tuesday.

New Orleans hung over him, a withered old woman who recognized him as one who'd tasted of her youth and left her behind. He'd come back, this prodigal son, no different than a thousand others, his carrion coach wrapped about him like a coffin, reeking softly of secrets and death. His sins were tucked away where he thought them hidden. But she knew. She knew them all.

She wrapped her blanket of night about him, slipping through the bug-smeared windshield to touch his hand, to brush the hair back from his brow, to taste the chill that haunted his lips. Somewhere nearby a church bell sounded one long mournful note; otherwise, all was silent. New Orleans pillowed Bill's head against her decadent bosom.

And he dreamed…

Kim took his hand and led him through the darkness. He followed, mesmerized by her beauty, aroused by the warmth of her hand. She was eighteen again. She wore a pale blue summer dress beneath which her breasts were firm, her stomach flat. Her hips had regained the sway that had first attracted him so long ago. Her shoulders and neck were the color of fine oak, lightly freckled by the sun. She hadn't worn her hair this long since high school. She smelled of honeysuckle and soft summer breezes.

"I thought I'd never see Mardi Gras again, Bill."

Her voice brought tears to his eyes. They spilled down his cheeks, fire against his cold flesh.

She waved her arm and a parade appeared in the darkness. Floats and people. Beads and coins arcing in the air. The smell of flowers and… gunsmoke.

"You know what all this means, don't you?"

"I—" He shook his head, uncertain what she meant.

She slapped playfully at his arm, then stood on her toes and kissed his cheek. "The parades, silly. Mardi Gras. Fat Tuesday." She cocked her head, raised an eyebrow.

"No," he confessed.

"Mardi Gras is the big blowout before Lent. Tomorrow's Ash Wednesday. Don't you know anything?"

"I don't understand." With so many important things he wanted to tell her, he didn't understand why they should be talking about Mardi Gras.

"Lent. The six weeks preceding Easter that are observed as a season of penitence. You know, time to feel sorry for your sins." She caught a strand of red beads, hung them about his neck. "No parties allowed during Lent, Bill. You got to do your partying the night before. The French knew it. They started Mardi Gras."

"What's all this got to do with me?" The parade had passed. Garbage lay in its wake. He went to kick at a piece of it, but stopped when he saw what it was. He turned away, refusing to acknowledge its existence, but the image persisted in his mind's eye: a blood-soaked tennis shoe with LADNER stenciled across the side.

"The French named it Fat Tuesday after the tradition of parading a fat ox through town. Everyone would follow in their party costumes. Surely you can guess what the ox was for, Bill."

"Sacrifice," he whispered. Something pricked his chest. He looked down and discovered the beads had become a strand of barbed wire.

Kim smiled, but did not answer.

"Are you their sacrifice?" Bill asked.

"No," she laughed.

"Me then?"

Somewhere she'd lost her clothing. Two holes, one centered between her breasts, the other just below her left collar bone, gleamed darkly. Her skin was pale and almost translucent. Beneath its thin veneer lay a roadmap of collapsed veins and arteries.

They'd come upon a stainless-steel table. Kim climbed up and lay down.

"Is it me?" he asked again, his voice weak with desperation—and hope. As he watched, the gentle rising and falling of Kim's chest ceased. He reached out to touch her face, but a voice stopped him.

"You stupid bastard!"

He whirled to find Charlotte at his back. Charlotte who owned Imago Decorations, the shop where Kim had worked; Charlotte who'd taken Kim with her to that convention in Memphis; Charlotte who'd told him…

"She was coming home to tell you she was pregnant! She insisted on surprising you, wouldn't call from the airport like I asked." Charlotte slapped at him, missed, and fell to the floor weeping. "She missed her period for the second time in a row, and I convinced her to take one of those E.P.T. things." She looked up, her eyes swollen and red. "The test was *positive*. She was coming home to tell you!"

Bill tried to say something. Nothing came out.

Another voice intruded: "Big time advertising executive, eh?" Mike Ford leaned across the table and looked down at Kim's pale corpse. "Left us behind. Showed us up. But you're still a dumb son of a bitch. Shot your own wife, didn't you?" He stuffed a finger deep into one of the dark holes in Kim's chest. "Forty-four magnum? Three fifty-seven? What'd you blow her away with Billy?"

Bill swung at him, just as he'd done at the reunion. Ford dodged the wild swing and popped him in the eye. Bill went down, his hand catching on a drain tube attached to the gutters in the table. The tube tore free and vile fluids—fluids that had once carried life through Kim's body—gushed out across his legs.

"Let's see," Ford mumbled. "What have we here?"

Bill looked up to find Ford dressed in white, his hands in rubber gloves, a mask across his nose and mouth, a scalpel at work on Kim's pale abdomen.

"Stop," Bill begged.

"Autopsy, Billy. We've got to determine what killed the old girl." As Ford opened her up, a fresh wash of fluids spilled from the torn tubing, flooding about Bill's hands and knees.

Ford laid the scalpel aside and used his hands to pry the corpse open. The sound of ribs popping and organs tearing free of the peritoneum echoed throughout the dreamscape. Ford reached in up to his elbows, dug around, and extracted a long string of Mardi Gras beads. "Not uncommon in patients of this age," he muttered. "Certainly not the cause of her death." He hung the gory strand about his neck where they proceeded to bleed down the front of his surgical gown. He dug around some more.

"Ah ha! I have it!" He pulled a tiny corpse from her.

"No!" Bill screamed, turning away, curling into a fetal ball.

"Oh yes," Charlotte insisted. "The test was positive." She grabbed his shoulders and shook him. "Look at it! Look at your child, you murdering bastard!"

He swatted at her from his protective ball on the cold floor. She shook him so hard his head rattled against the floor. She let out a long scream, like the wailing of a...

Train.

There was a train coming. Thundering and wailing, its mass shook the T.A. where it sat not ten feet from the tracks, rattling Bill's head against the car's cold window.

He sat up and wiped the sweat from his face. He was shivering. He stank. His body ached as if someone had clubbed him.

Glass towers to the east were ringed in a halo of dawn. New Orleans stretched beneath a sky dead grey, bruised with clouds that promised rain for Mardi Gras.

As the train roared past, Bill started the car and went to find a hotel.

The drizzling rain did little to dampen the Mardi Gras spirit. In fact, there seemed to be *more* people on Bourbon Street tonight. The barest sliver of a moon hung among the dark clouds, illuminating the faint beginnings of a fog. Beneath the street lamps, the wet streets took on an appearance of the macabre, as if they were bathed in the tears of a million grieving mothers. Lightning lit the sky just north of the interstate, followed immediately by the rumble of thunder, like drums in the distance.

Bill worked his way through the crowd, searching for Martin. He was tired. The hotel he'd found was comfortable enough, but his sleep had been filled with nightmare autopsies, prenatal fetuses, and accusations. He'd spent most of the afternoon in the hotel bar, drinking two dollar cokes and listening to a salesman's pitch on wind turbine generators, the power source of the future.

He asked himself why he was doing this. Why the Trans Am? Why the drive to New Orleans? What did he hope to find here? What missing element from his youth could he possibly hope to recapture?

You know what all this means, don't you?

"No, Kim. I don't."

A drunk patted him on the back. "S'okay, buddy. It'll—" He belched loudly. "—be starting an-eee minute now."

What? Bill almost asked. But he knew. The sacrifice.

On the final night of the celebration, blood is spilled to welcome in a six-week period of penitence. But why? For man's sins? A pagan equivalent of the crucifixion?

Bill was shoved aside as Martin Culpepper pushed past.

"Martin!" He caught his old friend by the arm and spun him around. Martin tried to pull free, but Bill hung on. "Martin, it's Bill. Bill Morgan. Don't you recognize me?"

Martin's eyes were unfocused—or rather, they were focused somewhere else. On something Bill couldn't see. Something Martin seemed to see by looking right through the milling crowd. There were circles dark as bruises beneath his eyes. His lips were swollen and cracked. His hair was matted, plastered to his head in knotted clumps. The shirt he wore, once white, now a dingy grey, had foul, ocher stains beneath each arm. The knees of his jeans were ragged and one of his sneakers was untied. He was bone thin. His hands shook like an alcoholic in need of a drink.

"Did you see her?" Martin asked.

Ice raced through Bill's spinal cord. His knees quivered. He *had* seen her. Last night. The smell of decomposing flesh suddenly assaulted his nostrils and for a second he thought he saw her cadaverous face looking at him over Martin's shoulder.

Martin was driving! a part of him screamed. *It was his fault.* His hand fell from Martin's arm and Martin slipped away into the crowd.

If there had to be a sacrifice, it should be—

Coward! He clawed at his face, drawing blood. If you'd gone to the police, told them what happened that night on the interstate... If you'd had the courage to face whoever it was in the house that night instead of blasting away...

He ran after Martin. He saw him turn the corner of Bienville Avenue. Bill followed. He was almost too late, just catching a glimpse of Martin entering a dark alley up the street. He yelled for him to wait, but there was no response.

The alley ran between a book store and a fast food dive, both closed. Twenty yards in, it turned to the right behind the book store. On the left was a high wooden fence closing off the alley behind the restaurant. Dead ahead lay the brick backside of another establishment. There was only one direction Martin could have gone.

Bill stopped, listening. The only sound was his ragged breathing. "Martin?"

Nothing.

The alley stank like a compost pile. He imagined a pile of rotting food just the other side of the fence: half-eaten burgers squirming with maggots, petrified fries, old lettuce and onions decomposing into a noxious sludge. He could almost hear the flies swarming about it.

He advanced halfway down the alley, repeated his call. No answer. His foot knocked over a bottle. Something darker than the asphalt bubbled out and ran thickly towards the turn in the alley. He followed it. Lightning flashed and the rain became a torrential downpour. He blinked fiercely to keep it out of his eyes. Turning the corner, he found the book store's dumpster. Martin lay face down in an overflow of sopping cardboard boxes.

Roxanne Ladner stood over him.

She was wearing a one-piece swimsuit and white sneakers—the clothes she'd worn that night at Wolf River. Her hair was gathered in a ponytail that reached halfway down her back, tied with a barrette made of bright balloons. The barrette seemed somehow painfully adolescent, reminding Bill that this was only a thirteen-year-old girl.

Barely ten feet separated them. At that distance, no detail was hidden. He could see puberty budding like a rose: the fine down of hair on her thighs; the small, firm mounds where her breasts were forming; the curve of her hips; the full, red lips. He thought of the years he and Martin had robbed from her. Tears joined the rain running down his face.

She was dry. The rain didn't touched her.

Their eyes locked. Hers were bitter blue, narrowed with accusation, laced with pain… and something else. It took him a moment to recognize it. Satisfaction.

Then she was gone, fading into the gathering fog as if she'd never been there at all, as if guilt and his shivering had somehow concocted her from the wind and rain, standing her there over his old friend just to scare the hell out of him.

He knelt beside Martin and gently rolled him over.

Martin's neck was slit from ear to ear. The wound gapped red and clean in the pouring rain, bone winking from its pink depths. Martin's eyes were open and wild. His mouth was frozen in a scream.

The windshield wipers seemed to ask the same question over and over. What now? What now? What now?

The wet expanse of I-10 slid effortlessly beneath the tires. New Orleans was just a smear of light on the horizon behind him. She hadn't tried to keep him from leaving. She had other souls to torment before morning.

He thought of Martin lying cold and wet in the alley. What should he have done? Call the police? Tell them a ghost slit Martin's throat?

"You could have told them you did it."

He turned his head to find Roxanne Ladner in the passenger seat. She smiled at him toothlessly. Her face was a mass of lacerated flesh and gleaming bone. One eye was gone. Her ponytail was wrapped about her neck, stuck in place with blood. Her chest was sunken, broken ribs protruding through flesh and swimsuit alike. Her legs—

The right tires went off the shoulder and Bill fought the car back on the interstate. He kept his eyes forward, focusing on the approach of a distant mile marker.

She ran her hand across the sun-weathered dash. "Nice car, man." Her hand left a red trail across the cracked plastic. "Needs a stereo though."

"Go away," he whispered.

For a time, she did.

Bay Saint Louis slid past in the night. He stopped at a rest area five miles further on, got out of the car and paced for ten minutes in the rain. When he came back to the car, she was waiting for him.

They pulled back out on the interstate. "What do you want?" he asked.

"Justice," whispered the rain beneath the tires.

A green exit sign flashed by: WAVELAND, PASS CHRISTIAN. Time had distorted, accelerating with the Trans Am till it seemed only seconds passed before the next exit whipped by. When he looked at her next, she was young and beautiful. Her hair shone like fire in the exit's lights.

She stretched her leg over the center console, sliding it alongside his until she found the accelerator pedal with her foot. His hand came down quite naturally on her knee, finding it soft and sensuous. She placed her foot atop his and pushed. He didn't resist as the T.A. picked up speed.

Roxanne leaned close, one hand finding his where it lay on her knee, the other brushing the wet hair back from his ear. Her breath was warm on his neck. "Am I pretty?" Her voice was a whisper, tremulous with insecurity, the voice of a girl struggling to become a woman. The car had begun to shake. The speedometer needle fluttered around a hundred.

"It's not so bad being dead," she told him. She reached out and took hold of the wheel. "You'll see." She directed the car over on the shoulder and held it there.

At the farthest reaches of the T.A.'s high beams, Bill could make out the bridge. She was steering the car on a direct course for where the railing sloped down to join the pavement. He imagined the car hitting it, ramping up and out through the darkness, arcing over Wolf River and finally coming down to impact against the far bank. At more than a hundred miles an hour there'd be little left.

She kissed his cheek. Her breath reeked of death and decay.

Bill took his hand off the wheel and lay back against the seat. He was suddenly so very tired. *Let Roxanne drive,* he thought. *After all, she knows the way.* He fought the urge to laugh hysterically.

She held the car's course, unwavering. The engine was screaming like… like the night he and Martin had pushed it up to 140.

As the bridge loomed nearer, she took his hand and put it on her little girl's breast. He could feel the sharp outline of fragile ribs beneath her soft flesh.

Suddenly, there was an ear-splitting explosion and the hood jumped as if struck an incredible blow from inside. Oil blew out across the windshield. Flame shot briefly from the hood scoop. The headlights flickered and died. The drone of the big engine was replaced by the soft whisper of the tires.

Roxanne Ladner was gone, the only reminder she'd been there a cloying hint of decay in the car and a chill where she'd touched him.

Deceleration pulled Bill forward. His eyes sought the bridge railing in the gloom. Would he still have enough speed when he hit it?

A hand fell lightly on his shoulder. He looked down and found delicate, familiar fingers, one adorned with the ring he'd bought her. In the rearview mirror he found her face.

"Stop the car, Bill."

Her eyes in the mirror were bright, loving. In them he found no accusations, no reproach, no condemnations, only love and understanding. Forgiveness too.

His hands found the steering wheel. His foot found the brake pedal. The wheels locked up and the car slid.

"Easy," Kim coached from the back seat.

He got the car under control, slid to a halt just short of the bridge. He rested his head against the wheel and shook for several minutes. When he lifted his head and looked, the back seat was as empty as the passenger side of the car. All his ghosts had left him. The Trans Am clicked and hissed, spilling its fluids out on the road, lifeless.

It was over.

A few minutes later headlights glared off the back window and someone pulled in behind him. Bill watched in the side mirror as a cautious highway patrolman got out and approached the car. He rolled down his window when the cop shone a flashlight inside.

"Car trouble?"

"I think the engine blew."

The cop frowned. "Just how fast were you going?"

"Don't know," Bill lied. "I think I might have fallen asleep at the wheel."

"Dangerous thing to do. You could have gone off the road."

"Yes, sir, I know."

The cop clicked off the flashlight. "Come on, I'll give you a ride to the next exit. There's a 24-hour service station there."

Bill got out, leaving the keys in the car, not bothering to

roll the window back up. The patrol car was warm and dry. He fought the urge to close his eyes as they went over the bridge, but the bridge was empty.

"Where are you heading?" asked the cop.

Bill had to think about that one. Finally he said, "Home."

The cop looked over at him. "Which is...?"

"Gulfport." He was surprised at how right it sounded.

They rode in silence until the cop looked at his watch. "Damn, look at the time. It's after midnight already."

"Wednesday," Bill muttered.

"Huh?"

"Ash Wednesday," Bill told him. "The first day of Lent."

AND THOUGH A MILLION STARS WERE SHINING

"It grieveth the sun ... to shine upon a man defiled by a corpse; it grieveth the moon; it grieveth the stars."
—Persian Zend Avesta

Bombay, June 6, 1906.

The smell of the gardens rises on the breeze coming in off the Arabian Sea, mingles with the tang of brine and tide much the way I remember the fine perfume of a lady will hang over a London street. The welcome wind is cool as it dries the sweat on my brow. I watch it toy with Kara's fine black hair and ruffle the dark sentinels that ring the tower's edge.

Yes... *sentinels*. I find no better name for them. Dark, silent watchers. Patience takes on new meaning in the depths of their unwavering eyes. Their demeanor is that of one acquainted with an infinite experience in the art of waiting. Though I am an unknown factor in an equation they've solved countless times before, they know how to deal with me. No one ever out waits them.

The majority of them are Himalayan griffons, the most common scavenger in this part of India. Griffons have served the Towers of Silence for centuries, their long, thin bills making short work of the Parsee dead. Pale-brown, sociable birds, they cluster in groups of six or more on the parapet, preening and pecking at each other, whispering among themselves. There's also a strong contingency of Indian white-backs, a few Indian and European blacks, and, remarkably, there's one monstrous lammergeier.

The other vultures have surrendered an ample stretch of parapet to the elusive lammergeier, as if they doubt his documented timidness. Perhaps they're among those who, as I, believe it was a lammergeier that tortured Prometheus for Zeus. Tibetan shepherds have named him "lamb vulture" because they don't believe him shy at all. Campfire tales warn of lammergeiers carrying off sheep and, worse yet, children. Looking at the wingspan on this one, easily ten feet from one primary to the other, and the wickedly curved beak and talons, the tales are not hard to believe. The warm russet of the lammergeier's under-plumage all but fades against the sunset behind him, so that for a moment I think he's left us, but the stirring of his massive wings assures me that he's still there. Waiting, like all the others.

Just last week, what wouldn't I have given to be this close to a lammergeier?

I pull Kara closer, with my arms seek to shield her naked body from their sight. Her flesh is incredibly cold for such a summer night.

As the sun fades, a full moon rises to bathe the hill of Malabar and its seven towers in pale, clean light. Before me spreads a view seen by none but the *Nasasalars*, the Parsee corpse-bearers. The maze of squat white buildings and crooked streets that is Bombay seems richer in this light—as if the buildings are silver; the running sewage, streams of gold; the waste dumps, the burial mounds of ancient kings.

But the Parsees do not bury their dead.

"The prophet Zoroaster taught us that the elements created by God are sacred, Nathaniel," Kara once told me. I recall imploring yet again that Kara call me Nate. Though she did not seem to mind my shortening her name, she always used my full Christian name, as if the word Nate were a Parsee curse of which I was ignorant. "Because the elements are pure, earth, air, fire, and water must never be defiled by a dead body. Our Towers are an efficient and safe method of handling a problem you British are loathe to even acknowledge."

"It's bloody barbaric is what it is, Karamiri!"

The lammergeier *huffs* and spreads his wings, agitated at

the sound of my voice. I eye him coldly. "You're free to take your leave at any time." Several birds do. But the huge lammergeier stays.

"You shan't have her," I hiss, and it seems his black eyes narrow slightly. *We shall see.*

Morbidly fascinated by the Towers and the Zoroastrian solution for disposing of the dead, I researched the issue while in Paris. I was there at the request of the French Ornithological Society to lecture on vultures, specifically those I'd been studying in India for eight months. My Indian assistant, Rajah, accompanied me. It was his first time outside of India, and to my surprise the usually reserved young Parsee found Paris deliciously decadent. While I spent hours buried in a library overlooking the Seine, Rajah did the town. The morning we were to leave, he looked to have been through the Apocalypse.

"You won't tell my sister?" he asked.

So he knew with whom I'd been spending most of my free time. But in his bloodshot eyes there was no anger. "What sort of friend would I be then?" I replied.

"You love her, Nate, don't you?"

Even then, before I'd once held her, before I'd kissed her and felt the velvet touch of her hair and brown skin, there was no doubt in my heart that I loved the delicate Karamiri. I suppose it was written just as clearly on my face, for Rajah had no need to wait for my answer.

"They'll never let you marry her," he said.

"We shall see."

The lammergeier nods his head as if in agreement. "*Gypaëtus barbatus*," I call to him. "Lamb vulture. Bearded vulture. Killer of Aeschylus. I know you." He shakes his wings, unconcerned.

Perhaps I should not be so offended by the Parsees' chosen method of cadaver disposal. Certain of the Kaffir tribes abandon their dead to the tender consideration of the jackal, as do nomads of the plains of Central Asia who even go one step further: they cut the body into small pieces first. In Siberia, the flesh of the dead is given to the dogs, while bones are preserved and religiously treasured. Packs of dogs are kept just for this. The rich have the privilege of owning their own "undertakers."

And what of those cultures who refuse to let go of their dead? In the Islands of Haiti the dead are smoke-cured, dressed in their finest, and hung in the homes of relatives. Egyptians and Etruscans mummify their dead and leave them in house-like tombs. At the monasteries of Krewzberg at Bonn and Capucine at Palermo the mummified bodies of deceased brethren, dressed in the habit of their order, are displayed in the vaults in various life-like attitudes, forming a horribly fascinating exhibition.

Who's to say what's right or wrong when it comes to relinquishing the dead?

The Parsees aren't unique. The vulture also plays a role in the ceremonies of Tibet. With the Himalayan ground frozen most of the year and wood too scarce and expensive to be squandered on cremation, the dead are taken to a "disposer of bodies." He cuts the flesh from the corpse and hand feeds it to Himalayan griffons. The bones are broken and set out for lammergeiers which are known to be especially fond of the marrow. The lammergeier's tongue is a strong, grooved tool specially formed for sucking the marrow from bones.

There are, I suppose, still worse ways to dispose of a cadaver.

Several griffons wheel about the tower in the last bit of light, finally settling among the others. "*Gyps himalayensis,*" I dub them. "I know you too."

The stars are just beginning to appear, dampened somewhat by the intensity of the full moon, but brilliant none-the-less. Bathed in their light, Kara's body is as sleekly beautiful as a gazelle.

"See," I whisper to her, "to the north there's Polaris, with Draco and Hercules." I trace their outlines in the warm air between us. "Leo and Virgo overhead. Gemini to the west. Serpens to the east. There's Hydra and Centaurus to the south. Look, you can see Venus and Mars. There. To the northwest."

And a million stars in between.

"Stars are eternal," she told me once as we lay beneath this same night sky, "like my love for you. As long as there are stars in the sky, I will always love you, Nathaniel." I remember holding her, smelling her hair, warm and content against the fragile curve of her body, satisfied with the fact that we'd always have stolen moments like this... oblivious to the dark towers rising above us on the hill, obstructing our view of countless more stars. "I wish we could be wed," she added.

I smiled at her there in the moonlight, kissed the down at the nape of her neck. "Your parents will eventually come to accept me, Kara. We need but wait another year or two."

But we weren't given that long.

One of the black vultures suddenly drops from the tower's low wall and hops several feet toward us. I hiss at him and he retreats, but he does not reclaim his original position. Several others join him. The lammergeier merely watches.

"How is it that I once found you so intriguing?" I ask them. Their bald heads and scrawny necks gleam in starlight that refuses to shine from their black beaks. Hundreds of impenetrable eyes, unblinking, focus on me. *Leave. We have work to do.*

"You shan't have her," I repeat.

A ruffling of feathers. A shifting of talons and a snapping of vicious beaks. They can wait.

Everyone wore white. They wouldn't let me see her. "The women will prepare the body," Rajah explained. Even so, I would not have been allowed to be alone with her. Zoroastrian superstitions. As soon as someone dies, the demons of corruption, the dreaded *Nasu,* take control of the body. Anyone near the corpse is in danger of corruption. The body is washed by women, dressed in clean white clothes, and placed on a stone slab to shield the sacred earth from evil. Throughout this process, no one is allowed to be alone with the corpse for fear they might be overcome by the *Nasu*. Sacred fires, fed sandalwood chips by Parsee priests, are burned to clear the room of infection and help keep the evil spirits at bay.

"Absurdities," I whisper to the night. "The four-eyed dog. The chanting from the *Zend Avesta*." Rajah explained that the sacred verses not only ward off demons, but remind the mourners of the shortness of life.

And then the *Nasasalars* came to take the body and lead the procession to Malabar and its solemn towers. The vultures, as if they'd known for days, were already gathering. The bed where

Karamiri had lain was disinfected with *gomez*, more of which was sprinkled behind the procession as it made its way through Bombay.

"Bull urine," I laugh hollowly. "What kind of people clean with bull urine?"

But I'd found them noble in other ways. Proud and beautiful. With none so beautiful as the woman now cold in my arms.

The procession wound out of the city and up the hill to the garden at the top. The most beautiful garden in India. The most beautiful garden I have seen anywhere. Through the iron gates, past the tall green trees… to the Towers of Silence.

The Towers rise thirty feet high, measure almost three hundred feet in circumference. Squat round fortresses, they were built to protect the living from the dead. Atop the towers, the dead meet the vultures naked and alone. Whatever barriers of wealth or birth may have separated individuals in life, they face this last ordeal as equals. In three days' time, the *Nasasalars* return to sweep the sun-bleached bones into the hollow center of the tower… where all becomes dust.

"When I die, and the vultures have consumed my body," Kara explained when she first fell ill, "I will cross the Chinvat Bridge which arches over the blackest hell to the mountain of paradise."

"Don't be silly, Kara. You're not going to die," I told her. "So long as there are stars in the sky, you're mine to hold. Remember?"

She smiled, but in her fawn-like eyes I saw that she knew I was lying.

I asked Rajah about the Chinvat Bridge.

"Wicked souls are met on the bridge by a freezing, foul wind and a hideous hag. The hag is their conscience made ugly by bad deeds done in life. For this person," Rajah explained, "the Chinvat bridge becomes narrower and narrower until it's as thin as a razor's edge, whereupon the wicked soul falls shrieking into the pit of hell. The dogs that guard the bridge howl and howl, sending the spirit deeper into darkness, into the House of Lies."

"And for the righteous soul?"

"They are met by a warm scented breeze and a beautiful young maiden. The dogs lead the righteous across a bridge that grows wider with every step until the soul steps into paradise."

Handed down from ancient Persians, Zoroaster's theology has become a part of the Parsee culture. In my research in Paris, I found the Persians to have a great fear of all burial grounds. They look upon the light of the sun and the purity of the air as a birthright from which, even in death, they refuse to be separated. The thought of walling up the body or placing it in the dark depths of the earth holds a special terror in their minds. They believe that, in death, the sun demands a return of the life-giving elements from each individual. What is decomposition, the Persian argues, save the natural process by which the material elements are given back to the sun from which comes all life? And the vulture, they believe, comes to bear the soul away to paradise.

"Her soul is mine!" I scream at the vultures. Those that have drawn near take to the air in a burst of black wings and startled cries. Briefly, they careen above the tower, settling in short order to their previous watch posts on the parapet, where they proceed to argue amongst themselves.

All but the lammergeier, which remains stoically silent. It's in his nature to wait. When the others are sated he comes for the bones and their sweet marrow.

Vultures are not without their myths and legends: Prometheus was sentenced to have his liver torn out daily by a vulture; it was a lammergeier that dropped a tortoise on the head of the poet, Aeschylus; the Greeks claimed the feather of a vulture would ease childbirth, ward off snake bites, and cure blindness; the Incas of Peru believed the vulture to be a messenger from the sun-god, lifting the sun into the sky each day; the dried heart of the vulture cures epilepsy; the vulture's eye, cooked and eaten, improves a man's eyesight; drinking vulture blood prolongs life. There are hundreds more.

"But you're just eaters of carrion," I tell the lammergeier. He cocks his head at me, the mask of black bristles about his eyes and beak waving in the wind. "You eat, you digest, you defecate. There's nothing spiritual about it. The Parsees think their towers beautiful, but I find them nothing more than foul rookeries coated in vulture dung and misery.

"With your eyesight—*seven times keener than mine!*—can you see where my Kara is going, lammergeier?"

The moon as it walks the southern hemisphere from east to west has caught a gleam in his eye, and it makes him look suddenly wise as he studies me across the tower. *Of course I know where she's going,* those owl-like eyes say. *She's going where we all go in time. With our help, she'll get there a little faster.*

I see it in my mind. The griffons will strip every ounce of flesh from her bones once the sharper beaks of the blacks and white-backs have begun the task. The lammergeier will hold back; it's the bones he craves. I've watched the merciless group strip a mountain goat in less than thirty minutes, leaving the lammergeier behind crunching bones.

I can't let that happen to Kara.

My love has grown heavy in my arms. My legs have gone numb against the hard stone. Already it is past midnight and nothing has come to me. Though the parapet shields me from the sight of those below, what did I hope to accomplish by scaling the tower? I wanted to hold her just one more time, and now I've done that. I wanted to say goodbye without chanting priests smothering me in sandalwood smoke, but there are no goodbyes potent enough to ease this great emptiness in my heart. I wanted to be alone with her, but the birds have made that impossible.

The vultures stir, begin again to inch closer.

"Would that I could have loved you an eternity, my Karamiri, my Indian princess." My tears fall and paint her face in opal moonlight.

I've but three days to love you. Three nights to share the stars and dream.

And then you'll be gone.

But none shall take you across that bridge save me.

I'll need help with the bones. I look to the lammergeier there at the tower's rim. He is ready... waiting.

THE SCISSOR MAN

When the green field comes off like a lid,
Revealing what was much better hid—
Unpleasant:
And look, behind you without a sound
The woods have come up and are standing round
In deadly crescent.
The bolt is sliding in its groove;
Outside the window is the black remover's van:
And now with sudden swift emergence
Come the hooded women, the hump-backed surgeons,
And the Scissor Man.

—W.H. Auden

Because there was nothing more they could do to ease Maggie on her way, and because he insisted so, the hospital allowed David Hunter to take his wife home to die.

Oddly enough, the same ambulance and paramedics that had transported her to the hospital took her home. It was a different ride. No lights, no sirens. No one taking vital signs and phoning them ahead to the hospital. The driver, who on that previous ride had spoken comforting words of encouragement to David, was solemn and quiet. No more "Everything's going to be fine, Mr. Hunter," or "We'll have her at the hospital in a jiff, sir; they'll know what to do." This was a different ride, at the end of which there waited no battle for life, no army of veterans in white masks, no miracle cure, no experimental drugs, no treatments, no therapy, no hope, no life.

This was retreat. This was surrender. And the only surgeon waiting for Maggie was Death himself.

The paramedics took her in the house and made her comfortable in her bed. Just as well that they'd brought her home, for David could have never carried her up the stairs of their tiny apartment. She weighed next to nothing, but after two weeks sleeping in the hospital waiting room or a chair by her side, David was beyond exhaustion. At sixty-two he felt himself an unfit opponent for the stress of Maggie's illness. It would have been better if *he'd* gotten the cancer. Dying, he could have dealt with. Watching her go was another matter altogether.

Either the ride home had tired her or the familiarity of her own bed was too much to resist, for Maggie dropped into a sound sleep before David had even shown the paramedics out. Tenderly, he covered her frail body with the comforter she'd made the summer before, her last comforter as it were. Then he went down to the kitchen to fix himself a sandwich and check their stock of soup for when she awoke. His mother used to swear by Campbell's Chicken Noodle. There was no sickness, she'd claimed, immune to the goodness of Campbell's. David remembered days as a boy curled up on the sofa watching television. The flu or an ear infection or some equally dreaded malady had kept him home from school. He'd drunk the soup from a mug, the warm broth coating his sore throat, the noodles slipping effortlessly from mug to stomach as if there was nothing between but a giant water slide. He remembered the lazy warmth of a full stomach of soup, the bloated, happy comfort that would lull him to sleep there on the couch.

I hope death comes for her like a bowl of soup, he thought. I hope it's warm and dreamy and as soft as that old sofa. Remembering the smell and the taste of death on Maggie's lips, he added, I hope that death tastes like Campbell's soup. I hope—

A knock at the back door startled him. Through the lacy mauve curtains Maggie'd hung, he saw their neighbor Carolyn looking anxious and concerned. Setting aside the knife he'd been using to spread mayonnaise, he went and let her in. P.D., their Schnauzer, dashed into the kitchen, barking and leaping frantically until David picked him up. "Hey, fella," he said, accepting several licks on the nose. "Did you miss me? Were you a good boy for Carolyn?"

"I called the hospital," Carolyn said, wringing her hands, "just to see if you needed anything. I was, you know, thinking I'd bring you some things when I came to visit this evening. But they said… they said Maggie'd been discharged."

David pushed the door closed behind her. "Yeah. They let me bring her home."

"Home?" Carolyn made it sound like a foreign country. "When does she… have to go back?"

"She doesn't," David replied bluntly, immediately regretting it because Carolyn had been their friend for over ten years, ever since her husband had died in an industrial accident and she'd been forced to sell her home and take the apartment across the courtyard. David put P.D. down and took her hands. "Carolyn, there's nothing more they can do." Watching as her eyes filled with tears, it all came rushing in on him. After thirty-seven years of Maggie's voice being the last thing he heard every night and the first thing he heard every morning, she'd be gone. After all those years watching her cook in this very kitchen, watching her climb those stairs to the bedroom, watching her sew in front of the television in the living room, she'd be gone. Just like that. Gone. The apartment would echo hollowly without her. He'd be all alone. Worse than alone, for he'd be alone with the memories of when he hadn't been alone.

"Maggie's come home," he whispered hoarsely, "to die."

And then he was sobbing on her shoulder, crying like a baby while she cried too. She stroked his back and told him it would be all right, but of course it wouldn't.

After Carolyn left, David ate his sandwich while watching the evening news. War and murder. Drive-by shootings and gang violence. Another corrupt politician and another bomb threat. Maybe checking out altogether was the right idea. Switching off the television, he was confronted by his own reflection in the black screen. He was surprised by how skeletal his visage had become. As if it were contagious, he'd acquired Maggie's wasted appearance.

The skeleton, he knew, was a long-standing symbol of death. With the erosion of time, the skeleton reveals itself. Death sullies forth. *We carry death inside us,* he thought. Death is ensconced in the body, lurking in our bones and tissues, becoming more and more apparent every day. As Plato proposed a suprasensible essence behind the surface of things in this world, so death would lie hidden somewhere behind the epidermis. Death underlies life, and time's purpose is to peel successive layers so as to render it ever more visible.

When exactly do we begin dying? At birth? In that case, life was a series of partial destructions strewn along the road of individual existence, culminating eventually in total destruction. It was a depressing line of thought, even in his present state of mind, but somewhere within him there was an evil chuckle that said it was all true. He tried to convince himself otherwise. *If life is a series of little deaths,* he reasoned, *then the final death would hold no terror for anyone.*

His sandwich was bland. When he offered it to P.D. and the finicky Schnauzer ate it without hesitation, he knew it was his taste buds and not the sandwich's flavor that had gone on hiatus. He gave the dog water and let him out in the yard. As the dog began making his rounds, David was unexpectedly overcome by a memory: "What'll we name him?" he'd asked Maggie after several days of calling him nothing but Puppy Dog.

"I don't know," she'd said. "What was the name of that funny dog on *The Little Rascals*?"

"Petey?"

"Yeah, that's the one. Petey. Let's call him P.D. Pee. Dee. The letters. Only say it like *The Little Rascals'* Petey. P.D.—short for Puppy Dog."

That was Maggie: creative. Nothing ever had one meaning with Maggie. She saw beyond the obvious, insisted on depth and originality in everything they did, even naming a stupid dog. If you asked her what color the sky was, you could expect anything but blue for an answer. She had the most incredible way of seeing *every* side of an argument. She was the only person he'd ever met who could disagree with someone by first admitting that they were right.

While P.D. was outside, David warmed up some soup in the microwave. Afterward, he locked up the house, gave P.D. a dog biscuit, and climbed the stairs, hitting light switches as he went. Maggie was still asleep, her breathing shallow and irregular. Because he hated to wake her—she'd gotten so little sleep in the hospital, what with all their needles and intrusive tests—he set the soup on the nightstand and got ready for bed himself. It wasn't until he was crawling into bed beside her that she awoke.

"Sorry, I didn't mean to wake you."

"That's all right."

"Are you hungry?"

She glanced at the soup with obvious disinterest. "No. Just tired. I feel like I could sleep forever." A shiver crept up his spine at those words, and Maggie saw his reaction. "Sorry." She reached out and touched his face. "Thank you for bringing me home, darling."

He shrugged. "This is where you belong."

A slight nod. "I couldn't stand another day of having those nurses waiting on me. You know how I hate having others in charge of me."

David kissed her on the cheek. "I know, sweetheart."

"At least the cancer won't outlive me. If nothing else, it's murdered itself."

He was quiet, as always at a loss for words when their conversation became dark and the subject was her dying. Silence reigned for several minutes. Because silence was what he had to look forward to and what he feared most, he felt compelled to break it, to hear her voice while there was still time. "Carolyn was here earlier."

"P.D.?"

"Downstairs, eating his biscuit."

"He likes those new barbecue ones."

"I know."

"I'm glad I missed Carolyn. Her first words would have been, 'How are you?'" Maggie rubbed at her eyes. They were already red and rheumy, worse when she was done. "God, what a thoughtless question. There's no acceptable answer to it, Davey. I can either tell her I'm fine, which is a lie, or I can tell her I'm dying, which is as brutal and unnecessary as it is true."

"Maggie—"

"It's as bad as the nurses calling out 'Good morning!' and throwing open the blinds every damn morning. They're just checking to see if I'm still alive. Carolyn, though she means well, is doing the same thing by stopping over. If she comes back in the morning, tell her I'm sleeping, Davey. I mean it. I don't want to see anyone. I'd really rather just be alone."

He wondered momentarily whether that included him.

"I can understand why elephants have a special, secret place for this."

He shuddered again.

Maggie took his hand. "I'm doing it again, aren't I? You'll remember me as a bitch if I'm not careful."

"Nonsense." He kissed the back of her hand. "Are you… are you in any pain?"

"No," she assured him, and then added darkly: "I think the cancer has mercifully eaten away my pain centers. I don't feel a thing."

He thought it more likely that the morphine shot they'd given her before she left the hospital was still doing its job. He made a mental note to check her again in a few hours. The hospital had given him codeine tablets for her to take when the pain set in. They'd also told him he could call the paramedics for additional morphine shots if the codeine wasn't effective. Relieving the pain was the only thing they could do for her now.

"I'm just incredibly—" She yawned. "—tired."

He kissed her again. "Sleep then, my Maggie May. I'll be here when you wake up."

A sweet smile. "I know you will, Davey. Do you think maybe you could hold me though?"

He took her in his arms, and she dropped off immediately. Though he was exhausted himself, sleep eluded him for some time. He contented himself by watching her sleep, feeling the warmth of her against him, the rhythmic movement of her breathing, the weight of her on the mattress beside him. He tried not to think about a time when it would not be so. The moon looked through the bedroom window and bathed her thin, haggard face in angelic light. P.D. came up the stairs and took up his usual spot on the foot of the bed. In time, David fell asleep.

There was no noise, no commotion, no tinkling of broken glass or the sharp crack of a forced lock to wake him. There was just a sudden overwhelming fear. A sense of wrongness. A foreboding presence that manifested itself in the fabric of his sleep and brought him screaming from the bed.

From their bedroom it was possible to look down over a wrought iron railing to the stairway landing and the living room below. Leaning out, David strained at the darkness, trying to determine what, if anything, had invaded his home and set his heart to racing so. The moon was pouring in the landing window and the stairway should have been well lit, but it wasn't. The stairwell was a black pool, inky deep and impenetrable. There was a thick, visible texture to the penumbra at the base of the stairs. As David strained to penetrate its nebulous core, he saw it was slowly, silently advancing.

He realized—no, *sensed*—that it was evil. More than evil. It surpassed evil. More than just the absence of good, this was an end to all things.

"Go away!" he screamed.

The shadows lengthened, stretching up the stairs in tendrils which swapped grey reality for black empty. It seemed now that he could see shifting silhouettes in the midst of the black: elongated, distorted limbs; clawed hands; gaping mouths and eyes darker than the surrounding gloom.

In the stand by the bed was his thirty-eight caliber revolver. He aimed down the stairway, shivering despite the warm summer night and the apartment's inadequate air conditioning. The barrel wavered uncontrollably, but by this time the darkness had spread, floor to ceiling, halfway up the stairs. There was no way he could miss it.

"Get out of here!" he shouted. "I'll shoot. I swear I will!"

The darkness advanced.

The roar of the gun was deafening. "Go away!" David screamed. As the presence continued to ooze up the stairs, he emptied the revolver. The flash from the muzzle lit the landing below, but failed to penetrate the intangible barrier coming up the stairs.

And then he was awake, sitting up in the bed, the sheets clinging to him with cold sweat. The soup he'd left on the night stand had been overturned. It was on his arm and dripping softly over the sides of the stand and into the carpet. Otherwise, everything was quiet and normal. The room was still lit by a brilliant, full moon. Though the recognizable shapes of his furniture were muted by darkness and the monochrome night, he could see everything—and *everything* appeared to be in order.

Careful not to wake Maggie, he slipped from the bed and peered cautiously down the stairs. The stairwell was empty. So, too, the stretch of living room at the base of the stairs. Nothing had invaded his home. The thirty-eight was still in the drawer by the bed, untouched and certainly unfired.

He'd had a bad dream. That was all. A nightmare. Everyone had them. And yet...

Death had come for Maggie.

He got a towel from the bathroom and wiped the sweat from his face. It wasn't until he was using the same towel to mop up the soup that he realized P.D. was missing.

Life advances by burying things. Dead things. Unwanted things. Debris, detritus, flotsam and jetsam. The things we cast off for one reason or another. The things we can't take with us.

When he was thirty-five, David buried his writing career, taking the three novels that he'd written, but couldn't sell, and burning them, a page at a time. He settled into tenure and committed himself to teaching other young hopefuls the beauty of English composition. None of them asked, *What have* you *published, Mr. Hunter? If you profess this mastery of language, why haven't you used it?* They were focused on their own futures and cared little about the greying man who might have been someone if only he'd found the proper voice. If only he'd found the right editor, the right publisher, the right agent. If only he'd had the money to write full time. If only he'd written the type of novel the public wanted to read, instead of the type of novel he had wanted to write. If only his manuscripts hadn't been *buried* beneath so many others.

Maggie had buried her dreams too. She'd buried the money they'd saved for her medical education in a vain attempt to get their son out of a Chilean prison. He swore the drugs weren't his, that he'd never seen them before, but the authorities had their own evidence and weren't inclined to believe him. It didn't matter whether David and Maggie believed him. It only mattered that he was their only son. In the end, all the bribes, all the political contributions (and weren't those the same thing?), had amounted to nothing. And when the day came when the embassy called and told them their son had died of pneumonia in prison, they buried him too. The money they'd saved was gone—and even if it hadn't been, Maggie's heart was no longer in it. So she settled on being an Emergency Medical Technician, which sounded exciting and important, but was in reality the grunt position of the emergency room. She emptied bed pans. She mopped blood and brains from the floor. She cleaned urine and feces from the bodies of the insane, the senile, and the just plain ugly. She buried her future in hours of drudgery.

When nineteen-year-old Christie Claremont sued David for an A in English Lit, they lost the house and were forced to take up residence in an old apartment complex where the only good thing was Carolyn across the courtyard. Okay, so the Claremont bitch had really sued him for sexual harassment, but he was innocent. He knew that. And maybe Maggie did too, but a piece of the trust that lay between them, however small a piece it may have been, was buried on the day the court ordered them to pay. They might have made it out of the red, but then Maggie got sick and was eventually forced to quit her job.

We bury these things and we move on. We try our best not to look back because going back and fixing them isn't an option. There is only forward—where there'll be still more things to bury. They're obligations and responsibilities that can't be shirked, these dreams we've yet to lose. We do our duty and we bury them and we try to forget, but Death has both a standing appointment and a sense of humor. When he comes, he digs them up, torments us with their recollection while he's reminding us that we're only human, and he is perhaps the *only* immortal.

When he comes, he never leaves empty-handed.

That morning, before the sun was quite up, before the apartment complex became a buzz of activity as people left for work, David Hunter buried his dog in the small wooded field separating them from the interstate.

Maggie ate some dry toast and a few mouthfuls of oatmeal with cinnamon. She was noticeably weaker and her color had gotten worse. Her skin had taken on an ashen grey hue that reminded David of an impending storm. Not the violent, lightning and thunder kind, but a storm that would drizzle softly, dying out sometime late afternoon with no one even noticing it had ended though they'd complained all day long about the rain.

The pain set in after she ate. Or maybe, as he really suspected, she woke up with it and suffered as long she could before she told him. He tanked her up on codeine, doubling the maximum recommended dosage because it really didn't matter if she became addicted. The pain subsided after about twenty minutes, but there was a stiffness to her jawline, a clenching of the teeth and a haunted look in her eyes that told him the pain wasn't completely gone.

She slept some more. He cleaned up the kitchen, climbing the stairs every so often to check on her. He called the university and spoke briefly with the grad student covering his classes. He watched television. He tried, but couldn't get her to eat anything for lunch. He paced. He watched out the window as kids on summer vacation ramped their bicycles over an old sheet of plywood set on some bricks. He picked some roses from one of Carolyn's bushes and left them beside the bed for Maggie. He vacuumed the living room floor. He dusted Maggie's collection of crystal elephants. He took out the trash, throwing in P.D.'s water bowl.

He tried not to think.

About.

Anything.

In this manner, the day slipped by. It took a lifetime.

In our dreams, we touch other worlds.

We can touch Heaven and Hell. People and places and times we've lost or never even known. We can fly. We can breathe underwater. We can touch the face of God and stand toe to toe with Death. In our dreams we can reach from here to there on some metaphysical level where the ethereal boundaries of the subconscious and the subliminal replace those of physical reality.

We don't always know or remember where we've been or what we've done. The subconscious has selective amnesia built in as a defense mechanism for the mind. Without it, if we always remembered the places we'd touched in our sleep, many of us would go insane.

David knew what he had done.

Death had come to claim its own, and David had met and withstood the Grim Reaper in some alternate dimension where dream and reality collide. Petulant, ever the sore loser, Death had taken P.D. instead.

There was no other explanation. The dog was still young, barely five years old, and in perfect health. There'd been no obvious injury or sign of illness. His heart had simply stopped beating. David had known as soon as he saw P.D. was missing from the foot of the bed. Finding P.D.'s cold, limp body on the living room floor had merely confirmed it.

In our dreams we touch upon that place from whence comes Death. Perhaps, we even touch Death itself. Who's to say how close we come to dying each and every night we lay down to sleep? Our hearts slow down. Our breathing becomes shallow and insouciant. David was reminded of an Ingmar Bergman film, *Wild Strawberries,* in which death is portrayed as sleep. The movie's last scene shows the protagonist in a deep sleep and everything seems to slow down. There was also a French poet, whose name he could not remember, who had said, *"Dormir, c'est essayer la mort."* To sleep is to try on death.

When we sleep, our minds reach out in an effort to find some focus, some temporary distraction for those hours in which the body, which must shut down and regenerate, is an inattentive suitor. And if in that quest for amusement, we happen to stumble in the path of Death on his errands, who's to say we can't sidetrack him? Lacking a physical presence, it is, after all, just a contest of wills.

While many people would have had trouble believing that they had confronted Death, David did not. Because of what he stood to lose, he had no choice but to believe. With Maggie's life at stake, he couldn't help but desire a repeat encounter.

Do you remember," David asked, "when we went to Fall Creek Falls in Tennessee?"

He'd been asking her things like that for several hours, holding her there on the bed. The questions were only to fill the silence, the memories they brought to the surface to fill her last hours with something pleasant. She didn't answer. She hadn't actually spoken since a little after noon. Her eyes were vacant and her pulse was shallow. Whatever battle she waged had turned inward.

It was his turn now, and while he awaited the opponent, he painted the dark room with memories of the good times they'd shared. The more of them he remembered, the more of them there were to remember, and he knew that despite all the hardships and buried dreams, they'd been happy.

"It was autumn, and we had almost the entire park to ourselves. Remember all the trails and the overlooks? We found that one overlook that was so secluded. You wanted to make love there on the edge of the world with all of the Smokies spread out before us, but I was too worried someone would come down the trail and catch us in the act."

He'd turned off all the lights. Moonbeams stenciled the room. The lace pattern of the curtains there. The perpendicular lines of the divided window on the far wall there. A distorted square splashed from the vanity mirror across the carpet. There was a geometric order to the night that he'd never before noticed. He took courage from this rhyme and reason, almost believing he'd imagined the night before. *This is absurd,* he thought. *Here I am waiting for the Angel of Death like it's someone or something I can reason with.* He laughed at himself and jokingly told Maggie she should be glad she wouldn't be around to see the men in their white coats come take him away and fit him for a special jacket.

"Remember that red Mustang I used to own when we were dating? I put more work into that car than all the others we've owned since. 'Course some of those nights when I said it wouldn't start, and we'd have to stay out until the engine cooled, you knew I was making it up, didn't you, Maggie?"

When the shadows deepened and the patterns lost their logic, when the moon-drawn lines bent and the squares of light folded in and swallowed themselves, he knew he wasn't crazy. Setting Maggie's head carefully on the pillow, he went to the railing and looked down on the stairs, braving the encroaching darkness this time without his revolver.

Am I dreaming or am I awake? he wondered. Or is this some place in between?

The turmoil of darkness was again advancing up the stairway.

"You can skip the melodramatics," David told the dark cloud. "I know who and what you are."

The demarcation of true night and false paused on the stairs, looking almost puzzled in its momentary hesitation.

"Show yourself for what you are," David commanded. "I'm not afraid—" (This, a lie that he hoped did not seem obvious.) "—and I don't intend to step aside." (Truth.) "Dispense with this facade and show your face."

He wasn't sure what he expected. A robed figure with protracted, skeletal fingers wrapped about the handle of a scythe? No, that was too garish, too cliché, too… Hollywood. He expected something simpler. Death revealed would be bourgeois. Death without his masks would be as inconspicuous as the mailman. Death would be the lovely actress Maria Casarès in Jean Cocteau's *Orpheus*. Death in black would not be skeletal, but rather like the character in Bergman's *The Seventh Seal*: dark of robe and white of face, but with nothing frightening or terrifying in his serene, regular features.

What he least expected was a crowded stairway.

There was a slim, dark young man in a black tux, an inexplicable pair of silver scissors protruding from his breast pocket. Behind him was a line of women, their feminine curves more accentuated than hidden by long, heavy robes, their faces concealed within the folds of dark hoods. Flanking the line of hooded women, was a line of surgeons, their hospital scrubs glistening with blood and gore as if they'd just come from some horrific triage, their rubber-gloved hands full of surgical instruments that appeared to have never been washed, let alone sterilized.

The man in the tux arched one Napoleonic eyebrow. "You've a reason for stopping me?" He withdrew a notebook from an inside pocket, flipped a few pages, and made a production out of consulting the data contained therein. "Hunter. David Allen." The dark eyes rose from the page to gaze up the stairs at David. "You haven't a great deal of time, Mr. Hunter, but your appointment was *not* tonight."

"You've come to take my wife," David stammered.

The dark man pursed his lips and snapped the notebook closed. "I see."

"I—" David forced his hands to release the wrought iron rail and rubbed absently at the painful indentations in his palms. "I can't let you have her."

"Can't?"

David swallowed. "Can't."

The dark young man indicated the remaining stairs. "May I?"

David shook his head. "I'd prefer you not come any closer." The absurdity of the situation suddenly set in. He fought an insane urge to bust out laughing. He hadn't expected Death to be so... polite.

"Then we have ourselves a dilemma here, Mr. David Allen Hunter." He glanced at his entourage, then at the moon shining through the window on the landing, then back up at David. "You've obviously realized that I can't proceed without your permission."

David blinked. Death needed *his* permission?

"I suppose we'll have to leave."

David shrugged and tried to smile, but it came out a grimace. "Don't forget to lock up on your way out."

No one laughed.

The tuxedoed man scratched his chin and leaned against the handrail with one foot a step higher than the other. For a moment, he held this pose, as if he were deep in thought. Finally, he looked up. "You love this woman?"

"More than anything."

"And you think she loves you?"

"I know she does."

"Hmmm... Interesting. What if I told you there were things about her you don't know. What if I told you she had lied to you for... let's see—" He consulted his notebook. "Ah, yes, here it is—thirty-seven years."

"It won't work."

"What won't work?"

"Your lies."

"Lies?" The dark man looked genuinely wounded. "My dear friend, there is nothing so honest as Death. Do you really know who I am?" He withdrew the scissors from his pocket and took a few practice snips at the air. "I am the Scissor Man, the Remover, the Collector of Spirits. I come for the soul. With these scissors—" He held the nondescript silver instruments up for David's inspection. "—I separate the spirit from the flesh. If you dissuade me, you condemn her soul to perish with her physical remains. Nothing, and I do mean *nothing*, of her will live on.

"You don't want that, do you?"

David found himself at a loss for words. What did he want? He wanted Maggie to be with him forever. He didn't think he knew how to go on without her.

While David hesitated, the Scissor Man advanced to the landing and several steps beyond, his entourage following close behind. David dashed from the railing to the head of the stairs to cut him off.

"You said you couldn't come any further without my permission!"

The Remover of Souls smiled sadly. "You gave it, Hunter. You don't know it, but you did." By this time, he had reached the top of the stairs. Despite his convictions, David fell back before him, terrified of the dark eyes, the dispassionate set of his thin mouth, the gleaming scissors.

"Please," David begged. "Don't take my wife."

One of the surgeons stepped forward and whispered something in the Scissor Man's ear. As he did, David got a close look at the surgeon's face. The skin was transparently thin and drawn, as if pulled by some inner vacuum until it was stretched like a worn rubber glove, leaving the bone visible beneath it. The surgeon's teeth were yellow and grey, held by more bone than gum. His ears were pale languets pinned to the side of his head by the band of a surgical cap. His eyes were protuberant, red-rimmed and pus-colored. He stank like road-rotted flesh. He moved as if his bones were linked with baling wire.

There was no way on Earth David was going to allow one of them near his wife.

The Scissor Man frowned. "You're probably right," he said to the surgeon. "Brutal, but right." He glanced at Maggie. "She must have once been a very beautiful woman, Hunter."

"Stay away from her," David hissed.

"Would you like to see her when she was… say, in her early twenties?" The Scissor Man indicated the hooded women who had by this time climbed the stairs and spread out along the bedroom walls. "These are Maggie's Memories. Each of them has captured some fragment of your wife's mind, some element of who and what she was, some piece of the events that made her Maggie."

"Vampires," David spat. He could easily imagine such monsters, the source for every case of Alzheimer's and senile dementia. "They're sucking away everything she was so that in the end there'll be nothing but a shell!"

"Oh, no, David. No. This is preservation, not theft. This has been going on since the day she was born. Let me show you." The Remover motioned and one of the hooded women stepped forward and dropped the dark hood down about her shoulders.

It was Maggie.

Maggie when she was about twenty-three years old, her hair full and dark, her skin smooth and firm and burnished with vitality and youth. Her eyes had that lapis lazuli hue that had first attracted him, but had faded over the years to the dull blue of twilight.

The Scissor Man motioned impatiently. "Go on, then, the robe too."

The Memory slipped the robe over her shoulders and let it fall to the floor. David gasped. He had forgotten how beautiful the bare flesh of youth could be. It was like a dagger through his heart, more powerful than any miracle they could have shown him. Still, some part of him felt like a dirty old man. This could be his daughter standing there before him. But, of course, it wasn't. It was Maggie.

She reminded him of Christine Claremont, and that sent another pang of guilt through him. For the first time he realized why he had wanted his student so badly, why he had fallen into the seductive snare she had set. Christine's youthful beauty had represented everything he was one day to lose. He hadn't known it then—at least not consciously. But perhaps some part of him had known that time would take it all away. Perhaps Christine Claremont had even seen that weak link in him from the first.

"She *was* exceptional," the Scissor Man exclaimed.

His words broke the spell. David looked away, embarrassed and ashamed. "Stop," he said weakly. "Make her cover herself."

The Scissor Man seemed not to hear him. "This is what you loved, Hunter. This embodiment of beauty. This sexual prize." He licked his lips, and for the first time David truly hated him. "Nice, very nice."

"Shut up."

"But it's only the flesh. You loved her for her flesh."

"That's not true!"

The Scissor Man pointed the scissors, "You never knew her for what she was. I can prove it."

David feared to say anything.

Another of the hooded women stepped forward and revealed her face. Maggie. Two or three years after they'd married. About the time she'd started college.

"Look into her eyes," commanded the Collector of Spirits and, despite himself, David was too fascinated not to comply.

Mirrors of the soul, they've been called. Windows on inner emotions, true intentions, and the deepest of torment. The eyes remember everything. In Maggie's eyes David saw a stainless-steel table draped in white paper. A woman occupied the table, her legs elevated in stirrups that supported her at calf and heel. There was a nurse to one side. There was a doctor between the woman's legs probing for—David didn't want to know what. When the woman on the table raised her head, he saw that it was Maggie. When blood flowed from her vagina, splattering the crisp, white paper, he saw that this was no simple gynecological exam. David turned away.

"I think," said the Scissor Man, "that they sell drugs for this these days."

Their son had died in a Chilean prison. By that time they were too old to have another child. They'd only had the one because Maggie was so determined, in those early years, to make a medical career for herself. But this... this was a child that could have been with them today.

"She never wanted a family, you know."

"Shut up."

"She would have aborted the second child as well, but you found out, didn't you?"

David suddenly remembered the intercepted phone call, the message he'd taken for Maggie. And he remembered how confused she'd been when she'd come home that evening, and he'd cooked her favorite dinner, complete with wine and flowers and candles. He'd told her how happy he was and at first she'd been confused. When she finally realized what he was celebrating, had she seemed less than excited herself? He couldn't remember. But maybe, just maybe, there'd been more resignation and acceptance than joy in her eyes that night.

Still, it didn't matter. She'd loved their son. In the end, she'd done everything humanly possible to save him.

"You never really knew her," mocked the Scissor Man.

David ignored him. "Dostoyevsky was right," he muttered.

"What? How's that?"

"There are things which we are meant to take with us to the grave."

"Dostoyevsky said this?"

"It's a story he wrote. It's about a dinner party where all the guests agree to tell something bad they did in their past. Everything's going well until one guest tells of an incident which portrays him in the worst possible way. The party is ruined and all the guests excuse themselves and go home. The thing that the man told was just too horrible.

"There are things which we should never reveal, even to those we love. There are things which we are meant to take to the grave."

The Dark Remover indicated the surgeons. "What goes to the grave is theirs, David."

"No."

"Yes. The spirit, the mind, and the body form the trinity." A snip of the scissors. "Her soul is mine. Her mind—her memories—are theirs." He indicated the hooded women. "But her flesh—"

"No!"

Again, one of the surgeons whispered in the dark man's ear. The Scissor Man motioned him away impatiently and, it seemed to David, with something approaching disgust. But the surgeon would not be put off. "Others," he hissed hungrily at David, "have had her flesh."

"What does he mean?" David asked before he could stop himself.

The Scissor Man let out a long sigh.

"Show him," said the surgeon, and the others quickly took it up as a chant. The words whipped around the room like a wave at a ball game, sour and tar-slick wet, doused with spittle and a gluttonous need that terrified David.

"Make them stop!"

The Scissor Man raised a hand and the chant died. Another of the hooded women stepped forward and dropped her hood. Again, it was Maggie, but this Maggie was in her late thirties. In her eyes David saw one of the young ER doctors she used to work with. David recognized him, had seen him at the hospital a time or two. Unable to look away, David watched as the doctor kissed, touched, undressed, and rode like a coquettish bitch the woman who'd been his wife for thirty-seven years.

David's legs tried to go out from under him. He stumbled back to the bed and sat upon its edge. Maggie hadn't moved. She lay there, pale against the white pillow, her face wet with perspiration, revealed to him for the first time.

She'd slept with another man.

He'd never even suspected.

The lines writ so dramatically on her face had concealed the loss of more than her youth from him. She had given a piece of herself to another man, and he had never missed it. How could he have been so blind? How could he have let this happen?

"You were never the man she thought you were," the Remover said softly. "She wanted adventure. She wanted a man who would have made love to her on that mountain top and to hell with anyone who came along, someone who'd take her in a coat closet or the back of a cab if the mood came upon them. She wanted an exuberant writer who took chances, one who wrote out-on-the-edge novels that publishers were afraid to publish, but published anyway because they knew they stood to make millions. She wanted—"

"You're wrong," David yelled, getting back to his feet. "She loved me. *Me*, goddammit! We were married for thirty-seven years and... if there were moments when things weren't perfect... when I failed to pay enough attention to her and she felt the need to—" He swallowed distastefully. "—to sleep with someone from the hospital... well, that didn't change the fact that we were man and wife, that she loved me, that I loved her, and—" He began to cry. "—that you *can't* take her from me like this."

Another of the hooded women stepped forward, but David shoved her back against the wall with such violence that she collapsed. "No!" he screamed. "You can't show me anything that changes the fact that we loved each other." He thrust a finger under the Scissor Man's nose. "You're a lying son of a bitch. You show me things that make her look bad, but for every one of those events, I could show you a hundred good ones. Where are those Memories, you bastard?"

The Scissor Man daintily wiped David's spittle from his

face. "Perhaps it's time to approach this from another angle."

"I've got an angle for you!" David whirled and yanked open the night stand drawer. Snatching up the thirty-eight, he whirled and fired. The Scissor Man stood firm as each of the six rounds thudded into his chest. When the roar of the shots died down, the room was silent except for several spasmodic snaps of the trigger recycling spent rounds. When those stopped, there was not a sound.

The Scissor Man glanced down at the front of his tux. The black material began to take on a darker, wetter shade. The Scissor Man probed one of the holes in his chest and studied the arterial red coating on his finger. "Fascinating." One of the surgeons reached out as if to sample the blood pumping from the Scissor Man's chest, but the Scissor Man snapped the scissors at his eyes. "You'd dare *this,* you foul eater of carrion?" The surgeon cowered back out of reach.

With blood dripping to the floor, the Scissor Man turned back to David Hunter. "Literature, old movies... you think in those terms, don't you, David?"

David dropped his arm to his side and said nothing. The empty revolver was dead weight in his hand. Forgotten, it thudded to the floor while David watched the slow puddle of blood forming about the Scissor Man's feet.

"Perhaps you recognize these lines from Auden?

Only now when he has come
In walking distance of his tomb,
He at last discovers who
He had always been to whom
He so often was untrue."

"'True Enough,'" David muttered, naming the poem.

"Yes." The Scissor Man seemed pleased. "So, you know now who you were to her all those years. Would you have her know who she was to you?"

David looked up from the puddle of blood. "What?"

"Shall I wake her up... show her some of *your* Memories? I

can do that, you know. I can show her the truth about Christie Claremont. I can show her all the things you would rather take with you to the grave." He looked to where Maggie lay on the bed. "I can wake her, not to do her a favor and take her soul, but to make her look into the eyes of your Memories."

David sank back to the bed, defeated. He loved her. He loved her more than anything. He couldn't stand to see her shown all the petty, weak, and ultimately meaningless moments in his life. She didn't deserve that.

"Maggie," he whispered, defeated. He traced the familiar lines of her face with trembling fingertips. "I love you."

"Let me save her soul then," the Scissor Man implored. "We can't leave it for them," and he indicated the surgeons.

"Take me with her," David begged.

"I can't," replied the Scissor Man, but as he spoke, David saw an incredible thing. For just a moment, the Remover's knees buckled, and there passed across his eyes a shadowed glimpse of weakness, as if he were about to pass out. His shoes, as he stepped to the side of the bed, tracked blood across the carpet. His hands appeared unsteady, hesitant… mortal.

The scissors came out again, pale, slender lances of moonlight. As the Scissor Man leaned over Maggie, David saw a ghostly aura strain up from her body, as if her very soul were eager for removal, as if the wasted vehicle on the bed could no longer bear the effort to contain it. Ever so carefully, the Scissor Man caught the aura at its edges and slipped in the tip of the scissors. There was a frailty about his movements, a slow grace that David suspected came not from a desire to be careful, but rather from a severe loss of blood.

David hit him with a body block, driving him against the headboard. Before the Scissor Man could react, David had taken away the scissors and now held them pressed against the Dark Remover's throat. "Bullets you might recover from," David hissed, "but I'll wager these barber's shears are as fatal to you as anyone."

"Let me go. What can you possibly hope to gain?"

David pressed the twin blades against the Scissor Man's throat until he was rewarded with the sight of a bright trickle of blood. The Scissor Man gasped as he felt the warm gush. "I've a bargain for you," David told him. "You forget your appointment book. We *both* go tonight. We go together."

"And if I refuse?"

"Then there'll be a job announcement in Hell's morning edition. Wanted, one Grim Reaper." David caught movement out of the corner of his eye. "Make them stay back!"

The Scissor Man's gaze shifted to the lurking shapes just over David's shoulder. "Do as he says." There followed a reluctant shuffling of feet, and what could have only been the scraping of surgical blades drawn across each other. The Scissor Man looked back to David. "You could make something of the years you have left."

"I give them all to you. Use whatever potential they hold to heal yourself when I'm gone."

The Remover nodded slowly.

"We have a bargain?"

"Yes."

"How can I trust you?"

"Death does not lie."

Morning found them together in bed, David's arms wrapped tightly around Maggie. His face was buried against her neck and his tears had soaked her hair. The sun tried in vain to warm her sallow cheeks, managing only to reveal their sunken depths and deathly pallor. Beneath the sheets, she was incredibly still. Her eyes did not flutter. Her mouth did not move. Her chest did not rise and fall.

David held her for some time, wishing that her cold would rob the warmth from his body, that her death would suck the very life from him.

Death was not to be trusted. Death lied. Death needed no one's permission, kept no bargains. Death, the Great Deceiver. Death, the end of all things. David suspected it had all been an evening's distraction, an amusing game for the Scissor Man and his entourage. He had taken what he'd come for. Maggie was gone.

Though he didn't want to get up and make the phone call

that had to be made, David was afraid to stay in bed with her any longer. He feared sleep more than anything. He knew that if he slept, he would see them. He would see the surgeons about their work. Cell by cell, they would dismantle what was left of Maggie. Time was their scalpel, and for Maggie time had become a speeding locomotive. The death she carried within her was about to be born, blossoming in putrescence and rot—the Scissor Man's surgeons by any other name.

A few years, the Scissor Man had said.

David found himself looking forward to seeing him again.

THE WOODSHED

The youth gets together his materials to build a bridge to the moon, or, perchance, a palace or temple on the earth, and, at length, the middle-aged man concludes to build a woodshed with them.

—Henry David Thoreau, *Walden*

My father took me out to the woodshed for the first time when I was twelve years old.

I had just broken a promise to him—not my first, but the first that he'd caught me at. I'd promised to have nothing more to do with Benjamin Conley, who had already gotten me in more trouble in the last year than all of my first eleven put together. I'd snuck out my window so Bennie and I could hang out with some of the older boys down at the drive-in. There'd been 'shine and pot, and enough of the older boys had taken a liking to Bennie and me so that we got samples. Daddy didn't catch me going out, but he caught me coming in just before dawn. The things he smelled on me had clenched his fists and narrowed his eyes.

The woodshed sat out behind our family farm in Hays, Kansas, nestled among the scrub oaks and junipers. The walls were roughhewn pine, dove-tailed at each corner. The planks seeped a sweet, sticky tar in the hot summer and glazed over like amber in the winter cold. The roof was shake cedar shingles, moldy black with age. I'd never been in the woodshed before because for as long as I could remember the door had sported the largest padlock known to man. And besides, "woodshed" was a misnomer. I'd been sent out after firewood often enough to know that it was stacked out back of the livestock shed.

Daddy's breath caught in the frigid air that morning as he fumbled with the lock. I'd never thought much about where the key to that lock was kept, and it came as some surprise to see him pull it from around his neck. Oh, I'd had my moments of curiosity about the woodshed. More than once I'd pressed my face against the walls and tried to peer through the cracks between the planks. But always, no matter how bright it was outside and no matter what the angle of the sun, within there was nothing but the deep dark of a root cellar. This little mystery became all the more inexplicable when I first saw the woodshed from the inside and discovered just how much light actually seeped through the unevenly spaced planks.

Daddy pushed me through the door first, then he stepped in behind me and swung it shut behind us. How do I describe what I saw? Where does one find the words to relate the impossible? I know at that moment I couldn't process what my eyes conveyed to my brain. All I could do was stand there, arms at my sides, eyes wide and mouth dropped open, and listen as my Daddy's voice broke the cold, still air in the shed.

"There are some things we say to people, son, that don't amount to a hill of beans. But there are other things, important things, that become promises which are marked against a man's soul like the devil's own scorecard. It's these promises you don't want to break, son. It's these promises that ride your soul to Hell and beyond. And guilt, well, guilt is the least of it."

There was a hickory switch leaning just inside the door, its four-foot length stained a rusty red. My father took the switch and stepped to the first man hung on the walls of the woodshed, a naked man of muscle and taut sinew, hairy thighs and knotted biceps. His eyes were wild, and he began to beg, twisting against the railroad spikes that had fixed him to the wall at wrists and ankles.

I watched while my Daddy beat that man. Watched as the man screamed and begged, as red welts rose on his flesh and then split open. Watched as blood trickled down his body to paint the clotted mud at his feet. I watched as my Daddy sobbed and struck again and again, his own stout frame flinching with every slap of the switch. "This man," Daddy wept, "this man broke a promise to your mother, son. This man slept with another woman."

When it was over, Daddy moved on to the next man, a frail, weasel-like character whose bones showed through his skin like the print on the backside of a Sunday paper. This one bit his lip and took his no less brutal beating in stoic silence. "This man," Daddy wept, "cheated his first business partner."

And so it went, around the four walls of the shed, until at last we'd come full circle and my Daddy stood there with blood running down that hickory switch and over his hand, blood splattered on his overalls, his shoulders slumped and his back bent like a man twice his age. He didn't look at the whimpering, sobbing, bleeding men on the walls. He didn't look at any of them… though each wore Daddy's face.

"Every broken promise, son," Daddy all but whispered, handing me the switch. "You lock them up inside and you live with them. You build a woodshed and you hide them best you can, but you know they're there. You know."

And my Daddy walked out, leaving me holding that bloody switch, staring at the things he'd done and regretted, at the weaker men that he'd been. I stood there for what seemed like hours, listening to them cry and beg for help, hearing the dripping of their blood. Finally, I dropped the switch and walked out, careful to lock the door behind me.

In the years that followed, I thought an awful lot about that woodshed. I wondered whether I really saw what I thought I saw or whether Daddy had simply pressed a rather horrifying metaphor so firmly into my impressionable young mind that I invented the whole thing. I asked myself why Daddy hung on to such a place, why he never just burned it to the ground, and I came to the conclusion—brought about more by hard experiences of my own than through any deductive reasoning—that there are some things for which you never forgive yourself. These are the things Daddy stored in his woodshed, not the petty betrayals of everyday life, not the meaningless lies that you forget with time. You carry these broken promises inside you and you torture yourself with them. Guilt, as Daddy said, is the least of it. The pain you inflict on yourself is far worse.

Why keep such a place? I believe that without guilt, without our woodsheds, we become monsters. Immoral men don't own woodsheds.

I'd like to say that I never saw my father's woodshed again, but I did. When my parents died, the farm was passed on to me. Among the personal effects returned by the mortuary was that key.

I went out to the woodshed with matches and a five gallon gas can in tow, meaning to burn the evil place to the ground now that my Daddy was gone, but curiosity is a tough meal to pass over. I wondered whether his tortured pasts were still hung there on the walls. I wondered what it would mean to set them free. I unlocked the door and stepped inside, expecting to see either Daddy's pitiful facsimiles or an empty room, but what I found was completely unexpected.

Already, hung shoulder to shoulder, were several of my own weakest moments.

I dropped the gas can.

Picked up the switch.

THESE ARE THE MOMENTS I LIVE FOR

He was part of my dream, of course—but then I was part of his dream, too.

—Lewis Carroll, *Through the Looking Glass*

Eternities of darkness...

and then, she dreams, and I'm alive again.

As the sun strikes the Bavarian Alps, it erases the last of the morning's blue shadows from Elaine's raven hair. Rebounding from the windowpanes of Kehlstein House behind us, its rays spark amethyst in her eyes and copper on her lips. She watches in silence as the lakes and chasms below come alive, one by one surrendering their phantom cloaks to the cleansing onslaught of light. The cobalt blue waters reflect the white-capped majesty of Zugspitze, the highest peak in all of Germany, and miniature copies of us perched on the summit of Zugspitze's neighbor, Kehlstein. On the slopes, a thousand shades of that singular ignoble color, rock, are born. The salt mines in the Salzbergwerk Valley reveal their hoards like bright diamonds, a scattering of brisance against the rock. Elaine's eyes take it all in—while I watch her.

"Elaine," I begin.

"Go away. I don't want you here." She doesn't look away from the magnificent view.

"Then why do you summon me?" The question is rhetorical, and she doesn't bother to answer. We've had this discussion before.

Long moments pass. Daybreak widens to a searing seam. In its pure intensity, I find the courage to try again. "Elaine—"

"Quiet!" she all but screams. "Can't you just enjoy the sunrise?" Then, as if to compensate for scolding me, she plays, as always, the tour guide, pointing out sights on the horizon. "Hitler, Goering, and Borman all maintained chalets here. Once they were connected by a network of underground tunnels and bunkers, but very little remains today. Only Hitler's Eagle's Nest remains intact." Her face echoes another place and time as she speaks of these things, for the moment clean of the emotions with which she continually wrestles. It's always this way, the magic of the tourist sights occupying her completely. I've never determined whether she's actually visited these places to which she brings me or merely dreamed of them, but I choose to believe the former. The details are too exact to be a fantasy. She *knows* the places we visit. "It's easy to see why Hitler built here," she adds. "The view alone is worth what it must have cost him to bring the materials so high."

I wonder if she includes in that figure the cost in human lives. From here, it's easy to see Munich and the town of Dachau with its infamous concentration camp—Nazi Germany's first. I've no idea how many perished in its shower-disguised gas chambers, how many souls were consumed in its belching crematorium. But then, I don't know how I know any of these things. I don't know who I am. Or even *where* I am when she does not dream of me. Memories to me are *deja vú* hauntings in the back of my mind, nagging premonitions and wraith-like suppositions. Like now: a little Carmelite convent outside Dachau; continual prayers for Dachau's victims; the lighting of a single blood-red candle before an altar. These things are a mystery to me, as unfamiliar, yet proper, as the face that I wear, as the role I've come to play in Elaine's dreams.

Tentatively, I touch the bare slope of her arm. Before she slips out of reach, I see her tremble. A pale rose climbs her throat, and her breath catches. As for me, the contact of my fingertips on her flesh brings on such a feeling of gestalt that, when broken, it momentarily occludes the rising sun.

"From here you can even see *der Führer's* native Austria," Elaine continues, fighting to ignore my advance. "In that direction, on a clear morning, I bet you can see Ludwig's castle."

I can see it in my mind: the Castle of Neuschwanstein rising above a forest near Füssen, the castle that earned King Ludwig II the title of Mad Ludwig for its extravagance, easily the inspiration for every Disney castle since *Sleeping Beauty*. But I've never been there...Have I? Yet I know about Ludwig, can see him clearly in my mind as if we were friends in a past life (dream?). I know that he committed suicide, drowning himself just days after they officially declared him mad, and Prussian Chancellor Otto von Bismarck drew Bavaria into the German Empire. Does Elaine create me complete with these memories? Do I know these things only because she has given them to me? Or is there an innate source for my nebulous past?

Eyes glowing, she turns from the spectacular view to face the Eagle's Nest, now a restaurant which the Germans insist be called Kehlstein House. The building looks to me as if it's hiding against the landscape, as if it's ashamed of its place in history, its granite blocks as cold as the grey dawn, as cold as the compound in Dachau. "I'm going in," Elaine declares. "I think I'll have a *gebirgler frühschoppen*."

"A what?"

"A mountaineer's morning pint," she answers, "the traditional drink of Berchtesgaden. I think I'll have a sausage with it: *Weisswurst, Stadtwurst, Bratwurst, Blutwurst* perhaps. I'm sure they have all of those and more."

The thought of Bavarian sausage and beer makes me want to be sick. "Sounds wonderful. I'll go with you."

"No."

"Elaine, we can't continue like this. Whatever it is you think I've done, I can fix it. You know that I love you. You've just got to tell me—"

"You don't know what love is. And there's nothing you can say, nothing you can do, to fix this." She doesn't retreat as I reach for her and, though I recognize the cruel set of her eyes, I offer no defense. It's a scene we've played more than once, in Paris, in Yellowstone, in Caracas, Jerusalem, Australia, and Palermo... wherever her dreams have taken us.

Placing her delicate hand against my chest, she shoves me

back… over the railing.

I see her face as I fall, deathly pale, eyes like dark pools, paladins to secret fears and desires. The set of her seductive mouth speaks of regret and satisfaction, a contradictory combination that would be indecipherable if I hadn't seen it so many times before.

She loves me. She loves me not.

Arms flailing, I fall into the thin air's chill embrace…

Sigmund Freud theorized the ego as mediator between the conflicting demands of conscience and society (embodied in the super-ego) and the urgings of instinct (the id). It's a tiring, watchdog assignment, requiring the ego to retreat from the battlefield each night to rest and renew. While the ego's vigilance is down, the repressed, unconscious urges in the id threaten to beat down the door of consciousness. By dreaming, the mind restrains the id, harnessing impulses that would terminate sleep and eventually wear down both body and mind.

Am I an id-driven impulse in Elaine's sleeping mind? When she pushed me from the cliffs of Kehlstein was she preventing my breaking through to her conscious mind?

Freud further theorized a dream censor that disguises dream content. It's this censor that generates the bizarre qualities in dreams: the nonsensical changes in time, place, and person; the plot, character, and action incongruities; the illogical content and organization in which the unities of time, place, and person do not apply and natural laws are disobeyed. These are universal dream characteristics which the censor convinces the mind to experience with uncritical acceptance, as though the episodes were normal everyday occurrences.

Am I a censor-induced disguise to keep Elaine's real demons from coming to the surface?

Freud had one last major hypothesis to make on dreaming. It deals with that other universal aspect of dreams: the amnesia-like way in which we tend to forget our dreams on waking. Freud postulated that even the censor-transformed and mutated content of a dream can be dangerous to the individual. Therefore, the mind pushes the dream back into the subconscious from which it originated, effectively hiding it from the dreamer.

It's possible that Elaine doesn't even know she's dreaming of me.

Night. This time we're underwater.

Elaine makes a most erotic mermaid. Her long dark hair rides the ocean currents, lifting to frame her face in mystery and seduction, revealing buoyant, bare breasts and a flat stomach. Her tail retains the shapely contours of a woman, like a tight-fitting, ankle-length evening gown. It's emerald green, shimmering with a million faceted scales that fade seamlessly into the velvet tan at her navel and the base of her spine.

As she tries out the tail, she reminds me of a child. Her face is split by the grandest of grins, and her eyes are brighter than diamonds. She's happier than I've ever seen her. I don't think she even knows I'm here. For a moment I'm loathe to interfere, content merely to observe and enjoy.

The dark sea is alight with a bioluminescence that sets everything aglow. Coral and fish shimmer like neon abstracts under black lights. Starfish and crustacea litter the reef in a kaleidoscope of brilliant color, quivering tentacle and wavering antennae marking time with the waves that ripple overhead. Dolphins cut the moon-drenched surface, shattering the opalescent mirror into a million sapphire fragments. The reef itself is a labyrinthine honey-comb, teeming with fairy fish and fantastical flora. Penguins. Sea lions. Parrot fish and manta rays. It's quite some time before I notice that I, too, have a tail.

There are dragons here as well, feeding on the kelp and bottom algae, slithering like snakes through the murkier trenches of the reef, dappled green in the warm yellow bands of sunlight scattered from above. For a moment, I think Elaine has created a realm of pure fantasy; then I realize where we are. There's only one place with such an ecology.

Galapagos.

A marine iguana studies me from its perch on a pinnacle of rock. Its tiny dark eyes track my movement as I experiment with my tail, blinking in amusement when I nearly collide with a frolicking sea lion. Only the sea lion's supple grace and lightning maneuverability prevent the collision; then, like a silent torpedo, it is instantly gone, paying me no more attention than the other gregarious sea life, leaving me momentarily alone with the iguana. Clutching the reef, the iguana looks like a gargoyle mounted on some Gothic rooftop, a prop perhaps in some Poe production. Its turquoise hue reminds me of copper gone green. It's like a tiny dinosaur. The saurian horns on its head and down the crest of its back are straight from the Mesozoic era.

"You're an anachronism," I tell the lizard, not in the least bit amazed that I can talk underwater. "Do you know that?"

The iguana releases the rock, twists about, and with one sweep of its three-foot tail shoots away through the water.

"It wasn't meant to be insulting," I call after it.

"What are you doing here?" Elaine demands.

I turn gracefully in the water, a delicate spiral initiated at the hips. *I could get used to this,* I think wondrously—then I see what discovering me has done to her face.

The smiles are gone. Her eyes have taken on the somber hue of the deeper trenches.

"Is there nowhere I can go to be rid of you?" she asks. With a powerful kick, she torpedoes away, disappearing in a passing storm of silver fish. For a moment, I've lost her, but then I see her emerald gleam in the foamy tidewater shoals. I follow, braving a sharp, intervening reef of blood-red coral. Over the reef, through the breakwater and down through a grotto, I emerge at last in a shallow pool populated by tide-locked manta rays. Elaine reclines among them, her gentle fingers stroking the ridge between their eyes, soothing, a promise of the rising sea and freedom restored. Again, I watch, amazed at her rapport with the environment.

"You always ruin everything," she says at last. I can barely hear her over the crash of the waves against the rocks around us.

"This man who you take me to be, Elaine, what is it that he did to you?"

"Quit pretending you're someone else!"

The broad surface of a patient manta serves as the backing for an impromptu mirror, and I study my face in the surface of the pool. It's completely unfamiliar. *This,* I think, *cannot be the face I was meant to wear.* Like everything else, she gives this to me. She creates me in the image she most fears.

Or most longs to see.

"Elaine, I'm here for a reason, but it's not to harm you. I could never harm you. Help me find the real reason I'm here." The sheer desperation in my voice is distressing, even to me. Until that moment, I hadn't truly realized how lost I was. I'd been so focused on *her* pain, that I'd been ignoring my own. Who am I? Why am I here?

Elaine slips back beneath the surface, but I intercede between her and the grotto to the sea. She's quick, but my arms surround her narrow waist. Tail to tail, we slip among the mantas, her hair sheathing us in a cloak of midnight. Her struggles cease and our lips almost meet. The sudden intimacy takes me completely by surprise, and I'm caught off guard when she slips through my fingers and out through the grotto. Powerful flukes disrupting the slumbering mantas, I follow.

"Go away!" she cries back over her shoulder. Inexplicably, there are tears on her cheeks, clinging there like tiny pearls. "I hate you! I hate you! I hate you!"

A second later, a massive moon-shadow passes over me. Too late, I realize that the dolphins and sea lions have suddenly vanished.

It comes out of the gloom, sleek and grey and, in its own way, beautiful. It doesn't hesitate. It doesn't think. It doesn't ponder the nature of dreams or the essence of existence. It doesn't question the distance between love and hate.

Its teeth are incredibly sharp.

Carl Jung was an early disciple of Freud's. Their opposing opinions on the interpretation of dreams drove them apart. While Freud admitted that some dreams do not display disguise and censorship, he thought that the most unique dream features reflect the operation of these concealing processes. Jung saw dreams as no less symbolic, but viewed the symbols as more directly expressive of human creativity.

I don't doubt that Elaine has read about and seen pictures of the marine life around the Galapagos Islands. The details were too carefully drawn, the colors too bright, the images too real. The merfolk aspect says a lot about her creativity.

But why place me in the dream if she doesn't want me there? I saw the look on her face. I've seen it before. What could have been a pleasant dream experience had become a nightmare because of my intrusion.

Why dream of me at all?

Unless... she has no choice in the matter.

The sand beneath my feet extends in all directions, rippled as if touched by the breath of the sea, colored as if saturated with the essence of life itself, a vast desert from which there rises a single tooth of granite upon which sits *la Merveille*. The inexplicable rock is Mont Saint Michel. Beyond all explanation, I know this for a fact. I know France lies less than two miles across the sand to the south. I know the Gulf of Saint Malo tidewater will sweep back and make Mont Saint Michel an island again within the next few hours. And though this is still just another of her dreams, I know that she did not give me this knowledge.

I *know* these things.

Elation rises within me, exploding as giddy laughter. *Deja vú* sings in my veins, a powerful drug. I have been here before. And I'm positive that it was *not* in one of Elaine's dreams.

She's standing not ten feet away, bare feet planted firmly in the sand, hair disheveled by the salt breeze. She looks wary and confused.

Above us, the monastery clings to the naked cliffs, a vast bastion perched on a summit one-fourth its size. Once, pilgrims desiring to pay homage to Archangel Michael were escorted across the sand by islanders who knew the lay of the quicksand. I can imagine the pilgrims' wondering, sun-reamed faces, hard used by poverty and bitter years. Now tourists scuttle across the raised causeway from the mainland, bright autos and rusting buses lining up like siege engines outside the sea-stained lower battlements. The islanders survive on tourism. Even here, a mile or so away, I'm convinced that I can smell one of Mère Poulard's renowned omelettes.

"Do you know this place?" Elaine's voice is all but lost to the wind and the calls of the seabirds.

"Yes."

"I've never been here. Of course, I know about this place… and I've *wanted* to come here, but—" The almost imperceptible quake in her voice tells me her confusion is rapidly succumbing to fear. "—I've never been here before."

I think of the other places she's taken me in her dreams. Why does this one scare her? "It's the details," I whisper.

"What?"

"You've wanted to come here. Maybe you've even read about Mont Saint Michel in a tour guide or something." Her face has paled, and I hesitate to continue. "But you've never researched it enough to fill in these details."

"Then where…?" Her face goes paler yet.

"*I'm* supplying them."

"No!"

"Don't be afraid, Elaine."

"You're *my* dream!" she insists, backing up in the sand.

"There's more to it than that. I know this place, Elaine. It belongs to Michael, Captain of God's celestial armies, golden angel who vanquished Satan." Inexplicably, I think, *I am Michael*. But that's absurd. Elaine is already terrified. What would telling her that do to her now? If I'm not careful, her fear will shatter the dream. Staring up at the Romanesque church and the towering pinnacle of the Gothic monastery, I know I don't want this dream to end until I've decided what it means.

"In 709," I stall, "Michael appeared in a dream to Aubert, Bishop of Avranches, and commanded him to build a shrine on what was then called Mount Tombe. There was a forest here then, before the English Channel swelled and claimed all this as its own. In the eleventh century, the church was built, and the island became known as Mont Saint Michel. In the thirteenth century, Benedictine monks built the monastery from native granite, an architectural wonder for that day and age. The whole is called *la Merveille*—the Marvel."

"You're making it all up!" She takes another step back. "I know what you're doing. You're taking over my dreams, just like you've taken control of my life."

"No! You're confusing me with *him* again. Give me what face you will, but I am no one but myself." I take several steps toward her, but suddenly there comes the sound of a blacksmith's hammer on an anvil. My ankle is pulled out from under me, and I pitch face-first to the sand. Looking back, I find my right leg chained to an iron spike in the sand. Chain and spike are secure; I cannot budge them.

"I'm here to help you," I insist.

"You will never hurt me again," she counters. Then she turns with a squelch of tortured sand and starts for the causeway.

"The quicksand, Elaine, be careful!"

But it is, after all, her dream. If quicksand lies before her, she walks right across it. Jesus on the water. In this realm, she's every bit the miracle worker. I watch her disappear through the gate of Mont Saint Michel.

In the distance, I hear the dull moan of the approaching tide.

In 1906, Ramón y Cajal was awarded a Nobel Prize for his work in neural anatomy. The father of modern neurobiology, Cajal made it clear that the nervous system is a collection of interdependent neurons, each functionally discrete with its own energy source and capacity for handling information. Consciousness arises out of the activity of this myriad of neural elements which, as an ensemble, possess spontaneous activity and information producing capabilities.

We know now that there are between twenty and fifty billion individual elements in the human brain. Each individual element is capable of communicating with its neighbors. By means of tiny extensions of the nerve membrane, axons and dendrites, each individual neuron communicates with at least ten thousand other neurons. Each of the twenty to fifty billion elements generates two to three hundred signals per second.

Neural communication is a continuous process. Night and day, awake or asleep, it goes on and on. With such an incredible system, it's inconceivable to think that it would not have awareness of itself. It's inconceivable to think such a system wouldn't have the best interests of its host in mind.

Such a system might conjure up anything.

Even a guardian angel.

I kneel and test the texture of the gray cobblestoned street in front of the Hotel Mouton Blanc. How many millions of feet did it take to wear the stones this smooth? How many dreamers have stood in this very spot? Elaine is some twenty yards ahead of me, looking into shop windows, trailing tentative fingers over the stone walls. The single road that winds its way up the slopes of Mont Saint Michel, from the gates at the causeway to the monastery at the peak of the mountain, is narrow and crowded. There's no room for vehicles or even carts. Those who make this journey are their own deliverers.

I didn't expect to wake here. Elaine's dreams have never repeated a location.

When she looks back at me, I see that she's as surprised as I am. She's afraid, too; I see that in her eyes. She knows I'm influencing her dreams. She knows I've brought us back here.

I catch up with her near the doorway of a small bakery. I take her arm, and for once she doesn't shrug me off.

"I'm here to help, Elaine. Let me help you."

"No one can help me."

"We wouldn't be here if I couldn't help you. People have come here seeking my help for more than a thousand years."

She laughs, a short, bitter sound that wounds my confidence. "You think you're the Archangel Michael?"

"I know I am." But the confidence I want is absent from my voice. I see my doubt reflected—no, *magnified*—in her eyes. Her eyes are the source of my doubt. Falling into them, I lose all hope.

"You're only who I dream you to be," she says, pulling away. She passes the bakery and enters the twilight of an alley between the shops.

It's my *dream,* I think, as I follow her. I can control this.

The alley is a dead end because I wish it so. Palms against the cold stone wall, she shivers, refusing to look back at me.

"I am the Archangel Michael, Captain of God's armies in Heaven. I'm here to help."

She shakes her head. "You are Azazel, once Chief of the

Grigori—the Watchers. You were cast from Heaven because you refused to bow down before Adam."

My heart stops. By simply speaking that name, she's changed everything. A veil has been removed from my mind. I know who I really am. I know what I did. I know how I came to be here, and why I wish I was someone else, someone like Michael.

"Do you remember what you said?"

I do. Oh, God, I do.

"Do you?"

She turns and shoves me back up the alley. I stumble and fall.

"What did you say?" she screams down at me.

"Why should a Son of Fire... bow to a Son of Clay..."

I said it. I remember it like it was yesterday.

"For that you were cast out. But there's more, isn't there?" Her finger jabs so deep that I expect to see blood welling up from my chest. "On Earth you disguised yourself as a man and changed your name to Eblis. Eblis showed the Islamic women how to use cosmetics and perfume and fine silks to inflame a man's passion. But whose lust did they inspire, Azazel? Who was lured into their beds?"

I swallow bile. I cannot speak.

"Your fellow angels. It was you who precipitated the Fall! You who—"

"Enough! I've heard enough!"

Because it's all true. I remember it all. And I know that my punishment for that second crime, for orchestrating the Fall of Dubbiel and Shenjaza and Sammael and all the others who'd once been my friends, for enticing the *bene-ha-Elohim* to bed the *benoth-ha-Adam,* begetting the *Hans-Nephilim,* is an eternity in Purgatory, in a black limbo where nothing exists and nothing survives, not even my own thoughts and memories. I'm not Michael. In fact, I'm as far from Michael as could be imagined, worse even than Satan-el, whose actions, in a sick, twisted way, had always been necessary, had always served God's ultimate purpose. Evil is an essential ingredient in any religion that preaches redemption. If one is to overcome evil and achieve salvation, there must, after all, be an evil to overcome.

I am worse than evil.

I am Azazel, he who carried out a petty vengeance on his own kind.

"You can't help me," she rasps. "You can't even help yourself."

She steps over me. As the sound of her footsteps retreat down the alley, the walls close in, screeching and moaning like the tortured souls of a thousand angels. I don't even raise my hands to fend them off as they gouge into my sides and compress my body. I don't scream. I don't weep. I don't ask her forgiveness.

I close my eyes and stir all those memories, now so fresh and revoltingly bare in my mind, watch as the hubris and the pettiness and the pride swirl like oil on water.

And there, somewhere near the thick ooze at the bottom, I find what I need to know. I find what I've found before, when a myriad of others have culled me from the ether of their dreams, to curse me or torment me or use me as an instrument for their pain. It's the knowledge of why I'm given these moments to exist in another's mind, and what I must do to one day earn my own salvation.

As my mind is crushed between stones laid in honor of my ancient captain and hero, I dream a dream of my own, that I might, for just a moment, be the champion that he was.

Modern research now shows that dreams are most often reflections of our daily lives—rather than random nonsense images caused by signals in the restless brain or, as Freud theorized, symbolic transfigurations of unconscious desires. Our dreams are often so closely tied to our waking lives that we can use them to resolve conflict.

Your unconscious knows and understands things that your conscious does not. The trick is to listen to it. And to understand what it's telling you.

Survivors of natural disasters, victims of accidents and crimes, and combat veterans relive those terrifying events again and again in their dreams. They punish themselves. And a select few, those with more control than others, learn to structure that punishment in such a way that they believe they are punishing others.

But the only one suffering, still, is the dreamer.

As I close the door behind me, Elaine turns in her wheelchair and glares at me, intruder in this last sanctuary of her mind, this place that most reflects her life, this lost moment between her dreams and reality. The small apartment is sparsely decorated: colorless curtains and dusty blinds, sun-blanched paint on the walls, and bookshelves whose lower reaches are crowded with much-used tour guides. There's very little furniture. The kitchen counters have all been cut down to accommodate the handicapped. There are scars on the doorframe where the wheels of her chair have rubbed. Tracks in the threadbare carpet. Rubber scuff marks on the linoleum.

"So," she says, "now you know."

I shake my head. "No. I don't, really." I cross the room and kneel before her chair. "You'll have to tell me."

There are tears in her eyes. Lines at the corners of her mouth. Scars down the length of her neck, disappearing beneath her blouse. She's older here, in this private place. Or perhaps it's the room that has stolen her vitality. The girl I watched swim with manta rays was in her early twenties, unblemished and vibrant. This is a woman approaching forty—with the eyes of a woman half again that age... and scars that transcend the visible.

"I've never been to any of those places," she says. "Never walked the miles of labyrinth beneath Palermo. Never climbed any mountains or stood before the pyramids at Giza or... never swam like a mermaid.

"Most of my life, I've spent in this chair."

I try to take her hands in mine, but she hides them under the coarse throw that covers the withered remains of her legs.

"I've read about them. Studied them in every detail. Dreamed of being able to visit them. I always wanted to travel. But I never have. I've been in this chair since I was sixteen."

Tenderly, I catch the tear that spills down her cheek. She doesn't pull away.

"Tell me what happened, Elaine."

"There was a man," she whispers. "He wore your face—"

I shake my head, but don't speak.

"He had your hands."

"No."

"He knew the lust that you brought from Heaven."

Her hands slip out from under the covers, and the steel bites deep, a sharp cold pain in my chest, an uncomfortable pressure between two ribs. When she tries to pull the blade out, I wrap my hands over hers on the handle and hold it in place. I can feel my heart thrumming down the length of the knife. Warm blood seeps between our fingers. Her hands are very strong from having turned the wheels of her chair all those years. Her knuckles are large and cracked. Our faces are very close now. As close as they've ever been. If I could stand the pain of another inch or two from the knife, I could lean forward and kiss her.

"For so many years I've wished that he only raped me," she continues. "Rape would have been so very easy to live with. But he didn't stop there. When he was done, he stabbed me with a kitchen knife just like this one. Over and over he stabbed me. You wouldn't believe the scars. His knife severed my spinal cord and put me in this chair for life."

Blood soaks the front of me, saturates her legs, pools on the floor around my knees. My heart is beating much slower now. It's hard to keep my eyes open. Her voice is distant. But I hold her hands where she clutches the knife, refusing to let her pull it out or shove it deeper, hanging onto the dream.

"Gone were my dreams of travel. Gone my chances for a husband, for children, for a normal life. Here I sit. In this room paid for with my meager disability allowance. Day after day. In my chair. I read. And I dream.

"And I hate."

"It's time… to let go of your hate, Elaine."

"How can I, when it's all I've ever known? Day after day I kill you for what you took from me. For the lust that you unleashed upon the world."

"Then give me your hate, Elaine. Let me bear it so that you can live in peace. Let me take it back with me, back into the darkness."

"It's not that easy."

"It's *just* that easy."

I pull her hands back, and the length of steel slides slowly from my chest, hurting every bit as much going out as it did going in. I can feel its edge drag across my sternum, can feel the red, glistening lips of the wound suck at the blade. Finally it is out. I shift our hands several inches to the right. Press the tip against my flesh.

"It's time to finish this, Elaine. Time to kill your past and move on."

Her hands offer no resistance as I shove the knife in to the hilt.

In the midst of the pain, there's the *snick* against bone, followed by a sharp release, a severing, and end to agony. I slump against her legs, my body dead and disconnected. Neither of us is holding the handle of the knife any longer. My hands are tangled in the spokes of her chair. Hers are on my back. As the knife spasms with the last beating of my heart, I feel her lips against my forehead.

She loves me. She loves me not.

And I understand her loneliness, understand the dichotomy that let a part of her crave my company every bit as much as she loathed it.

"I'm sorry," I whisper into her lap.

"I know."

"Forgive me."

She doesn't answer. As the all-too-familiar darkness returns to embrace me, I know that only time will tell if she's ready to get on with her life, to release her hate, to quit punishing herself.

Only my next dream will reveal if she's let her nightmares go.

Eternities of darkness…

…and then, someone dreams, and I'm alive again.

These are the moments I live for.

THE GROTTO OF MASSABIELLE

"I raised my head and looked at the grotto, I saw a lady dressed in white..."

—Bernadette Soubirous (1858)

It was Peter's idea to investigate locations where incidences of miraculous healing had occurred. "Maybe," he reasoned, "the truth is that there's someone like me waiting at one or more of these locations, someone who is performing the miracles." Julie argued that there was no single place where miracles had occurred in sufficient number to support his theory. They might just as well, she remarked with her usual cynicism, follow some tent revivalist around. Their argument went as most of their arguments did, with Julie winning and Peter doing what he wanted anyway. When he bought the tickets to France, she didn't complain. After all, she hadn't been to the country that had so inspired her father's lycanthropean quest since she was a little girl.

They flew into Toulouse, rented a car, and drove through the rolling green countryside to the base of the Pyrenees and the town of Lourdes on the Gave de Pau River. Of all the locations he had researched, this was the one that had most intrigued Peter because it had provided more documented cases of actual healing than any other.

The history of the place went like this: on February 11, 1858, in a grotto beside the river, a 14-year-old peasant girl named Marie Bernarde Soubirous (later Saint Bernadette), asthmatic daughter of a poor miller, saw a vision of a woman robed in white. The apparition would change the small town in southwestern France forever, eventually making it the greatest Christian pilgrimage center in the world. Up to three million pilgrims now pour into town each year, most of them hoping to be cured by the cold spring which Bernadette had uncovered within the Grotto of Massabielle. At first, Bernadette didn't know the apparition and would refer to her simply as *Aqueró*, meaning "that one" in the local patois. Rumors, loosely based on the decreased symptoms of Bernadette's asthma, quickly spread. It was said that the spring possessed healing properties. News of Bernadette's mystical encounters circulated through the town, across France, and eventually around the world. Crowds began to gather. Though no one else could see the lady in white, all who watched attested to Bernadette's entranced beauty during what they called her ecstasies. Local police and civic authorities, concerned by the commotion she was creating, interrogated Bernadette. They were unable to shake her conviction in what she had seen. The local parish priest, Father Peyramale, was initially skeptical and unsympathetic, but changed his attitude after the sixteenth apparition on March 25, when the lady dramatically revealed herself to Bernadette with the words, "I am the Immaculate Conception." Peyramale was shaken. The words referred to the Virgin Mary. It was not the sort of phrase that a simple, uneducated child would invent. To Peyramale, it served as authenticity. From that moment on, he was Bernadette's keenest supporter. Four years later, an inquiry commissioned by the local bishop of Tarbes confirmed Peyramale's belief that the Blessed Virgin had indeed appeared to Bernadette.

The sun had gone down by the time Peter and Julie arrived. Julie wanted to find a hotel in Lourdes and make their pilgrimage in the morning, but Peter insisted on going to the grotto immediately. The Domain of Our Lady was situated on a narrow parcel of land enclosed by the Pyrenees and the river. Dominating the site was the steepled spire of the white basilica rising above the three distinct churches, arranged vertically atop each other. Access to the churches was provided by two long, gracefully curved ramps rising up from ground level, mounted on aqueduct-like arches, encircling the grotto itself. Manicured lawns and trees, intermixed with statuary, beautified the grounds. Beneath it all, lay the Underground Basilica of Saint

Pius X, an open courtyard capable of holding 20,000 worshipers.

Julie wasn't sure what to expect, but she hadn't expected the crowd. The ramparts leading up to the churches were packed with a shuffling throng of people in ragged lines. Each visitor carried a flickering candle, the only light on the entire scene. It appeared as if the stars above had found some mirrored shoal below on which to reflect their beauty. A light breeze blew, tossing the tiny flames of the candles, bringing to Julie's sensitive nostrils the heat and odor of thousands. She felt nauseous and, for a moment, had to cling to Peter's arm.

"They must be having some sort of candlelight service in the church," Peter guessed. His eyes were big and his mouth was open. It was an expression she knew, one she had seen often enough to fear: a wide-eyed expression of compassionate naiveté. She'd seen it last in New York's Central Park at a gathering of AIDS victims. Peter had walked in among them. Just like that, he had touched one, felt the pain in the man's soul, so he said later, felt the death in his cells, and he had simply walked in among them all, touching and hugging, stumbling after a few minutes, going down to his knees eventually, but by this time they understood, and they'd begun to come to him. Hours later, Julie had fought them off and dragged Peter out of there. She had hailed a cab and asked the driver to take them to the nearest rental car dealer, where she rented a car and fled south. They'd spent one day in New York City. It had very nearly killed Peter.

She feared that this had the potential to be much worse.

From the railing along the ramparts, most of the healthier pilgrims looked down upon the massive line of people flowing around and to the right of the basilica where the grotto was situated beneath the churches. The walkway was crowded with wheelchairs and gurneys, walkers and crutches, and those who could only crawl. It was at the same time the most desperate and the most heart-breaking scene she had ever witnessed. Never had she seen such an assemblage of maltreated humanity.

"Peter, I think we should leave."

He said nothing. She followed as he made his way through the gardens to the end of the line leading to the grotto.

"Peter, this is a bad idea. Even if there was someone here healing people—and you have to admit the chances of that are pretty slim—you'd never be able to find him." She caught at his shirt sleeve, but he pressed on through the milling crowd until he'd run into the back of the procession and could proceed no further. Other pilgrims crowded up behind them, boxing them in. "I don't want to do this, Peter," she pleaded.

An old woman touched Julie's forearm, momentarily snatching it back at the chill she found there. "It's all right, love," croaked the old woman, her accent a heavy British. With obvious effort, she reached out again, this time taking Julie's hand. "The Virgin forgives you. Ask and you will be healed."

Julie smiled coldly at the woman. "Thank you, but I'm fine."

"Oh?" The woman glanced at Peter, turning loose of Julie's hand and reaching for his. "Your husband, then? Is there something wrong—" She coughed, and the hand which was reaching for Peter's went instead to her throat. She swallowed distastefully. "Forgive me, love. My throat—"

"Don't strain your voice, ma'am," Peter said. He reached out and placed his palm against her throat.

"Cancer," she whispered. "Taking my bloody vocal cords. I used to sing," she told him, but Peter wasn't listening. She placed her hand over his, there against her throat. Peter's eyes had that faraway look, and Julie knew he'd gone inside, that he was feeling the wrong in the woman and seeking to make it right. "I sang with the Philharmonic in London—that's where I'm from, dear, London." Her eyes sparkled brighter than the candle she carried, memories dancing like school children. "I could reach notes that most girls only dreamed of. I—Oh, dear," she faltered, looking at Peter, "are you all right?"

Julie reached out and pulled his hand from the old woman's neck. "Peter?"

Focus returned slowly to his eyes. "What? Oh. Yeah, I'm fine." He smiled at the old woman. "I hope you find what you're looking for here."

"Faith," she rasped through her tumor-clotted throat. "You've just got to have faith, son."

"Yes, ma'am, I know. I do."

A pretty young woman pressed in behind them with a wheelchair. The child in the wheelchair slumped lifeless in the chair, arms and legs twisted as if he were a puppet with all the strings drawn taut and twisted about him. His hair was as white as snow. His facial muscles were clenched in a grimace that hurt Julie just to look at it: mouth screwed into a feral growl, nose drawn back as if subjected to some foul stench, forehead wrinkled so that the brows were completely lost. One eye was closed; the other was an incredible shade of blue, as clear as a sapphire gem. The good eye tracked from Julie to Peter and back again, with an intelligence as lucid as that of any other child of ten. The eye gleamed with curiosity, a silent mental beacon in the wasted landscape of the boy's body.

"Please don't stare at him," said the French woman piloting the wheelchair. Her statement was as stern as it was rehearsed. The fact that she spoke in English implied that she'd run across more than her share of tourists in Lourdes. "Michael hates it when people stare." She adjusted a blanket around his deformed legs, tucking it in carefully around his waist. Her long blonde hair trailed across the child's cheek. For a moment, the hint of a smile straightened some of the grotesquery of his face. Julie could almost see him sigh at the caress of those lovely tresses.

Ignoring the woman, Peter dropped to one knee by the wheelchair. As the child's focus shifted back to him, Peter reached out to touch, but the blonde pushed his hand away. "Please," she said, "leave us alone."

"I meant no harm," Peter told her.

Julie took his arm and tried to pull him to his feet. "Peter."

"We just want to be left alone," said the woman. "We came here to bathe in the spring. We come here..." She faltered, her voice caught in her throat, tears capturing candlelight in the corners of her eyes. "We come here the first weekend of every month. Please just let us do what we've come to do, and then we'll go." Her eyes, despite the tears, were as hard as steel and completely unrelenting.

"It's all right, miss," spoke up the old woman with the throat cancer, "we understand."

"I'm sorry," Peter said softly.

"Just don't touch my son, okay?" She tried to pull the wheelchair back a few feet, but people had filled in behind her. "Michael doesn't like strangers."

"Is that true?" Peter asked the boy.

"I'll call a constable if you don't leave us alone," the blonde threatened.

"Peter," Julie tried again, "let them be."

But Peter was focused on that single sapphire eye in which, it seemed, there twinkled what could only be mirth. He reached to touch the boy, and again the woman batted his hand away. But Michael was obviously not frightened. As Julie watched, several of the boy's fingers uncurled like arthritic claws. His hand turned ever so slightly, as if he were trying to reach out to Peter. The blonde looked around frantically. "I'm calling for a constable now."

"Come on, leave the kid alone," growled a heavyset Frenchman behind the woman. He pushed past her and made as if to grab Peter, but Julie interceded with a hand on his bare arm. For a moment, the Frenchman stared at her, his face angry and confused. Then, he broke away from her and stepped back, clutching his arm. "*Puta in, elle me fout des frissons*!" he cried.

"Yes," said the old British woman with the throat cancer, "she made me cold, too." She stared at Julie suspiciously, suddenly worried, perhaps, that Julie's affliction might be something worse than throat cancer.

"Don't touch my son," the blonde repeated.

Another Frenchman, this one short, but wiry and heavily muscled, stepped up beside the first and glared at Peter, his hands clenched at his sides. "*Touche le gamin et je te casse la gueule*!"

"What'd he say?" Julie asked the old woman.

She grimaced. "He said he's going to break your husband's face. I think you'd better leave the boy alone. Why don't the two of you go ahead of me."

"Hey! You're holding up the line. Get a move on!" someone further back yelled.

Julie pulled Peter to his feet, thanked the old woman, and slipped on ahead of her in line. "Peter!" She turned his face so that he was looking at her. "You can't save all these people. You certainly can't save the ones who don't even want your help."

"She doesn't know what the boy wants," Peter countered.

"No, but she's his mother. If she doesn't want your help—"

"What are you talking about?" croaked the old woman.

"Nothing," Julie snapped at her. "Please, just let me talk to… to my husband." She forcibly turned Peter so he was facing forward.

The man in front of them had turned around and was staring at them with open curiosity. "So," he said, after looking them both up and down, "what is it?"

"I beg your pardon?" Peter replied.

"What is it? What's wrong with you?"

Peter hesitated. Then: "Nothing."

"Nothing?" The man appeared insulted. He was a big man, looked like he spent his weekend crushing beer cans on his forehead. Another Brit. "What the hell are you doing here then?" he asked.

"We just want to see the grotto," Julie told him, wishing he would turn around and leave them alone.

"See the grotto? Nothing wrong with you?" The man raised his voice. "Hear that, folks? Nothing wrong with these two Yanks. Bloody tourists is all!" He leaned close to Julie. "Want to know what's wrong with me, why I'm not just ducky? Prostate. Old Victor Fairbairn's got prostate cancer. Can you believe it? Radiation therapy isn't doing a bloody damn thing. All those years I worried about getting some sexually transmitted disease, and here I am going out this way. Want to know what the doc says he's going to do to me next Monday? Eh? Bet you can't guess."

"I really don't think it's—"

"The old bugger says he's going to cut off my balls. Won't that be a kick in the arse?"

The old woman with the throat cancer gasped and tried to become invisible behind Peter.

"Know what I think, though?" Fairbairn continued. "I think if this Saint Bernadette shit doesn't help me, I'm going to take a comfy seat in my crapper, put a gun in my mouth, and make my exit with my balls right where they've always been." He cocked his head and smiled like a madman. "What do you think of that?"

"I think you should turn around," Julie hissed, her breath wafting vapors in the warm air.

Peter reached past her and put his hand on the big man's shoulder. "We hope you find the cure you're looking for," he said softly, then his eyes went vacant, and he stopped breathing. Fairbairn reached up as if he might remove Peter's hand from his shoulder, but he suddenly hesitated. His breath quickened and his legs shook. One of the Frenchmen behind them hollered that they needed to keep moving, cursing them in French. The old woman with the throat cancer put her hand to her throat and swallowed several times. Her eyes narrowed and focused on Peter's back.

Julie caught Peter as his legs began to buckle. He took his hand away from Fairbairn without her having to tell him. The crowd pressed them all forward, Peter leaning on Julie for support, Fairbairn stumbling backward, his legs obviously as weak as Peter's. He looked confused. Reaching down to his crotch, he groped himself rudely with no apparent concern for the people crowded all around them.

"What did you do?" he sputtered to Peter.

Peter was incapable of answering.

"Please," Julie whispered to the man, "just move on before the men behind us get angry."

For a moment she thought Fairbairn would argue, then he frowned and turned back to the front, still groping himself.

Just ahead, through a series of stone arches, Julie could see the steps which led down into the grotto. There was a bath house below where the spring water was pumped up into long cisterns. *Just a little further,* she thought. If only she could keep Peter from playing God anymore. But Peter's head was up again, and his eyes were searching the faces around him. She knew what he was thinking. She understood the turmoil he was in. Not because she had endured it. She understood because she had seen him wrestling with his gift so many times before. She knew what he was thinking. That woman there, the one with the pale yellow sweater clutched beneath her throat, she was suffering from breast cancer—a five second cure for Peter. That man there: a thyroid disorder. That little girl on the stretcher: a quadriplegic after snapping her neck in an auto accident. The young man in the blazer had just learned he was HIV positive. The old man in khaki, emphysema. That young woman, Parkinson's. That one... Peter could cure them all with just a touch. Doing so might kill him. But not doing so was worse. Not doing so was breaking his heart.

"Maybe we should go," she tried again.

Peter shook his head. "We're almost there."

At the top of the steps there was a statue of Saint Bernadette. Carved in a pale pink marble by the famous French sculptor, Jean Montbéliard, she stood ten feet tall, her head nearly touching the arch, her eyes cast down on all who passed before her, her arms crossed over her chest as if she feared those in the crowd might attempt to touch her hands. Julie knew that neither the spring nor the Virgin Mary had saved the peasant girl. Harried by those who came to the grotto for years after the visions ceased, Bernadette left Lourdes in 1866 and spent her remaining years at the convent of Saint Gildard in Nevers, hundreds of miles to the north. She died there in 1879, at the age of 35, of tuberculosis. It would be 1933 before the church recognized her miraculous visions and Pope Pius XI canonized her at Saint Peter's in Rome. Marie Bernarde Soubirous became Saint Bernadette.

Poor girl, thought Julie. *She must have been incredibly lonely.* Much the way Julie Snow had been—before she'd met Peter Burke.

Clutching Peter's arm, she started down the stairs with him. There were nuns and nurses and local volunteers helping the weak and invalid into the baths. The walls were lined with endless racks of candles, tier upon tier, beneath which the dripping wax had created alien landscapes on the stone floor. The air was close—suffocatingly so for Julie, and she clung to Peter as much now as he was clinging to her. At the bottom of the steps, a nun stepped forward to help them to the water. Julie pushed Peter forward. "I'm fine," she told the nun. "It's my husband who wants to get in the water." Ahead of them, she could see the man with prostate cancer stripping to his boxers. People ahead of him were being helped out of the cold water.

The nun took Peter by the hands and led him forward. "Did you wish to bathe, *monsieur*?"

"No," whispered Peter, "just my hands, please. Would that be okay?"

"Oui," replied the nun.

Pressed by those from behind, Julie was crowded forward with Peter and the nun. She watched as he dipped his hands in the water, submerging them to his elbows. He looked back at her. "Cold," he reported.

Of course, Julie thought, *it's spring fed*. But she said nothing, merely watched as he closed his eyes and concentrated. She knew what he was doing. He confirmed it a moment later when his eyes, disappointed and distant, looked back up at her and he said, "It's just water, Jules. There's nothing here."

The nun gasped at his blasphemy, covering her mouth with one dainty hand.

Julie watched as Peter looked around the long, narrow grotto. The man with the prostate cancer, Fairbairn, was a few feet away, submerged to his neck in the cistern. The quadriplegic child was beyond him, being carefully dipped into the water by her parents while a nurse supervised. Others were climbing in or climbing out. Behind Julie, the old woman with the throat cancer was stripping down to a thin shift that did little to conceal her frailty, would do less yet when the water in the cistern worked its immodesty on it. The blonde woman had taken Michael from his wheelchair and was waiting patiently, the gnome-like child cradled in her arms. Peter looked at them all, then down at his hands. His eyes closed and his brow furrowed with concentration.

Julie saw him do something that she'd never known he could.

He reached out through the water. She saw ripples begin at his hands, though he held them motionless, save for a few tremors, in the water. She saw the ripples radiate out through the water until they touched each of the bathing pilgrims.

Tiny tendrils of steam suddenly appeared over the ripples, meandering in the flickering candlelight. Peter shivered. Sweat formed on his brow and upper lip. Fairbairn turned in the water and looked at Peter in awe. He knew. He had felt what Peter had done when he'd touched his shoulder, and he could feel it now. Julie watched as his face changed from awe, to terror, and back to awe.

The quadriplegic child suddenly screamed and kicked her legs. A woman beyond her shook her long, dark hair, showering the onlookers with holy water, and praised the Virgin Mary at the top of her lungs. A man to Peter's right clutched his milk-white eyes and began to sob. "Light," he cried, "I can see some light."

The nun reached out and touched Peter's shoulder. "*Monsieur*, there are others waiting." When Peter did not move, she turned to Julie. "*Mademoiselle*?" Peter was shaking uncontrollably now. His legs wouldn't hold him, and he had fallen forward against the cistern, his arms hooked over the stone rim, plunged to the armpits in the water which now roiled about him with churning energy. It might have appeared that Peter was creating the turbulence by stirring with his arms, except his shoulder muscles were flaccid, unmoving. "Please ask him to step back," the nun pleaded with Julie.

Up and down the length of the cistern, people were sobbing and thanking God, whispering prayers to the Virgin Mary. The old woman with the throat cancer had entered the water. Michael's mother crowded forward to dip her son. The blind man was splashing water into his eyes and weeping uncontrollably.

The nun looked about for help.

"That man's stirring up the water," an onlooker observed.

Fairbairn shuffled through the water to Peter. "Don't stop," he stammered. He looked as if he wanted to touch Peter, to hold him in place, but he was too afraid. His head swept left and right, back and forth, watching the miracle building all around him. He looked to the nun who was now trying to pull Peter back. "For the love of God, woman, leave him be! "He batted her hands away from Peter's shoulders.

"There are others waiting," insisted the nun. The frantic tone of her voice said that she was not blind to what was happening.

It was simply beyond her comprehension, beyond the normal routine of the grotto. She was unwilling to accept, that in this proposed place of miracles, that miracles might actually happen.

Julie touched her arm, watched as the nun recoiled and goose bumps sprang to her flesh. "Just a minute more. Please."

The blonde lowered Michael into the water with the help of two young nurses. Instantly, the turmoil in the water sought him out. One of the nurses leaped back from what she felt in the water, yelping in fear, whispering some incomprehensible litany in French. The other let out a gasp, but clung to the child, assisting his mother in dipping him completely beneath the turbulent surface. Julie could actually see energy in the water now, like the flickering reflection of the candles, only this light came from beneath the surface. It originated at Peter and shot out through the water in radiating lines that ended with individual bathers. Everyone else saw it, too, and now there was no one who didn't know what was happening. The boy, Michael, fought his way to the surface and screamed, arms flailing, feet kicking, twisting his head back and forth. When he looked over at Julie, both his eyes were open, glowing with reflected energy from the water.

The grotto erupted in chaos. Terrified bathers struggled to escape the water, while others refused to leave. Many of those awaiting their turn scrambled over the stone cistern and plunged in, fearing that the miracle would fade at any second. Nuns were screaming, trying to restore order.

Julie tried to pull Peter back from the water, but he was limp. She couldn't manage him by herself. "Help me," she asked Fairbairn. Fairbairn scrambled from the water, his briefs sagging. He hesitated until she pleaded with him again, then he grabbed Peter beneath the arms and hauled him back from the edge of the cistern. Instantly, the water went placid and the flickering lights vanished from its depths. There was an inexplicable sigh of wind that put out more than half the candles in the grotto.

Julie and Fairbairn supported Peter, dragging him through the pressing people toward the steps. "Wait," Fairbairn cried, "my clothes." He dashed back, leaving her struggling to support Peter, who was only semi-conscious. Hands pressed in around her, touching Peter, trying to pull him from her arms. Each touch was followed by a gasp or a cry in French. Julie lashed out, her cold hand slicing through the hot press of their hands. Cursing, she pressed through them toward the steps, shielding Peter as best she could with her own body.

The pilgrims on the steps had seen some of what had happened, but they weren't immediately aware that Peter had been the cause. They believed him to have been overcome by the miracle of Bernadette's spring. Still, many reached out to touch him, and as each one made contact, Julie felt a jolt go through Peter's body, saw their eyes go wide and their hands fly to whatever part of their anatomy served best as a focus for their particular ailment. By the time Fairbairn returned, his trousers hastily donned and the remainder of his clothing bundled beneath one arm, Julie had collapsed on the bottom two steps with Peter, struggling to keep the pilgrims on the stairs at bay. Those nearby knew. And the information spread like wildfire.

"I touched him and my hearing came back!"

"That man! That's the one. He healed me!"

The entire grotto had become a madhouse. Weeping. Praying. Screams and hallelujahs. People were running, colliding with those trying to press forward and see what had happened. Nuns and nurses were overcome by the chaos, accustomed to an orderly reverence. None of them had ever seen a miracle. In their years of serving at the Domain of Our Lady, the miracles they had heard of had been remote and slow-developing. A woman with cancerous lesions goes home and six weeks later her lesions begin to miraculously fade. A crippled child leaves the grotto and months later they hear he's managing to get around with a walker. Nothing like this had ever occurred before.

"Help me," a woman gasped, pressing herself at Peter. "Please help me, too." She hugged herself to his waist, pressing her face against his soaking wet shirt. Julie tried to pry her away without losing hold of Peter. She could imagine the crowd taking her from him, getting cut off from him in the press of bodies. She could imagine losing him forever that way. Could picture the crowd tearing him limb from limb or simply bleeding him dry. A moment later, the woman fell away from Peter, weeping and collapsing in a ball. "I'm healed," she cried. "Thank God, I'm healed."

Julie batted at the hands that were reaching for Peter as they reached the top of the stairs. Passing Montbéliard's statue, Peter reached out and placed a hand against the pink marble of Saint Bernadette's skirts. Where his hand lay, the marble bleached to an alabaster white. Screams ran through the crowd and people pressed for that hand. Even when they'd moved on, fights erupted for the chance to touch the white handprint.

"They're killing him," Julie told Fairbairn. "Please help me get him to the parking lot."

Fairbairn threw his clothes at her and ducked down, slipping one meaty arm up between Peter's legs. He lifted the limp man in a fireman's carry and surged forward through the crowd. Julie followed. Beyond the entrance to the grotto, the confusion was less. They outran not the news of the miracles occurring below, but the belief of it.

"What's happening?" people asked as they passed. "What's wrong with him?"

"People are going crazy in there," Fairbairn said as he forced his way through, "some bloody fool freaked and started complete pandemonium. My friend here got trampled." Julie followed, clutching their savior's clothing, wondering if she'd gotten Peter out in time.

Later, at the rental car, they threw Peter across the back seat and she checked his pulse. It was weak and distant, but he was alive. His face had gone ashen. His eyes appeared sunken. There were great hollows where his cheeks used to be, as if he'd lost twenty pounds that he hadn't had to spare. He was cold. His limbs trembled with unreleased energy. Once or twice, she thought she heard him whimper.

Fairbairn pulled on his socks and shoes. "Will he be all right?"

"Peter's strong," Julie answered. "He just needs time to recover."

Fairbairn pulled on his shirt and jacket, then ran a hand through his wet hair. "About what happened back there...

How? I mean, who are you people?"

Julie tried to smile at him, but failed. "I wish there was some way I could explain, but there isn't, Mr. Fairbairn." She wanted to thank him, but didn't know how. She finally settled for hugging the big man, which set him to shivering. "We can't stay here. They'll be coming up from the grotto, looking for us."

Fairbairn backed off. "Of course." He suddenly dug in his pants pocket and extracted his wallet.

"No," Julie said. "We don't need your money."

Fairbairn blushed. "No, that's not it." He extracted a business card and pressed it into her hand. "I live in Bristol," he told her, his voice cracking. "Investment broker." He shrugged sheepishly, as if embarrassed that he hadn't something more exciting to offer. "You ever need anything—*anything,* understand?—you just ring me up. Okay?"

Julie slipped the card into her shirt pocket. "Of course. Thank you."

She pulled away with him standing there in the vacated parking space, a big man looking lost, looking like he didn't know whether to laugh and jump and shout with joy—or break down and cry.

She drove west toward the coast, stopping only for gas and something to eat. Peter remained unconscious in the back seat, which was just as well because every radio station carried news that a strange American tourist had facilitated a miracle in Lourdes, that all who touched the water while his hands were in it, and all who touched him, were miraculously cured. So long as Peter remained collapsed across the back seat, no one passing by or at the places she stopped connected her to the American from Lourdes. By morning, she was dozing off at the wheel, a dangerous prospect on France's twisting country roads. She'd been following the coastline, heading north, for the last couple of hours. She found a small scenic park overlooking the Bassin d'Arcachon near the town of Arès. On a cliff overlooking the sea, she parked the car and slept.

Peter recovered enough that afternoon to sit up and curse the sun which had been burning the right side of his face. He was weak, sore, and starving, but he wasn't permanently injured in any way.

"We can't go on like this," Julie told him, their eyes locked in the rearview mirror.

"I know."

"Even if it doesn't kill you, it's tearing us apart."

"There's that thing inside of you, Jules. There's that, too."

"I don't know how to let it go anymore than you know how to give up your gift," she replied. "There's only one person who can answer those questions for us, but you refuse to help me find her."

Peter looked away. "If I help you find her, you'll give it up?"

"If you will," she whispered, her voice uncertain and distant.

He nodded without meeting her eyes in the mirror, his gaze locked on the waves pounding the beach below. "Then we'll find her. We'll make her tell us everything."

"And then we'll kill her," Julie added. Her eyes were as cold and hard as Antarctic ice.

He nodded again.

They drove to Bordeaux and caught the first available flight out of France. The journey ahead of them would be a long, hard one. They knew Wisteria would be as impossible to find as she would be to kill. All they had was each other.

ALL COLORS BLEED TO RED

In his peripheral vision, Jesse Sanders spotted a splash of color: one bright bit of blue contrasted against the muck of the creek bed. Turning toward it, he stumbled and fell as thick mud sucked at his boots. He managed to catch himself on the stalagmite-shaped stump of a long dead willow, nearly dropping his sample jars in the bargain.

He poked at the color with a stick. It was a dead bird. A blue jay with its beak buried in fetid slime. One feather, broken so that it stood out from the bird's wing like a pennant in the breeze, was all that delineated the poor creature from the pollution in which it lay. Some morbid tendency urged Jesse to pry up the carcass with the tip of the stick. The bird's breast clung to the mud, peeling back from balsa-fine bones cupped about an empty cavity.

The blue jay was gone. Only the shell it had once inhabited remained. *Like me,* thought Jesse.

He let the carcass settle back into the mud and tossed away the stick. There remained an obdurate film of slime in the palm of his hand. He wiped the ooze on his thigh, leaving long, green-brown stains on his khaki trousers. *Camouflaged,* he thought. *Thus I become one with the trauma to which Wilder Creek has succumbed.* On a whim, he bent and plucked the unsoiled feather from the dead bird. Though it parted at the break, what pulled free was most of the feather. He carefully tucked it away in his shirt pocket, stepped across the dead bird, and made his way through the cattails and sharp, high grass to the creek.

Wilder Creek was moving, though imperceptibly. Jesse had to stare at the water for several silent breaths before he was certain. The oil on the surface coalesced in the rainbow-hues of an abstract painting, like a mood ring shattered across the surface of a black mirror. It had a hypnotic effect and for a moment he couldn't pull his gaze away.

There was a small catfish floating just off the bank, its sleek, black body bobbing alongside a plastic tampon applicator. The catfish appeared to have only recently given up its struggle for life. He fancied for a moment that he saw its gills flare, but when it happened only once he was certain he'd imagined it. Beyond the catfish was something larger, something older, something that had occupied the foul water of the creek long enough to have lost its own discernability. Half submerged in the black water, the size of the thing was hard to grasp, but it might have once been a cat or a large rodent, or maybe even a puppy. Now it was a decaying cage of ribs and teeth and skull canvassed by a pale hide spotted with the last remaining tufts of grey fur.

Jesse shuddered, breaking his momentary apoplexy. He knelt amid the garbage to take his samples. The mud bubbled seductively about his feet, releasing an odor of pestilence and putrefaction. He filled the first of his three Mason jars and was screwing the lid back on when he saw the otters on the opposite bank, not a dozen feet away.

Stretched out in the mud, their fur clotted with oil so that it stood out in stubby porcupine spikes, the otters looked like bloated puffer fish washed up on the banks of Prince William Sound, their gills choked with Exxon crude, bristling and angry… but dead. Jesse shook off the image. He'd promised himself that northern Virginia was far enough removed from those memories. Besides which, the still shapes on the opposite bank were no member of family Tetraodontidae.

"Lutra canadensis," he said aloud, amazing himself by recalling not only the puffer's family, but the otter's genus and species as well. He hadn't forgotten *all* his zoology.

Startled by Jesse's voice, the far otter raised its head and studied him over the still form of its mate. Though he'd been taught that river otters are excessively shy, this one watched him without fear. Looking the animal over, Jesse realized that it might be incapable of fleeing. Worse, it might be incapable of fear. Jesse had seen that look before on the television, in the eyes of a Rwandan child whose head gaped wide, revealing gleaming bone and the edges of angry red tissue, the result of a blow from a Hutu machete. The child had lain for most of a day among the dead in a Roman Catholic church, not moving, barely breathing, knowing that if the life left in him were noted it would be succinctly snuffed out. The look on the child's face was one without the energy left to feel even pain, let alone fear. The look said that death might have been the saner choice.

The otter had that look.

Thus, thought Jesse, *do world events shape our perceptions.* A Rwandan child had taught him the look of hopeless surrender. And before the Exxon *Valdez,* he had believed in the sanctity of an absolute right and wrong.

The otter's eyes were coated with a murky film of white that was neither opaque nor transparent, but somewhere in between, like a thin, cloudy lacquer over black marble. Its ears and whiskers were pasted back against its head as if it were facing into a strong wind. The mouth remained a tight black line while it breathed through the nose in short wheezing pants. White fur that had once lined the underside of its neck, blending back into the darker brown of the body and tail, was now a charcoal grey, the color of smoke rising from a burning tire.

The otter raised a webbed foot briefly, part greeting, part dismissal. It was a pitiful gesture, and it brought Jesse to his feet. Forgotten, his two empty sample jars *plopped* into the mud.

Fifty feet upstream—if the stagnant creek could be thought of as having an *up*- or *down*stream—there was an ancient desk. There was also a dead rhesus monkey, a mystery that had occupied Jesse's mind for some time before the jay's feather had distracted him. Someone from White Post or Millwood had probably dumped the desk by the roadside, but he had no idea where the monkey had come from. A heavy rain might have swept the dilapidated office furniture to its final resting place, a good quarter mile from the road, where it'd become caught on some submerged log or sewer line. However it got there—the desk, that is—it lay astraddle the middle of the stream forming a bridge that, though incomplete, allowed Jesse to cross without getting water in over the tops of his boots.

He followed the creek back to the otters, moving as quietly as possible so as not to frighten them away. Stealth proved impossible, what with the mud sucking at his feet, the dry grass rasping against his jeans, and reeds snapping like number two pencils beneath his boots. He needn't have worried though; the otters weren't going anywhere. The far otter, the only one he'd seen move, had dropped its head across its mate's sunken side. Beneath their foggy shrouds, the otter's small eyes followed Jesse's approach.

"I won't hurt you," Jesse whispered as he knelt beside them.

He probed the matted coat of the still otter. And felt nothing. No heartbeat. No rising and falling of the chest. Nothing but cold, greasy fur stretched across a framework of prominent ribs. The other otter, which he decided was the male because it was larger, lifted its head and studied him, looking at him sideways the way a puzzled dog will do.

"I'm sorry," he told the male. "She's gone." It blinked ever so slowly. He reached out to touch it.

The otter's head turned, rattlesnake fast, and its teeth sank into the webbing of flesh between Jesse's thumb and finger.

From the *Washington Post:*

MONKEY VIRUS

Late Wednesday evening a strain of virus similar to that which was purged from Reston, VA, in 1989 was detected in African monkeys under quarantine at a temporary facility near Dulles International Airport. Local health officials were quick to announce that there is no immediate threat from this virus as it has been entirely contained within the quarantine facility. They added that, if the virus should somehow escape the quarantine facility, a scenario they view as virtually impossible, the virus is not easily transmitted and does not affect humans.

The virus, a relative of the highly lethal Ebola Zaire reported to have killed thousands in Africa, is one of several filoviruses (Latin for "thread viruses") under constant study by agencies such as the Centers for Disease Control (CDC) in Atlanta and the Army's Medical Research Institute of Infectious Diseases (USAMRIID) in Frederick, MD. When asked for comment, the CDC indicated that they had not yet been contacted by the Virginia State Health Department and were unfamiliar with the details of the incident. Both the CDC and USAMRIID were involved in the 1989 Reston incident in which several hundred monkeys were euthanized to contain the spread of the disease. Though unable to speculate, the CDC did reiterate local Health Department announcements that there was no danger to human lives, pointing out that there was not a single case of human viral infection during the 1989 incident.

A spokesman for the Health Department stated that some 16 to 20 thousand monkeys are imported into the United States every year for research purposes. Many are diseased. For this reason all monkeys are required to undergo a one month quarantine. He indicated that there is nothing unusual or alarming in the recent virus outbreak and that the quarantine procedures in place will contain it.

Jesse nearly ran into the Indian.

Startled, he realized he didn't know where he was—was, in fact, missing a sizeable slice of memory. Physical pain shut out the immediate fear of dislocation. Every joint ached. He was dizzy, head spinning about a fire centered somewhere just back of his eyes. He needed no thermometer to tell him he was burning with fever. His mouth was dry, and his lips were cracked. His hand was screaming a cacophony of pain. His legs were trembling, and he couldn't catch his breath.

The Indian looked to have been carved from cedar and allowed to stand, unfinished, in the weather for decades. Jesse wasn't sure he was real until he moved. When the Indian's gaze (eyes black as wormholes) dropped, Jesse realized there was something draped in his arms.

The dead otter hung like a sodden stole, head and tail bonelessly pointing to earth. Her thick coat of sludge was smeared across Jesse's shirt and trousers; his arms were black to the elbows. He felt something brush his leg and looked down to find the male had followed—how far, he had no idea. The male otter dropped at Jesse's feet, sides heaving, wheezing, a bubble of hemorrhagic blood erupting from its nose.

The Indian extended his hands for the dead otter. "She's dead," Jesse mumbled inanely, relinquishing her nonetheless. The Indian took her without comment, turned and walked quietly away. The male otter followed. Jesse stood for a moment, dizzy and confused; then he, too, followed the Indian up a gentle hill.

At the crest of the hill there stood a ragged hut of mud and reeds, its opening covered with some sort of animal hide. Smoke bled from the cracks in the mud. More smoke billowed out when the Indian parted the hide and entered. The hide slapped closed behind him, leaving Jesse and the male otter standing in the fast-fading twilight. Again, the otter lay down between Jesse's feet. Jesse used the time to examine the puncture wounds in his hand. They were swollen and red, with angry pus accumulating just beneath the surface of the skin. *It's infected,* thought Jesse, *I need to get some antibiotics.*

The Indian emerged from the tent without the dead otter. He seemed surprised to find Jesse waiting. "How may I be of assistance to you?" he asked in a voice that was as far from stereotypical as Jesse was from his antibiotics. The Indian was obviously an educated man. His careful enunciation belied the leather and beads and native trappings which he wore.

"I think I need help," Jesse mumbled.

The Indian nodded. "Will you enter the sweat lodge?"

"What?"

"A cleansing," the Indian said. "I can offer you that much."

"I think I need a doctor."

"I," said the Indian, "am a doctor."

"Oh," Jesse said, thinking, *Yeah, right.* Just what he needed, a native American medicine man.

"There is a price."

Of course. Jesse reached into his pocket, found the wad of bills he kept there. He wasn't thinking about why he should be paying an Indian who probably had nothing to offer him in the way of medical aid; he was running on automatic. Someone expected to be paid, and habit said pull money out and pay.

Maybe the Indian would call someone. Nine-One-One would do nicely. But before Jesse could pull his money free, the Indian laid a gentle restraining hand on his wrist and shook his head. *Not money then,* thought Jesse. But he had nothing else. There was the sample jar bulging in the pocket of his field vest, but Jesse needed to take that back to the lab at Alcor Chemicals.

"The creek is poison," said the Indian, as if reading Jesse's mind.

The only other thing in his pockets was the feather. Jesse pulled it free and passed it to the Indian. The Indian held it up so that it caught the last rays of the sun. "Fitting," he remarked, "that you offer me a lie."

"A lie?" Jesse's legs were fading fast. He thought they would buckle, but the Indian caught him by the elbow and held him up, his grip like iron.

"Like the sky, there is no blue in this feather. There is, in fact, little or no blue in the world. It's a deception."

Alveolar cells, thought Jesse, recalling more of his zoology and physics. Tiny, box-like, transparent particles in the jay's feathers bounce blue light toward the observer while allowing longer wavelengths to pass through. If Jesse's memory served him right, there's no blue pigment in any known vertebrate. His own blue eyes were not even really blue. In the sky, tiny molecules of gas do the same thing. Physicists call it Rayleigh scattering.

"Blue is a lie," said the Indian, "the only *true* color is red. All colors bleed to red."

"Look, chief, I don't have anything else to give you—"

"This will do," answered the Indian, and the feather disappeared into a leather pouch hung round his neck. The Indian pulled aside the flap and motioned for Jesse to enter the sweat lodge.

Excerpt from a 1990 report filed by USAMRIID's Chief of Epidemiology, Dr. Thomas Jahrling:

We can count ourselves extraordinarily lucky that Ebola Reston, though it exhibited the exact same appearance, structural makeup, and protein composition as Ebola Zaire, was not capable of multi-species transmission and amplification. Prior to USAMRIID's extermination of the specimens in the Reston Primate Quarantine Unit, no less than five civilian personnel had been exposed to the virus, up to and including exposure during necropsy. During the cleanup operation, several military personnel were also exposed as a result of breached Racal suits and gloves. Furthermore, during the initial investigation and prior to the positive identification of a level 4 hot agent, both tissue samples and complete specimens were transported under inadequate containment and safety precautions from Reston, VA to Fort Detrick in Frederick, MD, risking exposure to a large population group. Though we have no positive evidence that Ebola strains can be transmitted through the air, there is reason to believe, based upon experiments carried out with E. Zaire at this facility, that that possibility exists. Regardless, emerging viruses, in particular those identified as biohazard level 4, are known to mutate/evolve at extraordinary rates and must be handled as if they had the potential for airborne amplification.

An outbreak of E. Zaire or a similar hot agent in the Washington, DC area would have devastating effects and be extremely hard, if not impossible, to contain. The mortality rate among villages near the headwaters of the Ebola River during an outbreak in 1976 was ninety percent. An airborne strain would have species-wide, global impact, conceivably circling the globe in as little as six weeks. It's for these reasons that E. Zaire is the most feared agent at USAMRIID.

The fact that E. Reston did not exhibit the same multi-species transmission characteristics of E. Zaire, E. Sudan, Marburg, HIV, and other emerging agents, should not encourage an atmosphere of negligence in the handling of primate quarantines. When E. Reston next emerges, who's to say how it will have changed as a result of this one micro-break?

"Remove your clothing," the medicine man said as Jesse slipped through the hide-covered doorway.

Jesse was beyond arguing. Fever and fog. Things were shifting in and out of focus. His head was one dull ache, and he imagined he could actually hear his knees knocking together.

He stripped to his underwear. The Indian did not protest that last bit of modesty, merely draped a heavy robe over Jesse's shoulders. The robe stank and scratched at his skin. Jesse believed it to be genuine buffalo.

"Rub yourself down with this." The medicine man handed him a bundle of grass. "It is sage," he added when Jesse hesitated. When he had complied, the Indian motioned toward the central fire. "Sit and be cleansed."

"I think," stuttered Jesse, "that I need medical attention. Is there a phone nearby?"

"Sit," the Indian repeated, steering Jesse toward the fire. "You are beyond medical attention, my friend. I offer you a cleansing… and the chance to see the catalyst that you have become. No one can do more for you now."

The otter crawled into Jesse's lap as he sat beside the fire and stones. For a moment, Jesse was afraid, remembering the speed with which the otter had bit him the first time. Then he reasoned that the damage was already done, and there was nothing to lose. He touched it, stroking its oiled hide beneath his equally coated hand, scratching it carefully behind the ears. He found what appeared to be a bite mark on its hind quarters. Through hooded eyes that now looked as if they were covered with cataracts, the otter watched him. There was red arterial blood running from its nostrils, more seeping from beneath its tail. Jesse had seen cormorants and seals and even sea otters covered with crude. He'd seen them die from it. But he'd never seen an animal bleed like this. There was more at work here than Wilder Creek's pollution. What had Alcor been dumping?

The medicine man sat down across the fire from him. Of the female otter there was no sign. Her body might be hidden in the thick furs piled about the walls of the lodge; it was too dark for Jesse's eyes to probe every corner. From a wooden bucket, the medicine man ladled a thick soup of herbs onto the stones in the fire. Hiss and steam. A thick cloud that stung Jesse's eyes and burned going down his lungs. He thought of peyote and loco weed and all the westerns he had seen. He watched in silence as the Indian placed the blue jay feather into the fire. It did not burn, but instead withered and curled, the blue fading like a bruise to black. Its smoke rose pure white, mingling and disappearing into the steam rising above the fire.

Jesse's mind reeled with the vapors, soaring out and above himself for a moment. What he saw alarmed him. His eyes were red. There was a rash spreading across his cheeks. His hands shook and his breathing was labored.

A moment—perhaps an eternity—later, Jesse realized he must be hallucinating. The Indian was gone. A dense jungle had replaced the walls of the lodge and towering trees stretched above him where the lodge's dome-shaped roof should be. There came the calls of birds and nocturnal animals that had never set foot in Virginia. The smell of the jungle pervaded everything, a rich, moist odor of life and decay and smoldering creation. Jesse felt himself sink into the ground, melting. It felt as if he were dying, letting go of life oh so very, very slowly, returning a molecule at a time into the earth that had borne him.

Worms. Warmth. Waiting. Then a billion twisting strands struggling to snare a passing red globule. And then he was in. Replicating. The smells of earth and safety and comfort were replaced with a slaughterhouse stench of blood and death. This new realm didn't want him. There were bodies which opposed him, but they were weak, and he was incredibly powerful. Bursting forth again. Rushing headlong down narrow tunnels. Hunger. Incredible, all-encompassing hunger. Somewhere there was a drum beating the sound of a vast, echoing heart. It sounded tired, weak, wet. A pump spewing half its load.

Changing now. Subtle. Very subtle. A new strand here. A twist in the matrix. A protein minutely modified. Something screamed, and he recognized it as the cry of a monkey. The otter trembled on his lap, but it wasn't on his lap. He was the otter. He coursed through the otter's blood until—

Teeth.

Pain.

A new mutation.

This is evolution. This is creation. This is life older than time. There came the sound of air rushing through his lungs. Flight. He tasted freedom for the first time. He had been born again. And would be born again—

—with every breath.

When he opened his eyes the lodge and the medicine man were gone. He was alone with the cold morning air, a sky full of stars above, and the lights of White Post, Virginia, spread out in the valley below. Shivering, he stood and waited on the sun, cradling the otter carefully in the crook of his arm. When the sun topped the mountains behind him, it lit the slopes below, illuminating the stagnant creek, the road, and, right where he'd left it, his jeep.

Stumbling every step, he managed to make it down to the jeep. Crawling inside, he thought he heard someone whisper something from the shadows beside the road. But there was no one there.

Still, the words plagued him as he drove home.

It has begun.

From the *Washington Post:*

VIRUS-LADEN MONKEY MISSING

The Virginia State Health Department has reported that a rhesus monkey infected with a contagious virus is missing. On Thursday an operation was mounted to euthanize the diseased monkeys presently held in quarantine near Dulles International Airport. Though no one saw the monkey escape during the operation, the final count shows one missing. Health Department officials were quick to announce that there is absolutely no danger to local residents or their pets; however, sources within the Health Department, asking that they remain anonymous, have indicated that both the CDC and USAMRIID have been contacted. During a similar outbreak of monkey virus which occurred in Reston in 1989, a joint operation conducted by the CDC and USAMRIID was necessary to dispose of the infected animals and sterilize the facilities. For the moment, the CDC and USAMRIID refuse to comment, acknowledging only that they have been asked for assistance in identifying and containing the spread of the disease. Though all three agencies have emphasized that there is no danger to humans, it is interesting to note that the "monkey house" in Reston remains empty to this day.

The ringing of the phone woke Jesse. Rolling over, he managed to bring the clock on his nightstand into focus. The normally green numerals were hiding behind a red filter. Everything was red. The walls, the curtains, the carpet, the hand he held out before his face. Red. What had the Indian said? *All colors bleed to red.*

It was nearly five o'clock. Daylight still bled around the edges of the curtains. His hand had been bleeding while he slept. The Ace bandage he'd wrapped around it was soaked through, and there was blood in the bed. The otter was curled where he had left it on a folded blanket at the foot of the bed.

It took him a moment to figure out where the day had gone. He should have gone to the hospital, but instead he'd spent the entire morning in his basement running tests on the water sample from Wilder Creek. The water contained a high concentration of a benzene-derivative which he knew had to have come from Alcor Chemicals. He'd written his report and faxed it in to McLaughlin, his superior at Alcor. The pollutant, and more importantly the high concentration, was appalling, but it was not what was working at killing the otter or himself. When the report was filed, he'd taken the time to look at a sample of his own blood. What he'd seen there was as terrifying as it was confusing. That was his second chance to go to the hospital, but he'd been too exhausted.

The phone was a cordless model, and he took it with him to the bathroom. "Hello?"

"Sanders?"

"Yeah." The face in the mirror said he was lying. The face in the mirror could not be his.

"Steve McLaughlin. I just finished reading the report you faxed me on Wilder Creek. I need you to come in so we can discuss it."

"It's late." The rash had merged to form bruises. His entire face was black and blue and seemed to hang as if it had been detached from the underlying bone. He was wearing an expressionless rubber mask, and it was coming loose. His eyes were the color of rubies.

"I don't care how late it is. I want you in my office in thirty minutes."

"Hold on." He turned and vomited into the stool. Blood. Blood and tiny black specks like coffee grounds.

"Sanders?"

He wiped his mouth. "What seems to be the problem, Mr. McLaughlin?"

"The problem is the whole damn report, Sanders."

His nose was bleeding. He stuffed tissue paper into his nostrils, but the wads quickly soaked through.

"Sanders? Are you listening?"

"Go ahead."

"Page eighteen, Sanders. Where was the analysis done?"

"Analysis?" This wasn't making any sense.

"I checked downstairs. It didn't come from our lab."

"I ran the tests myself. Too sick to come in."

"We've got technicians for running those tests, Sanders. You're supposed to be a field agent."

"Yes, sir, but I wanted to verify the results myself." He used a towel to wipe away the blood that was pouring over his lips and chin. It wouldn't stop. "I've been sick," he confessed, spraying blood on the white phone. "I ran the tests at home. My equipment's mostly surplus government stuff and most of it's outdated, but it all works, and I'm confident of the results."

"This type of thing is supposed to run through *our* lab, Sanders."

"I didn't want to wait on Alcor's two-week lab queue, Mr. McLaughlin. I didn't think Wilder Creek could wait either."

"I can't forward these kinds of recommendations without some sort of second source verification. As it stands now, I don't even have our own lab's verification of the data!"

Jesse knew where this was leading. His data was about to get swept under a carpet. Write off Wilder Creek. There wasn't an entry for it in the fiscal budget books. It was time for him to bluff. "I sent duplicate samples to a friend with the EPA. I should have their results within a day or two."

"You did what!?"

"I sent a water sample to the EPA at Research Triangle in North Carolina—"

"I know where it is, Sanders! Who the hell gave you... Shit. Look, Sanders. You haven't been here very long. Perhaps you don't understand our procedures. You certainly don't understand all the issues."

"You mean the politics."

"Look, the EPA will see only one solution to this. They'll shut us down. Alcor employs—"

"More than eight hundred men and women in this area alone," Jesse interrupted. "I've seen the TV commercials."

"Don't get smart with me."

"Don't sit there and try to tell me that a creek contaminated with benzene is to be ignored."

"You don't know what you're dealing with. We're talking one pissant little stream."

"Wilder Creek empties into the Shenandoah."

McLaughlin nearly screamed. "You sanctimonious, little shit. Now I know why Exxon fired you. My office, Sanders. I want you here in thirty minutes. Is that clear?" The line went dead.

Jesse stood there for a moment, numb, the bloody towel pressed to his face, his vision pink bordered with red. He was sick again, vomiting a noxious concoction of blood and mucus into the sink. The smell of the stuff was overpowering. Worse than roadkill, worse than decay, worse than anything he'd smelled in his life. In the sink's mess, he thought he could see what he had seen under the microscope when he had looked at his blood. A million thread-like strands. Worms. Squirming through a battlefield of ravaged cells.

Devouring everything in their path.

From the *Washington Post:*

DISEASED MONKEY STOLEN

A representative from a local animal rights activist group calling themselves Humans for a Unified Tomorrow (HUNT) has come forth and admitted to stealing the rhesus monkey previously presumed to have escaped from a quarantine facility. The monkey carries what USAMRIID and CDC officials have now positively identified as a Reston-like strain of the Ebola virus, harmless to humans. Knowing only that the monkeys at the quarantine facility were ill, HUNT stole one hoping to prove maltreatment on the part of the monkey's owners. When asked to relinquish the monkey to Health Department officials, HUNT was unable to comply, saying the monkey had since died and been disposed of. Criminal charges against the animal rights activists are pending further investigation. Health Department and CDC officials are presently attempting to locate the monkey's corpse.

It seemed to take forever before the phone was answered. "Chris? It's Jesse Sanders."

"Uh? What time is it?"

"Sorry, I know it's late. I need your help. Pretend I'm a college freshman again and tell me about viruses."

The voice at the other end of the phone line sounded tired, as if he'd already put in more than his normal day explaining these things. "What have you gotten yourself into this time, Jess?"

"Nothing. I just need some background information for a report I'm putting together."

"You still doing field work for Alcor?"

"Yeah."

"Biotoxins?"

"Be serious, Chris, you know Nixon outlawed that kind of research years ago."

"Doesn't mean we're not doing it somewhere though."

Jesse had little time for patience. "Can you help me or not?"

"Sure, but I could give you the name of a friend who—"

"That's okay, Chris. You'll do just fine."

"You gonna tape this or what?"

"Right," Jesse lied. "I've got the recorder going now." All he was holding was the otter which had died a few minutes ago, venting blood from every orifice. Its body felt spongy and bloated, as if it had even bled out beneath its skin.

A long sigh from the other end. The sound of a pillow being slapped up against a headboard. "No, it's all right, dear. Go to sleep... Jess, where do you want me to start?"

"With the basics."

"Let's see. Virus. Virus. You mean like the flu or like HIV?"

"Both."

"Damn, buddy, you're asking a lot for three a.m., you know?"

"Sorry, Chris. I wouldn't ask if it weren't important."

"Yeah, yeah, I know. Your job's probably on the line or something. Let's see... okay. A virus is nothing more than a small capsule of membranes and proteins with one or more strands of DNA or RNA, smaller than a bacteria. Bacteria can even have viruses in them. Most life forms, in fact, carry viruses with them their entire life. In most cases, both virus and host have evolved to live quite comfortably with each other. You know about DNA and RNA, they contain the program for replication, same as in you and me. But that's all a virus lives for, making more virus. Stick one somewhere by itself, on the counter, in a Petri dish, pin it on your friggin' refrigerator with a magnet, and it'll just sit there. Nothing. The damn thing isn't really even alive. Call it stasis, call it hibernation, call it a nap. The damn thing just sits there waiting.

"Stick a virus in blood or mucus, and it comes to life. It's still waiting, but now it's waiting for something to come by. The surface of a virus has a stickiness about it and when the right cell wanders by—a cell whose stickiness matches the stickiness of the virus—then the virus clings to the cell. The cell thinks it's found a meal and it enfolds the virus. Once inside, the virus really switches on, and it begins to replicate itself using the cell's own materials and machinery to do it. A virus will build copies of itself until eventually the cell is full, and it explodes. Or sometimes the virus will bud through the cell wall, spinning off new virus particles to spread the infection—that's the way AIDS works.

"Viruses don't *want* to kill their host. It's not in their best interest, but sometimes they don't have any choice. Viruses are sharks, and they love to eat. Some of them have too big of an appetite, and they devour their host."

"Tell me about AIDS. Is it true that it came from monkeys?"

"Ah, that's what this is about. I saw on the news that you guys had a monkey scare going on there."

"Should we be scared?"

A long pause. Then, "I'm not sure, Jess. There's some scary shit coming out of Africa; HIV and AIDS are the least of it. You've got some good folks out that way though. The CDC's a bunch of idiots, but those Army guys know what they're doing. If they're saying things are okay, then they probably are."

"Do you know anything about this Ebola virus?"

"Only that you don't want it. It makes AIDS look like a Sunday picnic. It's believed that HIV and Ebola came from the same region around Lake Victoria. I've got a friend at Berkeley could tell you more. Want his number?"

"No, that's okay."

"You sure you're okay, Jess? You sound like you're having trouble breathing."

He was. There was blood in his lungs. He could taste and smell it with every exhalation. "Chris, if I told you I had seen an infected blood sample and that the viral organism looked like a clump of worms, would that mean anything to you?"

"Worms? Like maybe someone had dumped a bowl of noodles out on the floor? Like maybe a lot of twisted threads?"

"Yeah."

"My God, Jess, that's a filovirus. Marburg. Ebola. Where the hell did you see—"

"Tell me about mutations."

"Not until you tell me where the bloody hell you saw a blood sample contaminated with a fucking filovirus!"

"The monkeys, Chris," Jesse lied. "It's just these damn monkeys the papers have been talking about. Calm down, would ya?"

"You're scaring me, man. How the hell did you get involved with—"

"Mutations, Chris. Tell me about mutations."

"You really need to talk to my friend at Berkeley. These guys got a language all their own. They don't talk about the disease spreading; they talk about chain of transmission and amplification. They call 'em level 4 hot agents, and when it kills you, they say you *crash and bleed out.* They live in their own little world, Jess, seeking their own glory hunting these bastards down in the rain forest. You really want to know about mutations in that world, you should talk to an expert."

"Just tell me what *you* know."

"Shit, Jesse, what's there to tell? Viruses mutate all the damn time. Just look at the flu. You want a better example, look at HIV. It's believed that Ugandan monkeys carried a lot of unusual viruses. As the monkeys were caught, caged, and imported to support all the research done in the seventies, all these different viruses were brought together in kind of a big stew pot. They mutated or evolved—use whatever term you prefer—real friggin' fast. One of the end results was HIV. HIV jumped from monkeys to man, undergoing another series of rapid mutations so that it could establish itself. By the time we knew what was happening, it was so widespread that now you can bet that it's here to stay, just like the flu.

"But HIV was just a probe," Chris speculated, "Mother Nature's test case if you will. It's highly lethal, but not very infectious. Ebola's a whole new ball game and whatever mutation follows it will be a mother. The viruses are fighting back. We're destroying their ecosystems, the tropical rain forests. They've got to mutate fast and get out of the jungle, or perish."

"You make it sound intelligent."

"Viruses are one of the oldest life forms on the planet, Jess. Four billion years they've been here. They'll be here when we're gone. You want my opinion, Mother Nature has had enough."

Jesse thought of Prince William Sound, of the mess at Wilder Creek, of McLaughlin's callous attitude regarding the environment. They were but a small part of what was going on across the globe.

"Mother Nature is royally pissed," Chris continued, "and this is her way of telling us. She's getting ready to wipe the slate, starting at the top of the food chain. The really nasty viruses like Ebola didn't originate with the monkeys. Ebola burns out primate hosts too damn fast to be native to any of them. Somewhere deep in the rain forest is its natural host.

Epidemiologists have been hunting for more than twenty years now, and they're not even close. They can't find them, man. They can't find them 'cause Mother Nature doesn't want them found. She's getting ready, probing us, biding her time, building the perfect assassin. When it comes it'll be airborne.

"And it'll be the fucking end of the world."

From an unpublished document maintained by the Special Pathogens Branch of the Centers for Disease Control, Atlanta, GA:

A DESCRIPTION OF THE EBOLA ZAIRE VIRUS AND ITS EFFECTS ON THE HUMAN BODY

Biohazard Level 4 Hot Agent.
Filovirus: Ebola Zaire.

Ebola Zaire is named for the Ebola River, a tributary of the Congo, or Zaire, River. The first known outbreak of E. Zaire occurred in 1976 when it erupted simultaneously in 55 villages near the headwaters of the Ebola River. Additional microbreaks have been documented since that time, but reports are sketchy. Known strains of Ebola include E. Zaire, E. Sudan, and E. Reston. Together with Marburg, these comprise the filovirus group. Ebola is distantly related to measles, mumps, rabies, certain pneumonia viruses, parainfluenza, and respiratory syncytial virus. A primitive "life form," Ebola particles contain one strand of RNA and only seven proteins, three of which are vaguely understood and four of which are completely unknown. These proteins seem to target the immune system like HIV; however, Ebola does in ten days what HIV takes ten years to accomplish. Of the filoviruses, E. Zaire is inarguably the worst.

E. Zaire attacks every organ and tissue with the exception of skeletal muscle and bone. Early symptoms include headache, fever, back and muscle aches, and petechiae (red spots which are hemorrhages under the skin). Blood clots lodge in the capillaries where they shut off the supply of blood to various parts of the body, causing dead spots to appear in the brain, liver, kidneys, lungs, intestines, testicles, breast tissue, and all through the skin. Ebola attacks connective tissue with particular ferocity, multiplying in collagen (the protein which holds organs together). Collagen in the body softens and the underlayers of the skin die and liquefy. The skin actually separates from the underlying flesh and bone. Spontaneous rips appear in the skin, pouring hemorrhagic blood. The maculopapular rash merges to become huge bruises. The skin goes soft and pulpy and tears off under any pressure. The mouth, gums, and salivary glands bleed. This bleeding is a bright red arterial flow and it does not stop because the body's clotting factors have all been exhausted. The host literally bleeds out beneath the surface of his skin. The surface of the tongue turns brilliant red and then sloughs off, often during explosive vomiting of hemorrhagic blood resulting from internal bleeding. The back of the throat and the lining of the windpipe may also slough off. The heart muscles soften and the heart bleeds into its chambers. As the heart beats, it also floods the chest cavity with blood. The brain becomes clogged with dead blood cells. The lining of the eyeball is attacked and the eyes fill with blood. Victims may weep blood. The lungs fill up with blood and the host has difficulty breathing. Hemispherical strokes are common. Blood examined under a microscope shows that the red blood cells have been destroyed. Cells still under attack are fat with clusters of replicating virus particles.

Ebola triggers a spotty necrosis that spreads throughout the internal organs. The liver bulges up and turns yellow, begins to liquefy, and then cracks apart. The kidneys become clogged with dead cells and cease functioning. As the kidneys fail, the blood becomes toxic with urine. The spleen becomes a single blood clot the size of a baseball. The intestines typically fill with blood. The lining of the gut dies and is sloughed off into the bowels where it is defecated with large amounts of blood. In men, the testicles bloat and bruise. In women, the labia become blue and protrusive and there is massive vaginal bleeding. In both sexes, the nipples bleed. Pregnant women abort the fetus spontaneously. The fetus is infected with the virus.

Ebola destroys the brain. Depersonalization occurs as the

virus destroys the higher brain functions, leaving only the deeper, most primitive brain stem functions intact. Eventually even these are destroyed as the brain is liquefied. Victims often go into epileptic convulsions, thrashing and spraying blood everywhere.

Ebola multiplies so rapidly that the body's infected cells become crystal-like blocks of packed virus particles. The blocks appear near the center of the cell and then migrate toward the surface where it disintegrates in hundreds of individual virus particles which breach the cell wall and spread, continuing to multiply until all the body is filled with the virus. This amplification continues until a single droplet of the host's blood may contain a hundred million virus particles.

In the final stage, the host goes into shock and loses consciousness from loss of blood. Transfusions are impossible because the veins have collapsed. After death, the cadaver deteriorates quickly. The internal organs, having been clinically dead for days, dissolve. A meltdown occurs as the connective tissue, skin, and organs liquefy. The fluids that leak from the cadaver are saturated with Ebola particles.

McLaughlin called again, first thing in the morning, just before the Indian made his appearance. Jesse hung up on his boss. He tore the phone cord from the wall. He was tempted to do as McLaughlin said and come into the office. There would be a certain justice in sitting down across the desk from him, in sharing the death that explodes now from his body with every exhalation.

But Jesse used the very last of his strength to make one trip out to the garage and back. By that time he had lost all sense of equilibrium. Something had torn in his gut, leaving him with a bulbous, tearing pregnancy in his lower abdomen like a malignant child wanting out. He wasn't sure he could move anymore. A bare stretch of carpet in his living room looked comfortable enough, so he sat there. At least there was no pain. His nervous system was too far gone for that.

The Indian came back for the second otter, lifting it from the blood-soaked blanket and cradling it carefully in his arms. "Where do you take them?" Jesse asked.

"Home," answered the Indian, "to that place where I first created them."

"Will you also come for me?"

The Indian pondered the question for an eternity. Jesse thought he might have lost consciousness at least once in that time. He worried for a moment that he might have even missed the answer, but finally the Indian nodded soberly. "I will come back for you, Jesse Sanders, when your work is done."

And then the Indian was gone, as if he'd never been there, leaving Jesse to think about their first meeting.

I offer you a cleansing and the chance to see the catalyst that you've become, the Indian had said.

Jesse understood the vision of the sweat lodge. From jungle to monkey to otter... to him. A series of mutations in which the virus gathered intelligence and strength. A new strain of filovirus in the birthing. An airborne assassin now. Incredibly contagious and incredibly fast. The next transmission would be the last. Jesse is catalyst and cataclysm in one. The beginning and the end. The sacrifice and the promise: today for tomorrow. Mother Nature had done him only one cathartic favor, she'd given him the chance to see what he was delivering. And now she promised him a place to rest afterward.

He laughed, a sick bubbling of arterial blood flaked with tarry clots. It would serve McLaughlin right if he were capable of delivering it in person. From McLaughlin it would spread, unstoppable. A global cleansing. An end. And a beginning. The earth would survive. Time would march on... without mankind.

He couldn't do it. He couldn't even allow someone to find him like this. He refused to sell out his species.

Despite the dehydration, he was vomiting as much as ever. It poured from him, a concoction of blood and liquefied tissue and the microscopic death of virus particles. His clothing was soaked with it. It was in his mouth and his eyes and spreading out from where he sat, a black tide on the carpet when viewed through the red filter over his eyes. He seemed to be bleeding from everywhere. His home had taken on the odor of carnage and the color red.

All colors bleed to red.

The three-gallon gas can he took from the garage was half full. He hoped there'd be enough. He couldn't get on his feet to spread it around, so he merely sloshed it about, poured it into his lap, and splashed it over his head. No pain, even when it ran through the bleeding crenelations in his flesh. The vapors rose like red heat waves.

For a while, he sat there, forgetting what he'd set out to do, forgetting why it was important that he do anything. Then it took him several more minutes to remember where he had put the matches. His mind was going. Some distant, coherent remnant of who he had been before the intruder had converted so much of him to virus and liquid waste spurred him on.

He opened the matchbook.

Took one out.

Laid it carefully against the sandpaper striking surface.

Just a spark. That was all he needed.

The wet slap of the carpet across his eyes told him that he had fallen over. He had, in the terms of those who deal with such events, crashed and bled out.

Just a spark.

Please.

THE ENDLESS MASQUERADE

When Amy was eight, old Farmer Brandt sold his southern cornfield—the one that would flood every four or five years—to some big city carnival people.

Amy's mother said carnival people were trash, and if Amy's father were alive he'd have talked Brandt out of selling them that field. Amy was told to stay away from the carnival, but like most of her mother's orders, this one was ignored. As long as Amy showed up for lunch, her mother was too busy cleaning at the bed and breakfast all day to notice where Amy spent most of her time.

The carnival people came in trailers and buses, erected tents and plywood booths, shaping a midway there in the soggy bottoms along the Illinois River. The tents were dark canvas, round and bulbous. When they went up that first summer, Amy thought they looked like ticks on the back of some vast, foul-smelling hog. Ticks on the back of the Earth. Earth as an odious pig rooting through the cosmos—she liked that image. The shaven stalks of corn were its bristling, porcine hide. The mud and muck of the field were the effluvia in which the beast had rolled for so long that they had become the predominant components of its constitution. When the tents shuddered in the wind, the canvas billowing in and out like the heaving sides of some ravenous beast, it was as if they were sucking the lifeblood from the Earth.

The image was perhaps a bit excessive, but Amy was obsessed with parasites that summer. She had just become the victim of one.

The rides came next: great metal octopi, skeletal wheels,

abrasive music, and lights—more lights than in all of Tahlequah. Kiddy-car tracks were laid. Dunk tanks were filled. Gantries and gears were assembled to form apocalyptic leviathans from whose pinnacles could be seen the city people in their canoes and rafts on the river.

On a good weekend there were thousands of people on the river. Men with gymnasium muscles and blow-dryer hair. Women with French-cut bikinis and tans that could have only come from a booth or a bottle. The city regurgitated them every weekend, and they swarmed on the little river community like maggots in roadkill. By the thousands, the river brought them in. The carnival only made it worse.

One, or both, brought Kevin. He worked the river by day, hauling canoes and tourists up to the drop-off point, and by night he worked the carnival. Oh yeah, he *worked* the goddamn carnival.

She was attracted to him at first. No way for her not to be. She, an impressionable Okie who'd never been any further than the great metropolis of Muskogee. He, a suave college sophomore whose military parents had taken him around the world and back, settling finally near the Air Force base in OKC. They were the proverbial moth and flame. And by the time Amy was burned, Kevin had already convinced her that everything he said was true.

"I'll slit your throat if you tell anyone, Amy." He showed her the skinning knife he'd use to do it.

She was eight. She was as terrified as she was humiliated and hurt, more so perhaps. And she believed him. So she never told. It was, after all, only a summer. Come fall semester he'd be gone, and she could put it behind her. Now, almost thirty years later, she knows that problems are never resolved that easily. She knows that those who prey upon others never just *go away*. But the child she was that summer had never met the likes of Kevin.

When Amy was nine, the Illinois swelled in the spring rain and the carnival was forced to delay its opening by two weeks because of water standing in Brandt's field. Three tourists drowned on the river that spring... and Kevin came back.

College had disagreed with him. What had been a summer job was to become permanent.

That summer the carnival opened a makeup booth. For a dollar they'd paint your face. You could be a cat or a dog or a mouse, a mime or a superhero, even a hideous monster if that's the sort of thing you were into. Amy discovered that if she had her face painted, she could step outside herself while Kevin panted and shoved and tore at the tender parts of her body. With her face painted, it was someone else suffering the pain and indignation. She could watch: repulsed, but not really implicated in the events; disgusted—sick to her stomach even—but not filthy, not soiled with Kevin's semen and sweat like that caricature of a little girl with her painted face pressed against the vinyl seat of his car.

She stole the money from him. It took very little secrecy to slip a buck from his jeans while he lay gasping afterward, wiping at his flaccid penis with tissues from the box he kept in his car. She took his money, and she used it to buy a mask so that pitiful girl who he used so savagely could hide her face. She took the risk because she felt sorry for the little girl; though perhaps it was not so great a risk after all. Kevin may have known where the money was going. Kevin seemed to enjoy the painted faces.

When Amy was ten, the makeup booth expanded, adding colorful carnival masks with sequins and feathers and beads. They were handmade and exquisite, with died hair and painted smiles. For three bucks you could own one. There wasn't a masquerade or Mardi Gras to be found in the backwoods of Oklahoma, but Amy accumulated quite a collection of the bright disguises.

That August the Illinois flooded again and, as a river will sometimes do, it changed course. North of Brandt's field was a bend known as Slippery Shoals. For a hundred years, Slippery Shoals had kept the Illinois River from taking the easiest route south, the route through old Farmer Brandt's cornfield. That year the shoals collapsed, sinking under the weight of raging river, washing downstream to join the billions of other pebbles that had once been part of some greater whole.

There was very little warning. The carnival people had time to strike their tents and load their trailers. Within an hour, the field was under three foot of water. The Ranger's Station said the river would rise another six feet before it crested late that evening. The Ferris wheel, the rollercoaster, the Tilt-a-whirl and others were a total loss. Abandoned and deserted, they sat in the pouring rain like the half-submerged skeletons of some mythical sea-serpents.

Amy arrived that afternoon. She was a strong swimmer; she had, after all, lived on the river all her life. Though the swift current and pelting rain may have turned back someone from the city, Amy wasn't scared. She knew the field was clear of stumps and submerged branches that could pull her under. She knew to enter the water upriver so the current would do most of the work. When she reached the Ferris wheel, she scaled the slippery metal frame like a monkey. Just moments after she'd first plunged into the water, she sat in the wheel's topmost seat where she could see everything. This was the top of her world and, for that moment, she was its ruler.

Despite the rain and the treacherous current, there were actually a few canoes on the river. She guessed that they were locals looking for lost tourists or canoes that had been swept from the river's bank. The original course of the river was still open—probably would be until the water level dropped, and the river settled into its new path. The canoeists stuck to the original route, bypassing the flooded carnival grounds. Except for one.

When she saw Kevin coming, she realized too late that she didn't have a mask for the poor girl he was so fond of abusing. While Kevin tied off his canoe below, she slid down the spokes and collected black soot and grease from the hub of the wheel. By the time Kevin caught up with her, she had scrambled back to her seat. She huddled there, awaiting the inevitable, hidden behind her black war paint.

When it was over, they lay naked in the warm rain in an oddly tender moment, his arms around her, stroking her hair and back. "I think," he said after several long minutes, "that I have fallen in love with you, Amy." He tilted her head so that she was looking up at him. "Can you believe that? You're a kid, not even in high school yet, and I think I'm in love with you."

She realized at that moment that he was about to steal the very last thing she owned. He was about to take away her hatred of him. Lying there in the downpour, she could only pity him, this poor sick pedophile who'd not only failed at college, but at life. She was only ten, but she saw clearly her future from that point on. She saw how her pity would in time become compassion. How compassion would in turn lead to affection, how the rest of her life would be spent in service to him. Worse, she saw how the rest of her life might be spent *wanting* to serve him. She saw the masks eventually coming off. And she saw her face beneath the masks.

What she didn't see was the need which had already formed within her. The need to be possessed. The need to wear the masks. When she slammed the lap bar down over Kevin's head, both stunning and pinning him in one fell swoop, she didn't know she'd miss his touch, his ownership. When she slipped home the bar's locking pin and jumped, she didn't know he had already shaped her life as surely as if she'd let him live.

Because the Ferris wheel was one of the many rides she'd watched Kevin operate over the years, she knew about the hand crank used to turn the wheel when power was lost. It was hard to turn, especially with Kevin screaming like that the whole time, but she kept telling herself that it wasn't her murdering him, it was the girl in the mask. As Kevin's hands strained in vain to reach the bar's locking pin, she kept remembering the thing's he had done to that poor little girl in the mask. And she thought of the things he would do yet if she let him live.

Kevin's screams stopped when the seat that had been at the top became the seat at the bottom. He thrashed about for a few minutes because the water wasn't quite deep enough to cover more than his head. But, in time, he was still.

She unhooked the bar and let him float free. She capsized his canoe. He was a city boy, they'd say. He shouldn't have been out on the water in that kind of weather.

Amy still has her masks, quite a collection of them actually. They fill the walls of one whole room in the house she inherited when her mother died. She's found that most of the men she picks up don't really mind her wearing them. It adds a sense of mystery to the evening, an extra element of spice to the sex.

They're not so sure about the old cornfield and the rusted carnival rides though.

And she's had to cut back. The Illinois has been tossing up some of the bodies lately.

TO WALK AMONG THE LIVING

The life-support machines fell silent. No alarms; they'd all been disconnected at the nurse's station.

Shelby Lloyd, last of the Magnificent Seven save I, smiled at me as her murderer shambled from the room. Tears rolled off her cheeks and vanished against the reality of the hospital pillow.

"I love you," she whispered.

"Quiet," I told her.

"I'll never forget you." Her body spasmed as hungry muscles realized the delivery of oxygen had ceased.

"With any luck, we'll all be together again."

For once Shelby didn't remind me of her disbelief in an afterlife. "Kiss me, Johnny."

I placed my lips so close to her pale cheek that the illusion of contact seemed to satisfy her. She sighed, a skeletal rattling as her final breath slipped free. Her true face faded and was gone.

Repetition. A daily routine that became a monotonous totality of existence. For what seemed an eternity I'd lain abed, surrounded by the antiseptic purity of a room without a view.

Time could only be measured in bed changes and the metronomic drone of the ventilator. How often the nurses changed the sheets—Once a week? Twice? Every other day?—I'd no way of knowing. Time, therefore, was meaningless, marching to an end for which I was forced to wait… in miserable silence.

First there was darkness. No pain—that surprised me the most. Just the encompassing, cold black of the grave, a tight-fitting glove of isolation.

Later there came what I call my grey days: hazy visions; whispers from forgotten senses; dim hallucinations of childhood memories; and, finally, the beginnings of discomfort. Then, a slow dissolve from black.

Finally there was conscious light. And then... The Litany:

I will survive.

"How will you survive?"

I will cling to life as a parasite clings to its host, as a pit bull clings to—

"Why survive when the rest are dead?"

Because Death is my enemy. I shall not yield.

After The Litany, the long white existence. The monotony. The routine. Soon The Litany was forgotten, and the courtship with Death began. To woo, to entice, and finally to beg for that dark specter's visit.

Sometimes I dream of *that* night. Strange, waking dreams. Blurred images that interrupt my fading vision and play like poorly focused music videos. JTV, where the music is the discordance of squealing tires, folding metal, and exploding glass. Where the rockers give it all they've got. And all they ever had.

They're all dead. Mom. Dad in that silly hat he wore to keep his ears warm. My older brother Jason. Even Julie, golden youth, so looking forward to her sixteenth birthday just days away on that fateful night. All dead.

Had I seen the ice, I know it would have been black. Not the clear crystal innocence of water frozen on the overpass, but an insidious evil laid across the road's surface for a family such as ours. And had I seen the semi driver as he hit that black ice and lost control of his rig, slewing across all four lanes and into the path of our fragile car, I know whose face he would have worn.

Gleaming bone, rictus grin, and cavernous eye sockets. That's the face I would have seen. The same death's head that haunts my hospital daydreams.

The same face that refuses to come no matter how loud I scream.

Goodbye, Shelby.

I rose from her side and passed ghost-like through the door. Ward C was alive with Beverly Snider's cackling as she ran for the room at the end of the hall where my corporeal shell lay empty and dormant. I followed, leaving behind the rooms in which my six compatriots lay in peace.

"I'm coming, Father!" screamed the demented nurse.

Yes, Angel of Mercy, Goddess of Death, come for us all. Deliver us unto your kingdom. Fulfill our dreams. Grant us peace.

Alberto had been first. Alberto, whose motorcycle had been forced off an interstate overpass. Alberto who'd lain comatose for three years. He'd winked at me when Snider cut off his machines. His true face had worn a smile when it faded.

Initially I was entertained by those who came to study, but the visits quickly deteriorated to redundant episodes of asinine rhetoric.

The med students would file through, their lab coats suffusing the room with more of the hated white. They'd surround my bed, faces earnest, disciples embarked on a grand pilgrimage pausing for worship at the Shrine of the Unknown Patient.

"John Whitley McIver," the touring physician would intone, "victim of an automobile accident in 1988. We operated to remove splinters of bone from his brain. He never regained consciousness."

He'd explain the complex array of life support equipment, the machines that breathe for me, the tubes that feed me and remove my body wastes. Having heard the spiel an infinite number of times before, I'd tune him out, letting my mind drift with the rhythm of the ventilator.

The inevitable question would bring me back.

"Why keep him alive?"

"Look at his brainwaves," the doctor would answer. "Does he look dead to you?"

The med student would frown, his face betraying conflicting professional and ethical opinions.

"If your arm was broken," the doctor would ask, "you'd want me to fix it, right?"

"Of course, but—"

"This man's body was broken. I fixed it as best I could, however there are functions his body can no longer perform. The machines take care of those for him. The EEG proves he's not dead. If I let him expire because of the broken parts of his body, it would be no different than me letting you suffer, and perhaps even die, from a broken arm. Besides," and here he reveals the true medical motive behind my extended suffering, "the things we learn by sustaining his life are invaluable."

Once he's beaten the rebel down, once he's justified the unmitigated rights of his profession, the doctor would continue the lecture, pleased with the sound of his own voice imparting infinite wisdom on these pupils of medicine, these apprentices to human suffering. "Note the shortening of the limbs as the muscles, ligaments, and tendons atrophy. The nurses exercise him daily, but he's still drawing up in a fetal position..."

After Alberto, Snider had visited Donald.

Donald's all-expense-paid stay in Ward C served as expiation for the power company whose inadequate safety measures had gotten him electrocuted. Donald had been here the longest—a full seven years.

After shutting down his machines, Snider bent over him. "I love you," she crooned, caught up in the cocaine-overdose that had her believing each of us was her father. As her crazed-red eyes spilled waves of tears, I'd actually felt guilty for manipulating her. But there was no turning back.

Like Alberto, Donald smiled when death took him. His last words were, "Say goodbye to Eva for me," right after he told me how much he regretted not being able to hug me.

Every existence, however vapid, has its moments. Mine are with Eva.

Her routine runs like this:

She checks the long, transparent tube in my right arm—sustenance. I fantasize the IV to be a crystal serpent, Death's gatekeeper barring me from the beckoning darkness, from that well of warmth and comfort.

She inspects my catheter, another friendly tube, this one carrying away the waste my body mindlessly continues to produce. Despite the fact I haven't moved in... (What, a year? Three? Oh, God, more?) Despite the fact I have *never* moved since the ambulance brought me in, inflated bulbs within my bladder prevent the accidental extraction of the catheter.

She puts drops in my staring eyes, cleans my parched lips where they've caked around the ventilator tube, and gently strokes the fine beard covering my face.

Eva Schüpfheim. A synergism of copper skin, gold filigree hair, and nebulous blue eyes. I love the soft tease of her hair on my throat and the press of her breasts against my arm. Her cleavage is lined with a silky, blond down, so fine it would be unnoticeable were it not for the harsh lights above the bed. When she leaves, her presence hangs like honeysuckle in the tasteless air of the hospital room.

Headnurse Snider hated Eva.

Perhaps it was Eva's alpine beauty. Snider reminded me of a beached whale that'd lain too long in the sun. All of Eva could have fit in one leg of Snider's slacks. Snider's hair hung dark and lifeless, wet beneath the fluorescents as if weighted with oil. Her face was scarred by acne and her neck was wattled. Beneath each arm swung great pink excesses.

Perhaps it was Eva's dedication and empathy. Without hesitation, Eva goes that extra distance. *Every* time.

Case in point: My chart says I'm to be exercised daily, but most of the nurses consider me a lost cause. Why waste their time when there's gossip to spread, coffee breaks to take, and a television vomiting soap operas at the nurse's station? Eva's different. It's enough that the chart says do it. My muscles and joints are stiff and unyielding, but Eva persists, fighting their lack of elasticity with as much determination as I fight the tethers of life.

It was during one such exercise session that I first noticed the rift between Snider and Eva.

Eva's hands as she exercised me were cool velvet on my flesh. Her uniform was a pale blue, tight across the velvet swell of her bosom. I could smell her hair. Denied the comfort of

Death's welcome embrace, I was at least compensated with Eva's company. A would-be corpse couldn't ask for more.

Rhinoceros in heat is the kindest analogy I can find to describe Snider's sudden entrance. "Schüpfheim! I told you to quit spending so much time on that vegetable!"

"Doctor Monrowe's orders, Nurse Snider. He's to be exercised every—"

"I know what his chart says! And you know how short-handed we are."

"I'll be done in just a minute."

Nurse Snider screwed her into a scowl. "I don't know how much longer you expect to work here, Schüpfheim, but—"

"All right already!" Eva drew the sheet back up to my neck and stomped out of the room. Snider followed. I could hear the old bitch's voice as she followed my Eva down the hall.

Linda next. Linda, who had dreamed of being a singer before a brain tumor and surgery to excise it had put her here. To us who could hear it, her voice had carried clear and strong from the wasted woman on the hospital bed.

Just before her body failed her, she sang to me. Her voice was weak and quivering, but her eyes smiled.

Though I would gladly trade for Death's bittersweet kiss, sponge baths with Eva have long been the highpoint of my existence, serving as erotic interludes in banality. It was during one such bath that I learned there are always limits, even to silence.

The sponge left a tingling trail of warmth as it slid across my flesh. Eva's fingertips, riding the side of the sponge like outriggers on a canoe, were cool and soft. Her nails sent transparent shivers coursing the length of my body.

As the sponge slipped along my inner thigh, over my genitals, and across my lower abdomen, something triggered a reaction in her. I could see it in the startled look on her face. She saw something: some minuscule change in skin coloration, the twitch of an excited muscle, or perhaps a shift in the depths of my empty eyes. Whatever, I'd made that first contact.

She leaned close. "Johnny? Can you feel that?"

Oh yes, my Eva. I can feel the sponge where it presses warm against my belly. I can feel your other hand like fire on my thigh.

"You can," she whispered. And pulled back. There was doubt, and maybe just a trace of fear, on her face as she drew the sheet back to my neck. Quickly, she gathered up sponge, towel, and bath water. And then she fled the room, leaving me terrified she might never return.

Behind me, one of the elevators emitted a startling *ding!*

A second later, the doors slid open and out rolled a noisy mop and bucket, followed closely by one of the night janitors.

Snider spun, nearly pinwheeling off her feet. When she saw him, she screamed like a cat with its tail caught beneath a U-Haul and stormed down the hall. An orderly had left an IV stand near the water fountain. Snider snatched it up as she ran by.

The janitor spit several curses in Spanish and dove back into the elevator. As Snider charged by, the IV stand whirling bola-like about her head, I could hear his fingers stabbing frantically at the elevator buttons. The doors closed just in time.

"Hurry," I pleaded. It wouldn't take him long to get help.

Despite my fears, Eva returned the next day.

Her eyes were guarded. When she finally looked at my face, she froze, studying, wondering, searching for the empathy she'd felt earlier.

The desire to say something swelled in my chest and surged forth in utter silence.

Her face softened. She touched my cheek. "I wish you could talk to me, Johnny. I need a friend right now."

I'm here for you, Eva.

"It's this guy I've been living with." She ran her hands nervously over her face and looked fleetingly at the door. "We decided not to date anyone else—that's the only reason I agreed to move in with him. We weren't ready for marriage... too much of a commitment.

"But he's been seeing other women for some time. And now... Well, he's hurt me, Johnny." Her voice broke there at the end, and I knew that by *hurt* she meant he had physically abused her.

You deserve better, Eva.

"I know I deserve better. I should leave him, but then I'd be alone. And, there's this." She pulled a pill bottle from her side pocket. My eyes were too far gone; I couldn't make out the contents.

As if she understood, she explained. "This white powder has gotten a tremendous hold on my life, Johnny. Stronger than any feelings for that two-timing bastard, Clint. Stronger than even my love for nursing."

Cocaine?

"Clint started me on the coke. He keeps me supplied with it—Hell, I wouldn't know where to begin to look..."

The door slammed open, halting whatever else Eva was about to say. The pill bottle vanished back into her pocket. In the doorway stood Headnurse Snider, a shaggy blur to my failing vision, a hulking Neanderthal come for my Eva.

"I knew I'd find you in here again! This is my last warning. The next time I catch you spending all your time in here, I'll see that you're fired!"

As Eva slid past her and through the doorway, Snider bellowed after her, "And don't think I can't do it either!"

Letting the door swing closed, the hag crossed the room to stand beside my bed. "Goddamn vegetable. Why don't you do us all a favor and die already?"

Why don't you do me a favor?

Snider rested a wrinkled hand on the ventilator beside my bed. "You take space and time that could be devoted to important patients."

You can solve that problem.

She glanced at the door, not unlike Eva just before she'd opened her heart to me. But as Snider checked to make sure we were alone, her thoughts were as black as the ice that night on the overpass.

Do it, I begged.

Her hand rested on the large dial on the ventilator's front panel. I knew from clearer days that the numbered dial regulated the percent oxygen being supplied to my system. Shutting off the machine would sound an alarm; she couldn't have that. But she could turn down the amount of oxygen being supplied. It might take several minutes for me to expire, but it would work.

Minutes, even hours, seemed no more than a heartbeat to the eternity that I'd lain there.

Do it, bitch!

"I should do it," she mumbled, whether to herself or me, I couldn't say.

Her eyes were small black gems sunk deep in the blur of her face. Pig eyes, I thought. Kill me, pig.

"But you want me to kill you, don't you?"

God, yes.

"Dying's easy," she said, as if quoting some obscure text. "It's living that's really torturing you."

Her hand slipped from the instrument's dial. As she turned to leave, she laughed softly, cruelly. A second later, the door closed, and I was left alone.

Damn you, bitch!

That day, I dreamt clear, palpable visions of her death and dismemberment. A music video screaming with heavy metal. It was a wet video. Wet and red.

Just before Snider entered my room, she looked down the hall, almost as if she knew I was there. Her eyes were all white and iris, her pupils tiny pinpricks of midnight.

"Go on!" I screamed at her, terrified that I alone would be left alive.

After Linda, Snider had gone to Peter, the youngest of the Magnificent Seven. Peter gave us that name. Only nine years old, he'd spent the last two of those in Ward C.

Peter's older sister had pushed him out on a frozen lake. The ice had broken. Despite the most ardent of rescue efforts, Peter had been trapped beneath the ice for over an hour. When they'd recovered his body, a well-meaning paramedic had administered CPR. Peter's body had resumed a facsimile of life, but he had never regained consciousness. His parents had brought him here, hoping the experts could save their son, sentencing him to Hell with the rest of us.

The silence of the life-support machines had frightened the boy. He'd been even more terrified when darkness began closing down around him.

"It's all right, Peter. We'll all be together on the other side."

"You promise?"

"I promise."

"I wish you could hold me."

"I do too."

"Johnny?" His voice was distant and weak.

"I'm here, Peter."

"Linda's singing… there's… light. I—" And he was gone.

"I'll be right along," I promised.

I spent Eva's day off contemplating her addiction to Clint and the cocaine, concentrating with the absolute mental exertion only the comatose are capable of, as if sheer force of will could rid her of those two evils.

My efforts paid off.

"I did it, Johnny!" Eva's exuberance flooded the room, sweeping me up in a maelstrom of little girl giddiness and mirth. She flopped presumptively down on the bed beside me and laid a hand on either side of my face. "I packed my things and just walked out. Not a single backwards glance. Oh, you would have been so proud of me."

She stroked my beard and leaned close, searching, hoping. "I can beat that other thing too, Johnny. Just watch me." She swallowed. "And help me. I know you can."

Her eyes probed mine, their blue a commanding fire. "I know you're in there. I can feel you… *thinking* at me. I don't understand it. Empathy, telepathy—I don't know what to call it. But I know you're alive in there. Alive and alert, and in some way connected to me. I'll find a way to bring you out of this coma." Eyes locked on my soulless brown orbs, she pressed her lips against my cheek.

And shattered my world.

There was a sinking feeling at first, a tugging at the roots of John McIver. I felt as if the world had suddenly dropped out from under me. Gravity had failed, and I was plunging. But it was a uniform fall, not the gut-wrenching plunge of a roller coaster or the sudden altitude change of an airplane. *All* of me had suddenly been yanked aside.

I found myself standing just behind her. My vision was perfectly clear. I could see the way her hair flooded like silk over her shoulders. Her skirt had ridden up to reveal thighs that flowed like finely carved maple to meet sculpted calves and tiny ankles.

I barely heard her as she said her farewells to the empty shell on the bed. She walked right past me and out the door, blind to the miracle.

How had this happened? Like some Disney character, I found myself kissed and given new life, a Sleeping Ugly not entirely whole, for on the bed I still saw the real me. There lay the shell I'd become, stretched out like a collapsed two-liter bottle, wasted limbs like curling dry bones beneath the sheets. I hardly recognized the face as my own. Sunken eyes and hollow cheeks. Woefully thin. Yet, there was the crook in my nose where Nick Panzarati broke it in high school, there the scar where I'd fallen down the stairs as a child. Beneath a dark beard lay my arrogant jawline. My hair was long. One ear was mangled, and there were new scars on my forehead and left cheek.

But it was definitely *my* face.

I reached out to touch the face of the mirage on the bed, but my hand passed right through. Through flesh. Through pillow. Through mattress, frame, and everything between. One of us was not real. Which one, I could not with certainty say. But logic told me that *I* must be the projection and that… that *corpse* was the real McCoy.

It was too much. I stumbled to a corner of the room and collapsed, shuddering against the cold white wall.

Geoffrey next. Geoffrey had been the only one of us who didn't require life-support. Snider smothered him with his pillow. He screamed and raged and begged me to stop her. There was nothing I could do.

Drunk one night, Geoffrey had lost control of his 'vette on an interstate exit ramp. He'd rolled over an embankment railing and come down on the road below—right in front of a Toyota pickup. The husband and wife in the truck survived. Their two children, carelessly allowed to ride in the back, were killed.

"When they were released from the hospital," Geoffrey had told me, "they came to see me. The man spat in my face and cursed the coma that kept me from him. The woman slapped me, then wept and apologized."

"They should have never been allowed in here."

"Snider watched the whole thing."

"I'm sorry." I hadn't known what else to say.

"No need to be." He'd looked away then, his eyes ghostly as they hovered over the dead mask worn for the real world. "This is my punishment for murdering those two children, Johnny. I'll lay here forever, denied death, denied peace. Denied any kind of life worth living."

"I think those parents deserve some of the credit for—"

"*I* killed them!" he had screamed.

I had few conversations with Geoffrey after that. Because he preferred to be left alone, I never really got to know him. Pity, because as he died under the pillow, I never got to say goodbye to him either.

Of the many mysteries in our universe, some have ventured that the human mind is the single catacomb the depths of which mankind shall never fully fathom. Like the adrenal gland, the mind is a stronghold of incredible power… if only we knew how to tap it.

I've come to accept, for lack of any better hypothesis, that this presence, this shadow-McIver who walks among the living, is a mental projection. My mind, for so many years the single most exercised organ in my failing body, has broken whatever barriers kept it fastened within the confines of my cranium.

As I learned the first time I tried to touch my face, I lack the ability to interact with my environment. I pass through anything of substance: the wasted body on the bed, the door, the walls, the water fountain in the hall… even my dear, sweet

Eva. How fine it would have been to have held her just once, to have felt the warm velvet of her flesh against mine, to have stroked her hair.

But contact with the real world is impossible. Standing in my room, staring down at what time had made of me, I longed to terminate that tube-fed cocoon of a man. What would have then become of the *projected* me is anyone's guess. Would the projection have blinked from existence? Or would I have remained, forever, this ethereal affectation, this powerless ghost?

No matter, I'm doomed to continue this pathetic pretense, albeit no longer confined to the bed. Within a finite distance, roughly equivalent to this ward of the hospital, I can roam at will. Any further and I experience that sinking feeling, that pulling at every atom of John McIver, and I find myself back in the withered body on the bed.

Though I remain Death's most earnest suitor, my concept of that absent benefactor changed on the day of my resurrection. From the bed, I had zealously believed Death to be a god I could summon. But on the day I rose, I declared Death a distant effigy, impotent and uncaring. There is no Grim Reaper. No scythe-wielding savior whose succor I could call with prayer. Hence his absence despite years of cajoling. Death is merely death, lowercase D. A random encounter. A happenstance. Something that comes to each of us at some point in time, but by no predestined schedule. For surely if there was a schedule, I was long overdue.

I thought death beyond my control.

I was wrong.

The elevator sang out again. This time I was expecting it, so rather than a startling chime, it seemed soft, bitter. Snider couldn't hear it from inside my room. Nor could she see the three men that spilled forth when its doors opened.

The discarded IV stand, lying half in and half out of my gaping doorway, was all they needed to point the way. The two interns were young and fast. The rent-a-cop was old and wobbled as if one hip had been broken. He followed as best he could, but it was obvious who'd reach her first.

The next day I followed Eva on her rounds. That initial exploration was filled with many discoveries, first and by no means least of which was the realization that I was *not* alone. WARD C, read the sign by the elevators. As I followed Eva from patient to patient, it became clear what the C stood for.

I've since heard it called a number of names: The Coma Clinic, The Coma Research Center, The Research Center for Lethargic Illnesses… even The Dead Zone by a few nurses who had perhaps read a little too much Stephen King. By whatever name, the ward is a prison for those such as I, bound this side of the razor's edge separating life and death.

The realization that there were others would have been discovery enough for that first day, but it paled in comparison to the knowledge that I could communicate with them.

I met Shelby Lloyd first. She might have once had her pick of men, for even in the emaciated shell on the hospital bed there remained something of beauty. Her hair was burnished copper which Eva kept clean and brushed. It lay warm across the pillow, framing her quiet face in sunrise. Her eyes were the most startling pools of emerald green. As I watched over Eva's shoulder, I noticed that Shelby's gaze had fixed on me. I moved. Her eyes followed.

"You can see me!" I gasped, startling myself with the sound of my own voice. Until that moment, I didn't know I could speak.

"Are you Death come at last?" Her lips shaped the words as if unobstructed by the tube running down her throat. Her words were clear and musical, a voice to match the beauty that had once been Shelby Lloyd.

Eva gave no indication that she heard either of us, nor did she appear to sense anything out of the ordinary. She ran a washcloth over Shelby's face, cleaning lips I had just watched move.

"Not Death then," Shelby sighed when I did not immediately answer her. "A ghost? Have you come to taunt me, ghost?"

I shook my head and tried to lay a comforting hand on her shoulder. "I'm no ghost." The hand passed through, defying the answer I gave her. "Just another patient."

She smiled, and I realized that I saw two faces upon her pillow. One, the animated Shelby that spoke to me now, and beneath that transparent veneer of life, a second face, comatose, blank, staring blindly. Which of them was real?

"You're more than just another patient," she said. "How is this possible?"

"I don't know. One minute I lay like you, the next—"

"Can't wash your hair today, Shelby," Eva said as she gathered together her things and turned for the door. "I'm running behind and you know how Snider is. I'll do your hair tomorrow."

"Don't go," Shelby cried when she saw that I meant to follow Eva out the door.

"I'll be back." I laid one hand against her face as if I could touch her.

Tears ran down her cheeks, dripping off onto the pillow to disappear as if they'd never existed. "You'll never come back," she sobbed. I saw in her eyes that if I never returned, her Hell would be worse for having spoken to me once.

I leaned close. "I know your pain, Shelby. I *will* be back. I promise."

Shelby looked away, her eyes dark with distrust. Behind me the door was swinging closed as Eva left. There was nothing I could say to convince Shelby. I'd been in her position long enough to know that the only thing she took on faith was the continuance of suffering, the absence of Death. I turned and dashed after Eva, passing through the closing door as if it possessed no more substance than smoke.

So went that first afternoon with Eva, meeting the others, learning their stories. Until I stepped outside myself and walked from room to room, each of us had suffered in solitude.

Peter dubbed us the Magnificent Seven: Shelby, Alberto, Linda, Donald, Geoffrey, Peter and I. There were other patients who came and went, those who suffered from fugues, coma-like lapses, pathological amnesia, and more complex illnesses, but we were the true comatose. Those others were blind to us, as were all of the living. They projected nothing, even those who suffered occasional unconsciousness.

I was the Seven's nexus, the messenger, the binding element that held us all together, kept us sane until we figured our way out. Each of them, in time, asked me to end their suffering, to take up Death's idle scythe and do for them what he had never done for me.

"Johnny, you've been given this incredible gift for a reason," Shelby told me one afternoon. "I believe you've been sent to free the Seven."

Linda showed me how it must be done: "If you can't manipulate your environment, Johnny, you've got to influence someone who can."

Donald pointed out who that someone should be: "Snider'd kill each and every one of us if she thought she could get away with it."

Peter asked the important question: "Why does Snider hate us so?"

And Snider herself provided the catalyst to set it all moving.

I slid to a halt in the open doorway and watched as Snider reached for the ventilator beside my bed. Her hands were shaking uncontrollably, and it took her several tries to throw the recessed power switch. When she finally did, the machine died with a shudder. In the sudden silence, I could hear heavy footsteps charging down the hallway.

"They're coming!"

"Don't worry, Father." She took a fire extinguisher from the wall. "No one's going to stop me."

The nurse's lounge is not a place I'd frequent save for the fact that it's Eva's last stop as she leaves for home. She collects purse and coat, then departs. I follow her as far as the elevators where I say my goodbyes. In those early days, goodbye consisted of convincing her that she could get through another night without cocaine.

There were times when I was certain I'd lose her, when I feared she'd go back to Clint and the coke. But each night, she'd nod her head and promise, and though she had no idea that I stood right before her, she understood that I was speaking to her through that empathic bond we shared. Those first few weeks, her eyes were apathetic and bloodshot, her hair lackluster, her hands nervous, and her shoulders hung under a great weight. Though her love and care for the patients in Ward C didn't lessen, her energy and patience did.

Snider noticed. She might have searched Eva's locker on a whim, but I suspect Eva's withdrawal was obvious to any nurse with more than a few years' experience.

When Eva quit, she deposited that last vial of cocaine in her locker, a safer place than her apartment because she knew I'd never let her use it. She could have thrown it out, but that would have admitted she couldn't stand up to the temptation; it seemed important to her to face what she'd done to herself. Sometimes I think she might have planned to use that cocaine later to notify the authorities about Clint or his supplier. Whatever her reason, it all changed when Snider found it in her locker.

"Please, Beverly, I'm begging you. Nursing is all I have. Don't take it away from me. Don't turn me in." It hurt to see Eva supplicating before that fat cow.

"The blond goddess likes cocaine," Snider mocked. "Not so perfect after all, are we, princess?"

"I've quit. You've got to believe me, Beverly. Look at me! You can see the withdrawal symptoms."

Snider smiled like a shark. "What I see is the addiction."

"No! I've given it up. I—"

"Do you want to keep your job?"

"Without my job, I am nothing," Eva confessed.

And Snider's smile widened, expanding to the limits of her porcine face. "My silence will cost you a vial like this twice a week."

"What?"

"Twice a week you'll bring me cocaine."

"I can't."

"Three times a week then."

"No!" Eva wept. "You don't understand. Clint bought me the coke. To get more I'll have to go back to him."

"Shall we try for four times a week, Schüpfheim?"

Eva bit her lip and said no more.

"I'll expect your first delivery on Monday." That gave Eva one day, her day off as it turned out, to get more cocaine.

Snider knelt so she could look Eva in the eye. "Fail me, princess, and you'll be out of work." She pocketed the cocaine and sauntered out.

The room was silent save for Eva's sobs. I stood there unable to hold and comfort her, unable to go after Snider and—

Snider! Linda had asked, "Why does Snider hate us so?"

"Get up," I told Eva. "We can beat this."

"What can I do, Johnny?"

"We've got to see Snider's employee records."

Somehow, Eva got those records. She brought them to my room and read them aloud to the corpse on the bed, while I stood and read over her shoulder. She read them twice without finding anything she could use. But I found what I was looking for the first time through. It's true that our parents make us what we are. Beverly Snider owed her hatred of the comatose to her father. In a letter requesting assignment to Ward C, she'd listed her father's coma and her experience caring for him as qualifications.

As Snider braced to meet the three men, my fears were replaced with guilt. I remembered her meeting with a young resident that afternoon, and how I'd thought then how much she reminded me of a little girl, overweight and unaccepted by the other children. She'd only wanted the cocaine to buy her way into the hospital click, to belong for once in her pitiful life. She'd grown up tied to a father who was in turn tied to a ventilator, kidney machine, and tubes. From his cocoon, Snider's father had screamed in silence for half again Donald's seven-year sentence before his body finally resisted the machines and shut down.

The coke bought Snider an invitation to an upcoming party. She'd never experimented with drugs. All I had to do was encourage her to try the cocaine so she wouldn't make a fool of herself at the party. Since she rarely took time off, a night with only herself on duty seemed the perfect time.

From there it was not so difficult to encourage her to take too much. And then to convince her hallucinating mind that her father still screamed for release. To maneuver her into providing freedom for Eva and the Magnificent Seven.

The body on the bed convulsed. I felt drawn to it as if there were a thousand piano wires laced through my flesh.

One of the interns entered the room, his wide eyes registering the silent machines and shuddering body before they locked on Snider. She caved in his skull with the fire extinguisher. He went down with blood gushing from his head. Somehow, he was able to scream.

When he fell, he looked not at her, but at me. At *me!* I saw my guilt printed in jagged red lines across his glazed eyes. He hit the hospital floor with a sound that hurt, and his eyes rolled back in his head.

The body on the bed had become a black whirlpool, whipped by howling vapors. No one else seemed aware of the phenomenon. As I was sucked into the maelstrom devouring my body, the second intern stumbled over the first and sprawled at Snider's feet. She raised the heavy tank to strike him.

There was light at some point below, in the eye of that black hurricane. And more—there was music.

The security guard turned the corner. Warned by the scream, his weapon was drawn and ready. He saw the extinguisher descending on the second intern, and he fired. I could barely hear the .38 over the howling of the maelstrom and the song from the light below.

Snider jerked, an awkward, disjointed ballet on toes that could otherwise have never supported her. A crimson flower blossomed upon her white breast. She redirected her weapon at the guard. He fired again. And again.

She hit the wall hard enough to leave an impression. s she slid to the floor, I saw a calm ghost-face overshadow her twisted countenance. It was there but a second, then it was gone and her head dropped forward to rest against the bloody swell of her bosom.

There were grasping hands reaching from the light below. The song had grown louder, and I recognized the voice.

The intern scrambled across his dead companion and slapped at the switch on the ventilator. The machine kicked in with a great sigh and began to force air into my collapsed lungs. Helpless, they expanded. My traitor heart skipped once, then resumed its steady rhythm. The reaching hands brushed my extended fingertips and fell away. The tempest faltered, dissipated, and died.

I screamed, but there was no one to hear me.

Eva keeps me company.

Occasionally I walk the ward with her, but not very often… and I don't go in to see the new patients. I have no plans to go and meet them. Let another come to me this time.

And if not… nobody lives forever.

It's only a lifetime.

DEAD ART

"Works of art are of an infinite loneliness…"
Only love can grasp and hold and fairly judge them."
—Rilke

1. Artist and Canvas

He washes her first, a good, hard scrubbing that takes off the dead, top layer of skin. Ironic, that thought. As if part of her is more dead than others. As if death is nothing more than the inevitable collapse of all our defenses, so that the death we all carry on the outside eventually sinks through to our insides.

They brought her to him quickly enough, rigor mortis having set and gone already, leaving her pliant to his soapy brushes and sponge. He's careful to wash all her secret places: between her toes and behind her ears, the soft white crease under each breast, her navel, her nostrils, her eyelids and rectum and neck. With pliers he removes all her nails, then tenderly cleans the debutante-pink flesh he's revealed. With tiny scissors, he trims her now ragged cuticles, until each of her ten digits ends in a blunt and polished alien pad, smooth on top, concentrically crenulated on the bottom.

He takes a razor and begins at her feet. He shaves the fine pale hair on the top of her toes and her feet, moving onward and upward to meet the courser stubble of her legs. He's careful around the ankles and knees, mindful of the razor's edge against the thin, bone-taut skin there. The hair on her thighs where she traditionally stopped shaving is so fine as to be almost invisible. It slides away from the razor like a film of soap. With scissors, he removes most of the hair from her groin, then follows up with the razor, pulling on her bath-moist labia so that he can get at all the stubble in that tender region between her legs. He follows a trail of down up her belly, around her navel (where he finds a mole with a single dark hair that he plucks with tweezers), around the arc of her rib cage, and between her breasts which sport the same fine blond hair he encountered on her thighs. Her shoulders. Her neck. Her face. With shears, he removes most of the hair from her head. The razor completes the job.

Then he turns her over and does the other side.

When he's done, he washes her again.

She's now clean and pristine. The only hair left on her body is her eyelashes and the hair in her nose. The latter he leaves. Her eyelashes, he plucks one by one. When they're all out, he sews her eyes shut with surgical thread, pulling it from the inside where it can't be seen. He does the same with her mouth.

By this time, he's been bent over the table for three hours and his back is killing him. He's not as young as he used to be. He curls up on the damp, soiled floor beneath the table, shivering now that he's not working, not occupied with his art. His joints ache with arthritis as much as fatigue. He's spent too many years in this freezer. But once started, he never leaves them. If there were room on the table, he would sleep at her side. Lacking that, the concrete floor will do. They're not meant to be alone, these souls in his trust. He can only imagine their terror at being alone, at being incapacitated, impotent, abandoned… dead.

Two hours later apprentices bring him food. Simple fair. Cold cheese and sausage. A glass of milk—which is all he allows himself when he's working. While he eats, his apprentices set up the inks and needles. Another begins the base layer of acrylic. They should really pour the acrylic in a cleaner room, but he insists it all be done here under his supervision… and hers. It means more work for the apprentices; they'll have to clean and polish the surface of the base before she's placed upon it and the balance poured over her, but it's a minor inconvenience.

When he's finished eating, he lets his hands roam her flesh, learning what he can. There's a small scar on her chin (a childhood spill from that first bicycle?) and another on one knee (long and jagged, as if made by the tooth of an angry dog). He noticed them both while preparing her, but now he truly studies their topography: the way the original flesh flows around the swollen tissue of the scar, the arrangement of pores, the texture and color variations. He plays phrenologist, exploring the shape of her skull. He shifts her breasts for best effect. Arranges her hands. Explores her intimately and surmises that she never bore children. Her palms reveal no hard use. He knows she came from money—otherwise she would never have been brought to him—but still, sometimes, you find that even the rich enjoy a callous-rendering hobby. So she was pampered and kept (the soft deposits around her middle tell him that), fit for another five or six years, he estimates, before life would have caught up with her and she would either exercise or endure liposuction.

He starts with her head, working the inks under the skin with his needles, dabbing with paper towels as she bleeds preservatives, following finished patches of the mosaic with swipes of a Vaseline coated tongue depressor. He injects her flesh with color, painting her life as it had been told him by husband and friends, as it had been interpreted by his questing hands and artist's intuition. Her colors are bright. No earth-tone woman, this. No mother. No auntie. This was a woman of parties, of late nights, of cocktails and sequins and bright lights. The strokes he uses are bold and presumptuous, as forthright and *in-your-face* as he knew she must have been.

Time passes. When he's tired, he sleeps. When apprentices bring him food, he eats it. Beneath the unwavering fluorescents of the freezer, it's impossible to tell how long it takes, but its span is measured in days, not hours. He paints every inch of her, turning her this way and that, the images following the contours of her body but telling of her soul. When he's done, he kisses her painted forehead, then stands aside as the apprentices move her to the waiting slab of acrylic.

He supervises as they put up the forms and carefully—oh so carefully, lest there be air bubbles—pour on the remaining acrylic. Through the translucent forms, he can still see her, but her image is murky and cloud-puffy with hardening polymers. Hardly the work of art her husband commissioned. But when the forms come off and the encasing, sheltering, *immortalizing* acrylic runs clear as glass, she will be perfect… forever.

The apprentices leave him alone with her and he collapses, beyond exhaustion. His vigil won't end until her cocoon has cured, another eight hours. There remains, however, one final task. He retrieves needles and ink, removes his shirt, and looks for a bare stretch of skin on which to remember her.

2. Art and Audience

The multitude of voices in the gallery don't penetrate the acrylic, but the stares do. Faces file by, linger with open-mouthed awe. Hesitant, near-reverent fingers trace the crystal block as if they can feel the lines of tattooing. A crowd gathers, and as their lips move, it's easy to imagine what they're saying:

"It's a genuine Ransom, isn't it?"

"Oh, yes! Much better than those imitations across the hall. The guy's a genius."

"Genius? You ladies oughta have your heads examined." The two women appraise this cowboy-type who has come to the fore, their eyes as sharp and cold as the diamonds adorning their digits, wrists, and necklines. "Tell you what I think—" They both knew he would; it's written on their faces. "—I think he's a goddamn psycho!"

"Oh, no sir, not Herbert Ransom. Now Moog… Moog, he's psychotic. All those *rearranged* pieces. Butchery is all it is. Moog acts out his fantasies on cadavers."

"God, Moog *is* disgusting. Katie, did you see the guy with the penis where his nose should be?"

"Sick! And what about Chapman's *reanimated* series? Did you see that? Or Pruitt's 'Study of the Amputee?' How do some of these artists sleep at night?"

"It's all sick, ladies." The cowboy runs a beefy finger along the brim of his hat as if making some minute adjustment. The one called Katie watches the gesture with sudden fascination. She looks as if she's just realized where she misplaced something valuable. "The dead should be used for fertilizer, not mutilated and displayed."

"Oh, no. This is *art,* people." A new face crowds up to the acrylic's surface, this one in an Italian suit and hundred-dollar tie. The only thing he probably has in common with the cowboy is the money in his pocket. "You're all three missing the point. Think of the talent it took to transfer that penis. Not a single seam. To look at it, you'd have thought the guy was born that way."

"I still say it's sick. What I wonder is what sorta people contribute their loved ones for these things?"

"Moog probably collects homeless beggars and files disposal rights. If no one comes forward in ten days, the corpse is his, isn't that right, Betty? Betty knows these things, she works down town at the Bureau."

"That's right. It all started with those damn organ donor laws. Find a body, get a new kidney. Kinda says something about society, doesn't it, Katie?"

"No more so than this tattooed nightmare," retorts the cowboy. "I certainly wouldn't want my daughter, or sister, or mother—or whatever she was to the person who commissioned this—used for some sick paint-by-numbers exhibit." He's moved closer to Katie and she to him.

"No, you just don't get it. Look at her. It's all there in the ink. Her whole life. It's like some sort of spiral galaxy, the events and the connections and the components of her life swirling out around her. She's the center. All these other people, all these incidents revolve around her. She was the center of their universe… and now they are without her."

"Shit, what we got here is one of them dead art impressionists, ladies. Kinda fella thinks he sees purpose in a pile of dogshit. I'm leaving before he spews some on my boots."

"Katie, you're not going too, are you?" There's an unspoken level of communication between the two women as they separate, a *meet-you-at-the-bar-in-a-couple-hours* relayed on some telepathic level. Betty understands that Katie and the cowboy have reacted to the exhibits on some instinctive level. Death dares them to defy his presence, to deny his breath on the neck of every visitor in the packed gallery. Sex is an instinctive defense. See me, Death? If I can enjoy this, you're a long way from being on my appointment book.

Betty is disappointed that she is left with the art critic, the thinker, the one too aesthetically sensitive and hormonally insensitive to recognize that she's also ready to leave. With him.

"Let them go. They don't get it. They don't see that whoever asked Ransom to do this loved this woman more than anything in the world."

"And wanted us to see her like this?"

"Maybe not. Maybe he had no choice. Part of Ransom's standard contract says he gets to display the work for an initial period. She'll be here a week, two at the most, then she'll be secreted away somewhere where only the people featured in these tattoos can view her."

"But to shave her and… display her nude like that—"

"Don't you see that Ransom needed every inch of canvas? This woman was connected to a lot of people."

"And all of them marched into Ransom's studio and posed for this? I think the guy's a genius, but I'm only willing to go so far, pal. Come on, he makes these images up for those of us who don't know any better."

"They say he's intuitive, empathetic even. He interviews everyone he can before he starts the job, but in the end he takes most of what he needs from the corpse. They say he has an 'intimacy with the dead.'"

"Creepy."

"Yeah. Perhaps that's what makes his art, and all the art in this gallery, so popular."

"Maybe we're looking for the opportunity to touch death?"

"Or immortality."

"She looks so young. How do you suppose she died?"

"Didn't you see it in the paper and on the news? She drowned in some kind of boating accident."

"Oh." As if that explained something. She taps the acrylic with a manicured fingernail. "How long will she last in there?"

"No air… pumped full of preservatives… I'd guess, maybe, forever."

3. Loneliness and Judgment

The night holds the garden in a skeletal silence so complete it seems even the insects are loathe to intrude upon it. Herbert Ransom has come like a thief over the garden wall to his customer's study. He stands now outside the open veranda door, in the shadows, in the half light, in the judicial black of the monochrome realm where he, the artist, comes like a god, a god of color. He watches as his customer inspects the acrylic block, running tentative, trembling fingers across the polished surface. Herbert Ransom runs his own hands beneath his shirt, feeling the landscape of textures spread across his stomach and chest. Where his shirt gaps and the flesh beneath is touched by the light from the study, colors are born to challenge the night.

The customer weeps, spreading his tears across the acrylic surface. The tears bead there, dispelling the illusion that he and his dead wife are separated by a foot of water. He shudders and begins to weep uncontrollably. "I'm sorry," he whispers, but not so low that Ransom can't hear.

Clearing his throat, Ransom steps from the shadows.

The husband looks up, wiping at his eyes. He seems unsurprised to find the artist at his door.

"Is the work satisfactory?" Ransom asks.

"Satisfactory?" The husband touches the acrylic and methodically moves from scene to scene across the tattooed panorama. "How could you have known all these things?"

Ransom doesn't answer.

The husband gestures toward the face of a dark and attractive man occupying real estate on his wife's chest, just above her left breast, that spot where she would place her hand if asked to put it over her heart. "How could you have ever known about him?" The dark man's face is caught looking back over his left shoulder, his eyes and mouth set in an expression of incongruent surprise and expectation. It was exactly the way she remembered him best. Exactly as he'd looked that first night she'd called him back when he'd made to leave the bar.

"I wasn't going to keep her, you know," continues the

husband. "I was going to send her... to *him*. I thought that... that when you were finished and all the important things about our life together—our life before he came along—were laid out there on her flesh, that I'd send her to him. See what you did? I would ask. You destroyed all this. You were nothing to her. But," he sobs and slaps angrily at the tattooed face of the dark man. "There the son of a bitch is and... how can I send her to him now? Right there he is. Right there near her heart.

"And it's me who's left to ponder my own significance in her life." He looks up then and finds some strength in the ambivalence writ upon the artist's face. He wipes his eyes, screws his face into an indignant frown, and asks, "What the hell are you doing here anyway?"

Ransom removes his shirt and lets it drop to the floor.

"Oh my God."

There, on the artist's breast: the long, gondola-like boat, the moon and the swamp and the backlit cypress trees, the pole in the husband's hands, and the white turmoil where the pole enters the water. Beneath the water, at the end of the pole, a face twisted in terror.

THE TROUBLE WITH THE TRUTH

"The truth is a snare: you cannot have it, without being caught. You cannot have the truth in such a way that you catch it, but only in such a way that it catches you."
—Søren Kierkegaard (1813-55), Danish philosopher

Sri Mani's bullet clipped a twig near my head, punched a perfectly symmetrical hole in the broad red leaf of a plant that closely resembled a poinsettia, and hissed off through the forest. A couple seconds after its passage, the dull thunder of the musket reached me, shattering my reverie. For no apparent reason, I'd been thinking about Kyle. Remembering the way he used to hold our hands and swing between Connie and me while walking through the shopping mall. I was trying to remember why it used to aggravate me so. But something about that fifty-caliber musket ball breezing past my ear reminded me that Sri Mani and Nanda, his assistant, were no longer hunting honey.

They were hunting me.

It hardly seemed important to wonder why I hadn't appreciated Kyle when he was alive, not with the echo of that shot whispering in Nanda's raspy voice, "You are next, Bahktur. Pholo will make forest of you."

How long to reload? Another ball. Powder. Something for a patch (I pictured Nanda using that wicked Gurkha knife of his—the one I'd seen him use to dispatch a full-grown boar—to cut small rags from the hem of his woolen wrap). Then the rod from the underside of the barrel packing it all down. Replace the percussion cap—how many of those did Sri Mani have? Surely they weren't cheap. Surely he couldn't afford many, not when he had to go all the way to Kathmandu for them. And finally, I could picture him raising the musket back to his shoulder, lining up his eye with the sights, lining up one dumb fucking American who'd come to Nepal because he believed it was the last place on Earth for the truth to ever catch up with him.

One dumb fucking American—AKA *me.*

I ducked into the nearest brush, wincing as the course branches tore at my face, and scrambled away, keeping low, limping. Waiting for the bark of the rifle again. Knowing that by the time I actually heard it, it would be too late and the lead ball might already be buried in my back.

Ten feet and the ground pitched out from under me. I slid, bruising shins and tearing my palms on jagged rock, coming up short against a storm-ravaged stump. It wasn't much of a fall—leastwise not when compared with Nanda's cutting my safety line this morning. The stump tore my shirt and gouged a furrow in my side, further aggravating my bruised ribs, but the shot I'd been waiting for didn't come. Looking back, I saw why. For the time being, the edge of this shallow ravine hid the two honey hunters from sight.

For at least as long as it took them to rappel down the cliff face and climb back up through the valley and over this verdant peak, I was safe. I had some time to think. Some time to recall how I'd come here. And, more importantly, to figure out how I was going to get out alive.

The village of Bahadur was hidden so deep in the Himalayas as to discourage any contact with the outside world. Tourists didn't visit. Pilgrims and holy men en route to the monasteries to the northwest found easier routes along the Brahmaputra River. The Zangbo and mainland China lay over the peaks, impassable. Kathmandu was four days away through dense forest. Mount Everest was more accessible by air. There was, in short, no reason for *anyone* to visit Bahadur. Only those who'd become truly lost ever found themselves there.

Lost is exactly what I was.

I'd been lost for over three years when I came to Bahadur.

I was still mourning the death of my son. Full of self-loathing. Still reeling from the bitter hatred I'd last seen in the eyes of the woman I loved. When she told me to leave, I don't think Connie realized just how far I'd go. Or perhaps she did; she'd been married to me long enough to know my extremes. Perhaps she simply didn't care.

I first found myself in Sri Lanka at the home of another writer I knew from my days with *National Geographic*. When I wore out my welcome there (even the best of friends tend to tolerate heavy drinking and self-pity for only so long), I crossed the Bay of Bengal and lost myself in India. I drifted up the coast for two years, accepting work when it was offered, and I could keep my senses about me long enough to collect a paycheck. When I couldn't find work, I stole what I needed to survive. I was a wreck, clad in filthy rags no better than the *lungis* wrapped about the waists of beggars (with whom I'd spent a fair share of my time). I'd gone from pickling myself on my friend's expensive liquor to the cheap and readily available *apang*, a fermented grain concoction that tasted like goat's piss and took several gallons to put me into my usual stupor. By the time I'd pass out from drinking the stuff, I would have crammed so much of it into my bladder that I'd wake up floating in a puddle of my own urine. Worse, I'd generally roll over and go back to sleep, beyond even caring.

But it wasn't until I reached Calcutta that I hit rock bottom. I lost thirteen months in Calcutta, doing what and with whom, I still can't recall. Drugs replaced the alcohol. There were injections. There were pipes. There were exotics that stank of cobra venom and opium and God knows what else. There were months that I never saw the sun. Weeks that the only waste leaving my body came up through my mouth and nose. It wasn't until I woke one morning in a feces-clogged gutter behind a brothel, a toothless old man in fine yellow robes bending over me with several rupees in his hand saying, *"Baksheesh, baksheesh,"* that I began my fight up from the bottom. I didn't want to know what I'd done to earn that tip. I didn't want to know why I was naked in an alley in Calcutta, or why two men tried to drag me back into the brothel, or why I was down to 140 pounds, or why my hands shook so bad that I couldn't hang on to the coins, or...

I found a monastery, hoping to seek sanctuary among the monks there. They beat me with cane poles and chased me out into the streets. Children took up the assault from there, harrying me northward out of the city, pelting me with stones, kicking me in the ass as I scrambled about on all fours. North of Calcutta, somewhere on a dirt road rutted by busses and littered with llama dung, I curled up to die beside the steaming carcass of a yak. There ensued several days of heat and flies, starvation and sunburn and pestilence. I was delirious with fever. Wracked by substance withdrawal. Travelers rolled me from the road and into a ditch. Insects laid their eggs in my eyes and beneath my skin. The mud of the ditch sucked up around me, while rodents nibbled at my extremities, and the dogs who came to fight over the yak waited for their turn at me.

But death did not find me.

Eventually I found my feet and continued northward. I stole some rags. I begged for food. I ate raw corn from a farmer's field and eggs from his hen house. By the time I reached Jamshedpur, I was beginning to resemble a human being again. I had bathed in a pond and shaved with broken glass. I found work clearing brush from a construction site. A Frenchman named Montbéliard gave me a hundred rupees and a ride to Patna near the Ganges. With Montbéliard's money, I bought used, but sturdy clothing from a street merchant. In the Ganges River, I washed away the last of Baxter Lewis. With the dirt and blood and dead skin that flowed away from me down the river went the truth of who and what I'd been, the sins that I'd committed, the man that I had come to hate. I wasn't sad to see any of it go. I wasn't interested in the truth any more than I was interested in returning to any semblance of a normal life in the States. But neither was I any longer interested in death. I'd taken my best shot at killing myself and failed miserably. It was time for something other than self-destruction.

I continued north, through the town of Varanasi and up into the foothills of the Himalayas. The roads grew steeper, then disappeared altogether. Goat trails drew me ever higher, into thin air, moist clouds, and thick, damp vegetation. Where the forests hadn't been cleared and sold off as lumber, the overpowering essence of life that dripped like honey from every Nepalese leaf and limb took root in the poisoned pores of my flesh and flowered, rejuvenating my soul. I was alive again. The higher I went, the less of civilization I saw, and the more alive I became.

When I finally stumbled on Bahadur, it was Nanda who spotted me first.

"*Drokpa*?" he asked in that cancer-clogged rasp of his.

"Yes," I whispered. I am indeed a nomad. A wanderer. An exile of life. There is no past. There is no future. There is no truth. There's only here and now. Here, at the end of the Earth.

"Bahktur," he called me, unable to pronounce my name.

I nodded. Yes, that's right. Baxter Lewis is dead. Only Bahktur remains.

If only it had been that easy…

The Gurung of Bahadur allowed me to settle in a corner of the *namghar,* their communal hut. Nanda showed me where to gather bamboo and how to build a privacy screen of sorts. I was given a straw mattress, a bowl with which to beg food, and free run of the village. For the most part, the *namghar* was mine, having been built for the occasional wedding or village meeting. The Gurung rarely met as a group—most of them working until nightfall in the fields of corn they carefully cultivated in the rich nooks and crannies nestled in the mountains. They were a simple people, prone to bland foods and earth tones. Their skin was of a color and texture best compared with a dried riverbed, cracked and hardened by the sun. Their eyes were dark and impenetrably Asian, revealing whites only when excited or startled. Their hands were as gnarled as old roots. Their feet were wide and heavily callused, with black nails and flat soles. With the exception of Nanda, none of them spoke any English. Though they were kind, they rarely smiled when I was around, but I would often catch them when they thought they were alone, and in those rare moments I'd observe the love of a mother for her child, the laughter of siblings at play, the teasing of the men as they went out into their fields: emotions and actions as universal as man himself. They fed me without reproach, ridicule, or scorn, and never once asked where I'd come from or what I'd done. They did not care why I had fled civilization.

Clear-headed for the first time in years, it didn't take long for me to become bored, to begin to feel useless. I asked Nanda if there was something I could do around the village to help out.

"Men work the fields," he said.

I shook my head. I'd no interest in being a farmer, certainly not at an elevation in excess of ten thousand feet. I simply wasn't up to it. But not all the men worked as farmers; Nanda and Sri Mani were hunters. The forest was alive with wild goats, yaks, boars, hares and foxes and marmots. I'd been eating stews provided courtesy of Sri Mani's musket since my arrival.

"I could hunt," I ventured.

"Pholo smile on Sri Mani," said the Nepalese. "Pholo does not know Bahktur."

"You could introduce me to your forest god."

"Bahktur does not know how to pray to Pholo."

I'd seen the *chorten*, the shrine that they'd made to Pholo. Nanda and Sri Mani never left the village without making an offering. In as much as I'd long ago forsaken my own god, I saw no problem with accepting theirs. I touched Nanda's shoulder, startled to find his bare arm as hard and dry as rock. "Teach me, Nanda."

He searched my eyes. I've no idea what he was looking for, no idea what he found. His eyes were as deep and unreadable as always, a thousand years lost in the heavy creases of his wrinkled brow, his lips set like stone. There were old scars on his cheek, barely distinguishable from the less traumatic but equally hardened weathering of time. Finally, he blinked.

"We leave at dawn, Bahktur. If you not farmer, Pholo will see what kind of man you are."

I found them near the shrine, a chicken struggling its last in Sri Mani's strong hands. The breast of the chicken had been split open, the white downy mantle now slick with blood, its organs dangling from the gaping cavity… like some morbid high school lab experiment, minus only the straight pins and paper labels.

Nanda gave a curt nod when he saw me. "Sri Mani say Pholo smile on us today. We will hunt."

The chicken was placed on the altar, still struggling feebly against the evisceration that had yielded Pholo's blessing. Sri Mani wiped his bloody hands on the grass, picked up his musket, and started off into the forest without a word. Nanda pointed to a massive bundle of bamboo fiber rope, several long bamboo poles, and a large wicker basket lined with goat hide.

"You carry," he said.

Before I could complain that the load would be too much, he shouldered his own load, a huge bundle of rope and bamboo that was at first a mystery, but as I studied it I saw that it was a long ladder, coiled about itself into a bundle some thirty inches in diameter. It must have weighed more than half as much as the man himself. With a strap that he looped over his forehead, Nanda braced the heavy load on his back, leaning far forward to balance the weight. He didn't watch to see if I would follow. He simply started off into the forest on the heels of Sri Mani, who carried nothing except the musket.

I gathered up the ropes, poles, and basket, strapping as much of it as I could on my back, gathering the rest in my arms, and struggled after them.

The day waxed hot and humid. The air grew thinner as we climbed higher. It was a struggle to breath. Twice I nearly lost sight of the Nepalese hunters, who did not slow their pace for me. In a rare moment when Nanda was within shouting range, I called out to him.

"Isn't there plenty of game below? Nearer the village?"

"Not the game we seek, Bahktur" he replied, without turning his head.

"And what game is that?" I asked.

He didn't answer.

We stopped for an afternoon meal of *tsampa,* a Tibetan staple of roasted barley flour, cheese, sugar, curd, and butter rolled into small balls. We washed it down with cool water from a nearby stream. I leaned against the coils of rope, my feet up and braced against the trunk of a tree because I seemed to remember reading somewhere, a million years ago, that it was good to keep the blood from flooding your feet while resting on a hike. I was still breathing heavily, a combination of the thin air and the exertion. I was beginning to wonder if I'd ever catch my breath. Sri Mani stared at me openly, his gnarled, fastidious fingers stroking the long gray whiskers on his chin. Finally, he turned to Nanda and said something. Nanda just shook his head.

"What'd he say?"

"He say you are weak. Too weak to be hunter. But your baby face remind him of his son, so he like you."

"Oh?" I tried not to sound insulted. Sri Mani's remark was based on the fact that I had continued to shave each day, despite the fact the razor I had bought in Patna was long since dull, despite the fact that none of the Gurung men were so inclined to bare their faces. "How old is his son?"

"His son is dead," said Nanda.

I looked away, suddenly too exposed by their dark, unwavering eyes. I didn't want to hear about dead sons. I didn't want to know the truth.

Sri Mani huffed, shouldered his musket, and rose to his feet. Within seconds, he had disappeared into the forest.

"Not far now," Nanda said. No compassion. Just a simple statement of fact.

I gathered my load and set out after them, determined not to fall behind.

The cliff face dropped away some four hundred feet to a rocky, scrub-clogged ravine below.

"Runs from there," Nanda said, nodding up at the peaks of the Himalayas lost in the clouds, "all the way down into India."

The rock face was dove-gray, striated with meandering bands of white and cinnamon. Its edges looked to have been specifically sculpted for breaking skin and bone. The jagged boulders peeking through the thorny scrub brush below seemed poised to receive a hurtling body, to crack it open and spread its fluids amidst the leaves and lichens. While Sri Mani leaned far out at the cliff's edge to peer below, I hung back, shaking, trying to convince myself it was due solely to the exhaustion. But that first glimpse over the edge had been enough for me. My stomach was in knots. My knees were weak. I felt lightheaded and nauseous.

Nanda made one end of the rope ladder fast to a tree and hurled the remainder over the edge of the cliff. It uncoiled smoothly, spilling down the face of the rock, stopping some seventy or so feet short of the bottom.

"We're not…" I couldn't even finish the sentence.

Neither of them bothered to answer. Sri Mani set his gun aside, gathered two of the bamboo poles I'd carried, and vanished over the edge, walking down the ladder as nimbly as a circus performer. The fact that he had set aside the gun baffled me. Just what exactly were we here to hunt?

Nanda extracted several coils of rope from my bundle and shoved several more at me. "Ties those to basket. Like this," he said, indicating the rim of the basket, "so the basket does not spill."

"Spill *what*?"

But he'd already turned away and started tying other ropes to the trees at the top of the cliff, casting their free ends out over the edge. With a shorter length of rope, he fashioned a harness about his body. "Watch," he said, as he tied the knots. "Now, you." He slapped at my hands. "No. Like this. Pholo will make forest of you, Bahktur, if you do this wrong." When the harness was complete, he showed me how to loop one of the main lines secured to the tree through the harness and around my waist. He showed me how to brace my hands. One in front. The other back against my hip. "Like this," he said, showing me how to brake the rope. "Walk down side of mountain. Easy."

"I think I'll just hang out here."

He shook his head. "Farmer Bahktur, then. That is what I call you."

Then he took the basket and, lowering it behind him, backed over the edge of the cliff and disappeared. For a moment, I was alone. The only sound was the wind and the snickering leaves.

"Fuck."

So long as I didn't look down, it wasn't all that bad. I focused on the face of the rock just a few feet away, pretending it was the ground, hiding the truth that the ground was some 400 feet behind me. Nanda saw me coming and laughed softly.

"Are you sure these ropes are safe?" I asked. They were quite obviously handmade. Nothing but bamboo fibers. Sri Mani had the ladder, which seemed much safer, distributing his weight across two lines and all those bamboo cross-pieces. Why he got to use the ladder, while Nanda and I had to rappel…

"Tree," said Nanda, pointing. "There. Tie a second rope. Make you feel safer. Ropes only break once in a while."

"Once in a while?"

He merely smiled.

I side-stepped over to the tree. It was a stunted, twisted thing, the sort of tree one finds in a desert, but its roots were firmly anchored in the cracks of the cliff face. There seemed little chance it would come loose soon, even if tested with my weight. I took a second line from those I'd looped over my shoulder and made a safety line some thirty feet long, tying one end securely to the tree and the other to my harness, looping it again around my waist just in case the harness broke, too. If my main rope snapped, I'd fall, but not as far as the bottom of the ravine. I might snap my spine at the end of the rope, but I'd live to talk about it afterward. This became my standard practice on all such hunts, hanging safety lines as I made my decent. Safety first, as they say. It seemed absurd when considering what I'd come through to get there.

My fear somewhat checked, I became aware of a loud droning noise. I dared to look down, and there was Sri Mani, sitting on the ladder, his hands occupied with those two bamboo poles. He was prodding at something back up under an overhang. The noise came from whatever hung up under there and from the cloud that swarmed all around him, enveloping him in a black, shifting mass of sound. Fighting my terror at the drop waiting on the other side of Sri Mani, fighting to focus my eyes only on him and not on the terrifying open space beyond him, the cloud took shape. The individual layers of movement segregated, took form, came into focus… became black, bulbous bodies swirling around Sri Mani, lighting on his flesh, coating his back and shoulders and head.

They were bees. The largest bees I had ever seen, each as big as my thumb.

"Bahktur!" Nanda shouted over the noise. I realized it was the second or third time he had called for me. "You go lower. Put basket under hive. Hold steady."

I looked down into that shifting, angry cloud of black and shook my head adamantly.

"Hive too far under cliff," he explained. "I have to pull ladder toward rock, get Sri Mani closer. You hold basket for honey."

"No. I'm not going down there."

"Pholo blessed this. Sri Mani ask bees not to sting."

"And they'll just listen to him? No thank you."

He shook his head as if to show I was a disappointment. Then he took the basket and rappelled down into the swarm. I was left hanging there, waiting. The cloud below became so thick, I could barely see the two honey hunters. The droning sound went on and on, insinuating itself into my brain, one long monotonous song whose meaning and origin had been lost a million years ago with my ancestors. The sound was hypnotizing. Before I knew it, I'd been hanging there ten or fifteen minutes. My hands were tired of bracing my weight against the rope. I began to think about climbing up. Easier to wait on the escarpment above. Besides, I felt the need to escape the sound of all those bees.

It was then I discovered that I wasn't strong enough to pull my weight up the rope.

Below me, the bees were an impenetrable cloud, a near solid, shifting mass of bodies and noise. Through the swarm, I'd occasionally get brief glimpses of Sri Mani, trying to swing his ladder in toward the cliff face so he could reach the hive. Bees had become a black mantle on his shoulders, flowing down his back like a cape, covering his head like a hood.

I didn't know how much longer I could hang there, holding my weight against that great fall and certain death. If I waited too long, would I have the strength to lower myself? Could I count on Sri Mani or his assistant for help?

I had no choice.

I slowly lowered myself toward the swarm. They landed on

my boots first. Then the legs of my trousers. Anxious, the bees flew up to meet me, their wings fanning my face. They were nearly the size of hummingbirds. The noise of the swarm had become tactile now, a thrumming vibration in the air. There was no escaping it. I couldn't cover my ears and, even if I could, I had a feeling it wouldn't work. I was certain that the droning song of the bees was a sound to penetrate any barrier. I closed my eyes and bit my lip and backed my way down the cliff face, fighting the urge to scream as they pelted my body.

But they didn't sting me. Soon, I was through the worst of it.

Looking up from beneath the swarm, the hive was clearly visible. It hung suspended from the overhang, as large as a minivan, millions of bees crawling across its surface. It consisted of two parts: the honeycomb, which was attached to the cliff, and the brood comb, a lower crescent burgeoning with pupae, eggs, and larvae. It was frightening in its immensity. The noise was terrifying and loud. I seemed to recall reading about them once. *Apis laboriosa,* the world's largest honeybee, found only in Nepal. Reading about them and encountering them were two different things—worlds apart. There weren't words to describe the black, motile mass of all those bees or the revulsion and fear that shifted prehistorically within my gut. The truth embodied in actual contact could not be told.

Nanda had rigged the basket to catch the honey. Then he'd gone below to pull the ladder in under the overhang. Sri Mani assaulted the honeycomb, carving into its side, using the poles like giant chopsticks. He scraped great slabs of the honeycomb into the goatskin-lined basket. By the time the basket was full, it must have contained some fifteen gallons of honey. From the brood comb, he scoured great slabs of beeswax. As I slipped past Sri Mani and dropped below, warm sticky drops of honey dotted my arms and face. I took a dab of it on my finger and put it to my mouth. I hadn't tasted anything sweet since leaving the States. The honey's nectar was overpowering, like a drug. I reached for more as it dripped past.

"No!" Nanda yelled.

When I looked down at him, he shook his head. Evidently, I wasn't supposed to eat the honey. Terrified, I looked up, expecting to see the swarm regrouping for an assault, angered that I'd dared consume the gift in their presence. But nothing about their behavior had changed. Their song remained the same. Later, Sri Mani would examine the honey closely and hold it cupped in the palm of his hand to see if it tingled. Often, Nanda said, the bees visit poisonous plants, and those who eat the honey can become sick and even die. Supposedly, Sri Mani, who has hunted honey all his life, as did his father and his grandfather before him, can tell by sight and touch if the honey is bad. After everything I had witnessed that first time harvesting the honey, this was but one more small miracle that I was willing to believe.

I continued down the cliff face past Nanda, discarding and rigging safety lines as I went. At some point the bees left me, all at once, as if by some silent agreement they'd decided I wasn't really a part of the proceedings anymore. Why I wasn't stung, I can't say. The only explanation Nanda offered was that Sri Mani had asked them not to.

When my feet touched the ground, I collapsed in exhaustion, gasping on the much too thin air, while dollops of honey spotted the rocks around me. Sometime later I heard Nanda calling my name. He threw down all the safety lines that I'd left hanging on the cliff face. Through gestures, he indicated that I was to follow the ravine toward a crumbled gap in the rocks where he thought I could probably climb up to meet them. I gathered my wits about me, collected the ropes, and followed the ravine…

…and it was then that I found the first bone.

Bleached white. Long and supple. Delicately curved. It looked like the rib of some small animal. I saw it in an oddly utilitarian light, something I could fashion into a tool—as if I had survived by making such things all my life. Bahktur, the Neanderthal. Fashioned into something useful, it might make a gift for Nanda or one of the Gurung women who often fed me. I slipped it under my shirt and… for a while… I gave it little thought.

It was but the first of many bones I'd find in the ravine.

That had been two months ago.

A mynah bird scolded me from the trees, and I realized that I'd been resting in the shade for far too long. Sri Mani and Nanda had probably rappelled down the cliff face by now. Months of hunting honey had made me lean and strong; it had only taken me twenty minutes or so to climb the other side, but it would probably take them even less time. I got to my feet and started downslope, limping on the ankle I'd twisted in the fall, holding my bruised ribs.

Nanda had seen me pick up my latest find, a bone so obvious in its origin and design that there could be no doubt as to its species. A quarter of the way up the cliff face (I'd been re-ascending for several weeks by then), he'd simply leaned out with the Gurkha and cut my line. I'd plummeted, coming up short a second later at the end of my safety line, gasping to draw air into my wracked chest, dazed and terrified. Above me, Nanda walked across the cliff face and stopped by my secondary line.

He set the curved blade against the bamboo fibers and called down: "Throw it to me, Bahktur."

Above us both, dangling from his ladder, Sri Mani looked startled and confused. Nanda's action had taken him by complete surprise, too.

"I don't know what you're talking about," I croaked, hugging my chest, wondering how many ribs I'd broken.

"Under your shirt," he said. "Take it out. Show Sri Mani what you found."

"Leave me alone. I don't know what you're talking about," I repeated. "Have you lost your fucking mind?"

He drew back the Gurkha as if to strike the safety line in two.

I held up a hand. "Okay. Wait. I was going to show you later anyway," I lied. The truth was that this was the capstone to the monument I'd been building in my private corner of the *namghar.* There in the dirt beside my bed, I'd carefully arranged each piece. I'd no intention of showing anyone. This was private. Personal. This was between Pholo and me. This was the truth

I'd come to Nepal to escape and, if I could confess it to my new god, perhaps he would do what my old god could not. Perhaps it would take the truth and set it right.

"Show it!" Nanda rasped.

I pulled it out from under my shirt and held it up. Sri Mani gasped, the whites of his eyes revealed to me for perhaps the first time.

The Nepalese sun gleamed from the tiny skull. The lower mandible was missing, but the skull's dome was bleach-white and nearly perfect, marred only by the gaping fracture which ran from the outer rim of the right occipital ridge around and down to the base of the skull. It had been a grievous injury, one which had surely cost the child its life. The fracture could have been made by a blow—perhaps even the slash of a Gurkha knife—but I knew differently. The injury had been the result of a fall.

I had let him fall.

"Throw it to me," said Nanda.

The trouble with the truth is finding someone to tell it to, someone who actually wants to hear it. And then there's the possibility that you'll never live long enough to tell the truth, that you'll take it to the grave with you, because for everyone who might want to hear the truth, there are ten or twenty who want to suppress it. No one really wants to hear the truth when it doesn't fit in their nice, neat ordered lives. Some people would rather see you dead than listen to it.

The truth will bite you on the ass if you let it.

Everyone has their own version.

The truth can get you killed.

These are the basic truths about the nature of truth itself.

"How did Sri Mani's son die?" I asked Nanda over the crackling of the campfire one night. We'd been hunting late, too late to return to Bahadur before dark. Sri Mani had already curled up in his woolen wrap and gone to sleep. The sound of that afternoon's hive still echoed in my skull. At times now, it almost seemed as if I could understand their song.

Beneath my shirt, cold against my belly, was a tiny femur.

Nanda shrugged. “Boy get sick. Die before we can take to Kathmandu to see doctor.”

“Does Sri Mani have other children?”

He shook his head, his dark eyes catching the firelight and reflecting… nothing.

“Who will hunt honey for the Gurung when Sri Mani is gone?”

He shrugged. “Perhaps you, Bahktur?”

I shook my head. “The bees frighten me.”

“The bees know Sri Mani make them strong.”

“What?”

“When Sri Mani cut into the comb, many are lost, but the strong survive.”

I was surprised to find the basic principles of Darwin’s theory alive in the Himalayas. And for Nanda to suggest that the bees understood it, that they permitted it? It was absurd. But the fact remained that the bees did not attack Sri Mani or his assistant.

“Once,” said Nanda, “we harvest six hundred hives a season, between the time ravine floods in spring and first snow on mountains. Now we lucky to find eighty. Many forests gone. Many hives destroyed.”

He was lamenting the death of the environment and their culture, the wasted landscape I’d walked through to get here, the end of Sri Mani’s occupation and all that they knew, but I heard something else. In the spring, the ravine ran with melt-off from the mountains. That explained the dispersion of the bones I’d been finding, the reason why the femur I’d found that afternoon had been twenty miles or more from the rib I’d found that first day, or the finger bone I’d found a week ago, or those vertebrae, or…

“Sri Mani’s ancestors have always hunted the honey, always had Pholo’s blessing and protection from the bees.” He shook his head sadly. “But I don’t know for how much longer there will be honey to hunt.”

A thought came unbidden to me then, as if extracted from the very drone of the bees that still rang in the back of mind: As long as the bees desire to be hunted, there will be honey hunters.

I slipped the skull back under my shirt and shook my head. "You can't have it," I told the honey hunters.

Nanda didn't hesitate. The Gurkha flashed silver in the sunlight. I clung to the cliff face like an insect, my fingers and toes wedged into the cracks I'd sought out while we were talking. My safety line tumbled down and past me, dangling at the end of my harness, its end still twenty feet short of the ground. Nanda seemed shocked that I hadn't fallen. In truth, so was I. His shock lasted only a second, though, before he started descending his own rope toward me. Sri Mani took the opposite tact, climbing up his ladder. The musket, of course, had been left at the top of the cliff.

It's amazing what you can do when your life is threatened. Though it felt as if razor blades had been embedded in my rib cage, I scrambled down the cliff face, managing to make it halfway to the ground before I slipped and fell. The slip saved my life, because just as I came away from the wall, a musket ball—first of several shots Sri Mani would take—skipped off the rock in front of my face and passed between my legs into the vegetation below. The echo of the musket followed me down.

I landed in a patch of brush, just missing a massive boulder. Fighting the pain of a twisted ankle, I scrambled through the ravine and began my ascent up the other side, while Nanda yelled for me to stop. I looked back only once. Sri Mani was reloading the musket. That was all I needed to convince me not to stop.

"Sri Mani asks if you have any children, Bahktur."

I looked across the melting pot at the two of them and said nothing. Nanda was straining beeswax through a fine mesh of grass fibers. It was my job to take the hot, filtered wax as it cooled and shape it into cubes which would be sold in Kathmandu.

Sri Mani rattled off something else.

"He say is not good to leave this world without someone to carry on in your place."

"No," I agreed, "it's not."

"So, do you have children?"

"Just a son," I said softly.

Nanda relayed the information to Sri Mani. "How old?" he asked.

"Five," I replied. He'll forever be five.

Somehow, Nanda circled around and cut me off. He was strong and fast. He probably knew an easier route up from the ravine. I don't know how I had expected to escape him. This was his home, his forest. And Pholo had been with him since long before I'd come here. What made me think the Gurung's god cared whether I lived or died?

"Give to me," he said, brandishing the Gurkha.

"Which one of you killed him?" I asked, showing him the skull. "*Why* did you kill him?"

"He fell."

"And for that, you want to kill me?"

He smiled, but it was a transparent expression. The knife was still in his hand. "No, no, Bahktur. You misunderstand. No one want to kill you. We just want skull. Skull is ours."

You're wrong, I thought. The skull is mine. This isn't Sri Mani's son. This is mine. Because of my coming here, because of my praying to Pholo, Kyle sleeps beside me each night. There on the ground, so carefully arranged, so quiet and peaceful and... forgiving.

Some element of the old Baxter Lewis, some remnant of civilization and rational thought, peeked out from the dark corners of my mind and laughed at what I was thinking. The word schizophrenia surfaced, but it was a word beyond Bahktur's comprehension.

"You lied to me," I told Nanda. "You told me the boy was sick and died. That's the same thing you told the village, isn't it?"

He said nothing.

"That's why you don't want me taking this skull back to Bahadur. The Gurung will know that you lied. The Gurung will know the truth. You killed the boy. Why?"

He let the knife fall to his side. He relaxed. His shoulders slumped, and he looked defeated. "All right, Bahktur. You win.

Yes, Sri Mani kill boy. Sri Mani want to end the cycle."

"End the cycle?"

"Is no life for boy, hunting honey. Is no life for boy's son when boy grow up, or grandson, or... You see? Pholo will never let Sri Mani and his family go. Sri Mani's family serve bees forever."

For as long as the bees desire to be hunted...

"Sri Mani make them strong. Bees know this."

Suddenly, he lunged, the Gurkha slashing at my gut. I stumbled back, away from the wicked slice of the knife, and struck him across the temple with the skull. As he stumbled, blood spilling down his face, I caught the wrist that held the knife. We went crashing through the underbrush like that, a deadly dance for possession of the blade. I was bigger and stronger than the little Nepalese. The years of abuse I'd inflicted on myself had been sweated from my pores hunting at his side, hiking and climbing through the forests and the thin air. Despite my bad ankle and tortured rib cage, I managed to overpower him. I slammed him against a tree trunk. The knife flew off into the leaves.

It was then that I heard the bees. I looked up, and there they were, a dense cloud coming through the forest. Framed within their dark, shifting mass stood Sri Mani, the stock of the musket against his shoulder. As he fired, I spun Nanda in front of me. The ball caught him in the throat, splattering his blood across my face. I fell to the ground with him, his life pumping hot across my forearms. He made gurgling noises. Rolled his eyes back to beseech me for help I didn't know how to give.

"I tried to save you," I whispered.

But it was a lie. The car had rolled, had come to rest there on the cliffs overlooking the sea, and I'd been thrown free. Kyle, buckled in his seat as always—*safety first!*—had reached through the shattered window for me. For a period of perhaps five seconds... with the ground shifting out from under me and shifting out from under the car, with the sparse trees that had temporarily held the car in place popping free of the ground, with Kyle's cry of "Dad!" and that outstretched hand... the world had simply stopped. I saw him release the seatbelt. I felt the snap of roots beneath my feet. I saw his hand… there… so close. And I felt the world fall away.

There was time then, in that last fraction of a second, to grab Kyle's hand, or to turn and grab for the shattered railing at the top of the cliff.

"I wanted to save you," I told Nanda, who wasn't Nanda at all, but just another fragment of the lie that Bahktur kept selling himself.

Sri Mani approached, reloading the musket, the great cloud of bees at his back, their song so anciently familiar, a sound that had heralded man's first decent from the trees.

I hadn't even been drinking, though Connie never believed me.

The truth was that Baxter Lewis had chosen life over death. He could have taken Kyle's hand. He could have gone over the edge with him. There wasn't time to pull him free—at least that's the truth that I've chosen to go with. There was only time to take his hand and follow him down.

Not a day's gone by that I don't regret my decision.

Sri Mani pulled the packing rod from the barrel and fumbled at the pouch on his belt for a percussion cap. I pushed Nanda's corpse aside and got to my feet.

"Is this what you want?" I asked, holding up the skull.

It was Kyle's skull. I'd killed him. No matter how carefully I reconstructed him in the dirt beside my mattress, no matter how hard I tried to make myself believe that he was there sleeping beside me… he was gone. Nothing could bring him back.

"Is this what you want?" I screamed at Sri Mani.

Behind him, the great mass of bees seemed to pause. Their song changed. Though it remained as indecipherable as always, it seemed that a different chord had been taken up. Sri Mani heard it, too. Musket raised and sighted, he hesitated, looking back over his shoulder at the bees.

"They know," I said. "You killed your son to escape them. And now they know, Sri Mani."

He dropped the gun and tried to run, but the bees were far faster than he. They harried him through the woods, covering his body like a black mantle of death, at one point actually lifting him from his feet. Their stingers broke his weathered old skin, plunging their venom into his veins. They scrabbled at his eyes and filled his mouth, wriggled their buzzing bodies into his ears where their song must have been deafening indeed. His screams went on for a very long time, bouncing back and forth between the Himalayas and the trees. It would only be later that I'd discover how he ended his own pain by throwing himself from the cliffs.

And me?

I'm still here in Bahadur. I will stay here for the rest of my life, of that I am certain. The bees will never let me leave. The villagers have never truly believed the odd series of accidents that killed both Nanda and Sri Mani on that hunt. But they really don't want to know the truth, now do they? Besides, using Sri Mani's musket, the musket that his father passed to him and his grandfather had used before that, I continue to provide for them. And I bring them the honey that breaks up the monotony of their simple lives.

I've taken a wife from the Gurung. She is pregnant with our first child. I am hoping for a son.

But he will be my second son, for my first still sleeps in the dirt beside my straw mattress. Carefully arranged, every fragment of truth in place, his head pillowed across one arm and his legs tucked up like a sleeping baby, he waits for me to join him when all my truths have finally caught up to me.

His half-Gurung brother, of course, will be a honey hunter when I am gone. I have promised them that. The bees sing their song, Pholo smiles on me, and I seek out what hives remain, never stopping to consider what the bees ultimately have in mind. The symbiosis allows me my illusions... my semblance of the truth.

OUT THE BACK DOOR

Long after his heroes were ghosts, the very old man decided to take his leave. Because his jailers were watching the front, he decided to risk the tangled weeds and crumbling concrete in the back. Better a broken ankle or cracked skull than the tearful embraces and pleas that would hold him back. He had made up his mind. Screwed on his most courageous face. Put the minute affairs of what had once been his life in order. And made his decision.

He was determined that he would not be swayed. Not this time.

The house, his prison, reflected all that was left of his life. The barren rooms and peeling walls. The musty drapes and cobwebbed corners. The threadbare carpet, empty picture frames, and sagging kitchen cabinets. The echoes. The shadows. The emptiness.

He would not be swayed. Not this time.

They'd stopped him before. Love, in her gossamer gown and opal shoes. Youth, with his wild hair and ragged jeans. The twins, Passion and Lust, with their touch and their kisses and their sweet-scented breath. Friendship, Courage, and Joy. Glory and Promise and Hope. They were Memories—the good ones, at least, those which he hadn't long since locked away in the room upstairs. They were *his* memories. And they were his jailers.

The door opened easily enough, creaking on its rust-crusted hinges. He winced at the sound, glancing back toward the front room where the Memories held congress.

"Remember when..." they would say in turn, those two words the preface for every recollection; more, for their very existence. The ballfield where he and his friends played as children. That one glorious touchdown in high school. The first time he laid eyes on Betty. The births of his children. The birthdays, holidays, sunsets, and wines. All the memorable moments comprising the sum total of who and what he'd been.

Except the bad Memories. Those he'd trapped in the room upstairs, forgotten now, quiet. Too quiet, for at times he found he missed even them. Pain and Suffering. Sorrow and Grief. Loss and Boredom, Melancholy, Despair, and even Hate. These Memories, too, were a part of his life.

The outside of the house was no better than the inside. The paint was peeling away from the weathered siding. The weeds choked at the crumbling foundation, cutting away at the very roots of his life so that those early Memories, many now lost, were the dimmest and most feeble.

He stepped across the threshold to the small concrete step, a springboard from here to there—wherever *there* might be. The door closed easily enough behind him, but the snap of the latch seemed incredibly loud. He imagined the conversation in the front room coming to an abrupt end as they realized he had snuck away. He imagined their frantic flight through the kitchen to the back door. He knew he didn't have long, but the figure on the back lawn had frozen him in place.

Death.

He wore the appropriate black, but there was no scythe and his face was soft and kind. The frame concealed by his robes was thin, but by no stretch of the imagination skeletal. His feet were firmly planted in the weeds. His eyes were a quiet turquoise.

Death extended a hand and bade the old man come with him.

There arose a racket from the kitchen window. The old man turned to find them all crowded there: Love and Youth; Glory, Passion, Lust, and Joy; Camaraderie and Friendship; Courage and Vitality and Desire. They pounded on the window glass and begged him to come back into the house. Their tears broke his heart.

"Take my hand," said Death.

"I cannot leave them," cried the old man. "Without me, they

will perish. It is I that keeps them alive, even as they keep me from you."

"You're wrong," Death replied. "Their fears have made you blind to the truth. Take my hand, and they will follow. Where you're going there'll be those with whom you'll want to share these old friends."

There was something in Death's voice which denied all doubt. And what, wondered the old man, is more honest, more true, more *real* than Death? Only life. And that was fast crumbling behind him.

He stepped carefully down into the weeds and reached for Death's hand, but at the last second drew back. "Wait."

"What is it?"

"In a locked room upstairs..."

Patiently, Death smiled. "I've already set them free."

The old man nodded. That was as it should be. With only a slight trepidation, he took the offered hand.

BRIAN HOPKINS AND "THE GREAT & TERRIBLE GOOD"

BY JOHN PUERTO WISKE

My dear Boy,

To be great and good, is a worthy ambition for any boy or man under the sun. But not all of us are born to be great: and while I gladly wish you greatness and goodness both, I would have you remember that any one may be good, and however desirable greatness may be 'goodness is better!'

Ever your friend and Pastor
Henry C. Potter
Troy, N.Y. January 1st, 1863[1]

As to the question of "greatness," I leave that to each reader to decide. This is not the first time I've spent time thinking about Brian Hopkins's ample qualities as a writer, and my opinion on that point is easily available to anyone who cares to engage the powers of his or her favorite search engine. But what of "goodness?" And in Brian Hopkins's hands, is it *really* better?

Trying to deconstruct the magic of authorship (especially when one is not an author himself) can feel a little gauche and counterproductive, like explaining someone else's joke and quantifying how hard the audience should laugh at the punchline. It's in especially poor taste if the audience hasn't

---

1 An inscription to C. M. Wiske by Henry C. Potter, who would become the 7th bishop of the Episcopal Diocese of New York (in office 1887-1908). The wonky punctuation is original to the inscription. I guess the rules were different then…?

heard the joke themselves. Or, perhaps in language that is better suited to this collection, it's like eviscerating the goose to see how it makes its golden eggs. In any event, if you're one of those readers that consumes all the ancillary material first (*mea culpa*), please, stop. Start at the title page and work your way forward. If you still have the energy when you get back to this page, we can pick up where we left off.2 Also, to the degree that I may subsequently veer into the territory of anserine vivisection, I offer a preemptive apology.

The stories here (and throughout Hopkins's catalog) are about broken creatures. This is not a fresh observation; Yvonne Navarro beat me to it 20 years ago in her original introduction to this collection. On its face, it's not even especially unique in the world of dark fiction. I suspect "damage" is the central theme for all existentialist fiction, all the way back to Horace McCoy's *They Shoot Horses, Don't They?* (even if it predates the "existentialist" label). But "damaged" isn't quite the same as "broken."

"Broken" here specifically gives lie to the myth of the composed individual. This brokenness is not an emergent property of living, but rather a fundamental condition of life. In Hopkins's world, we are an ever-shifting jumble of urn shards, many of which don't seem to be part of a single, coherent whole. These parts of us are contradictory, manifesting schizophrenically and simultaneously, like Robert Mitchum's two warring hands that LOVE and HATE, and "are the soul of mortal man."3 Indeed, we should recall that Mitchum's switchblade hand—his killing hand—is actually the one that says LOVE. I have to wonder what may have been invisibly tattooed on the hand that pulls the trigger in Hopkins's "Shrovetide." Which brings us to the most salient fact about those broken pieces: all of those shards—even the pretty ones—have jagged and dangerous edges.

It's this implicit emotional paradox that creates the

2 Suggesting you might need to recharge at the end of this collection isn't a case of my being cute. Brian Hopkins's stories are *exhausting*.

3 Davis Grubb, *The Night of the Hunter* (1953).

conditions for goodness. I don't mean this in the simple "where-there-is-dark-there-must-be-light" sense, although my point is certainly derived from it. Self-awareness is only possible in view of competing impulses; single-mindedness precludes context. And "The Woodshed" gives us a glimpse of the transformative power of context. (Thank God it's only a glimpse.) As the story winds down, its narrator very obviously has a complex view of his father… and of the woodshed that houses the embodiments of personal failure. They are a source of confusion, revulsion, disappointment, and fear. And yet he also unwaveringly acknowledges the woodshed's necessity. An immoral man, the narrator rightly notes, doesn't own a woodshed. But his view of his own self is entirely uncomplicated. Armed with gas can and matches, he blithely casts himself as an avenging angel, charging into the woodshed, ready to wreak righteous havoc. It is at this instant that two things are revealed. First, despite his noble conviction that morality can't exist without a woodshed… we (and he) realize that, until this moment, he has been without one himself. Second, he is confronted with that existential truth, evidently and unceremoniously crucified like so many manifestations of Spartacus: he is Legion. Only in seeing our many selves do we know our singular self… as far as such a thing exists.

There is a corollary observation here: goodness isn't about doing the right thing; it's as simple as knowing there's a wrong thing. I already hear the objections from the bleachers about the low bar I'm setting, but please bear with me. Returning to the protagonist of "Shrovetide," is there any doubt that he was operating on autopilot when he pulled that trigger? Any doubt that he was immediately, soul-destroyingly horrified by what he had done? Of course not. He didn't *choose* to do something awful, he just *did* it. Inevitably. Redemption—temporary though it may be—does not conform to the gravity of the wrongdoing. No, his momentary respite is the small reward for *feeling* the profound awfulness of his failings.

The other problem here is that virtue competes with itself. There's never just one good path, and many of those nominally good paths are mutually exclusive, consistent with our fragmented character. Let's consider "All Colors Bleed to Red." Mankind poisons the world and is poisoned in return. There's a kind of peaceful (albeit unhappy) justice to it. It is a natural correction. It is good. In Hopkins's deft hands—the way he weaves technical and emotional verisimilitude—this "you-reap-what-you-sow" narrative is more than its eco-horror trappings would normally suggest. Specifically, Hopkins delivers a protagonist that is a hero/harbinger. Not an "or" dichotomy, but rather an "and" unity. With this neat little paradox, the story could end there, and it'd be fine. More than fine. But the magic is in showing us a *competing* good. Because at the last minute, another shard emerges in the mind of our hero/harbinger: he is a part of nature, but he is also a part of mankind. It's not the path he chooses which makes him virtuous, but rather recognizing the virtue in both. That is why desperate though his final moments may be, whether he saves humanity or dooms it, he'll be the hero—he'll be the *good* guy. And goodness is a privilege paid for in blood.

The price of goodness is amply demonstrated by Hopkins's series of Watchers/Timekeepers stories. For both watchers, they are condemned by their affinity to mankind to witness its relentless self-destruction. Their only solace is that they can commiserate with us, here. For what is the reward of Cecrop's final act of mercy? To be banished, *and still to witness.* It is a Promethean punishment that is probably familiar to the lammergeier that haunts "And Though a Million Stars Were Shining."[4] So, Dubbiel demurs from defying the Timekeepers, but how long do we think that will last? Because empathy—the heart of goodness—is a door impossible to close once opened.[5] Compassion always hurts, and we will be punished for daring to indulge that rarest of human qualities worth celebrating. But,

4 This recalls for me the sublime ending of John Carpenter's *The Thing* (1982), which tells us that, sometimes, winning means losing everything you have left.

5 Incidentally, this is a concept that is developed further in Hopkins's collection *Phoenix* (2013), where I see hauntedness as the ultimate, supernatural expression of empathy.

as the heroine of "Five Days in April" tries to remind Dubbiel, it's better than the alternative.

Which isn't to say it's an easy choice. For every balm that a little broken piece of goodness offers, it cuts you in a half-dozen new ways. "The Scissor Man" is one of my absolute favorite stories in any of Hopkins's collections.6 It is merciless without being unusually cruel. The story offers moments of light in the darkness, but doesn't shy away from reminding us that light also reveals hidden ugliness. The story ends with the protagonist deceived, anticipating the day he meets Death again. There is undoubtedly an element of despair here—a (not unreasonable) sense that his life's lost all meaning and death would be a release. Fine. We recognize this trope. But there are also elements of hope—remember: it's "all we have," according to the heroine of "Five Days in April." Here, we have the protagonist's predictable wish to be reunited with his wife. But I also detect a hopeful defiance, a desire to face Death again and not be fooled twice. And this is where I think Hopkins really twists the knife. Because for the obvious horror that despair represents, this dual reading of hope demonstrates that there is also horror *in* hope. The protagonist's wishes are both low-probability outcomes here. But, if forced to choose between his two hopes, do we *really* think the protagonist would choose its most wholesome incarnation? Would he choose to be reunited... or revenged? And so, we find that even such a vaunted quality as hope has been tattooed with LOVE and HATE.

Does "And Though a Million Stars Were Shining" show us that goodness itself breaks us into ever more jagged pieces? Is "The Endless Masquerade" a tragic exploration of the corrupting power of good? Does the ember of good at the heart of guilt—and at the heart of "The Trouble with the Truth"—create a fire that will consume the guilty and the innocent alike? And how much more draining than rejuvenating is the healing touch in "The Grotto of Massabielle?" But no more... I promised some restraint in dissecting this exquisite collection. I'll leave it to the

6 Don't ask me what the others are because the list may prove long enough to sap some of the impact of "absolute favorites."

reader to take up the scalpel, if it so compels.

Death lies. Thanks to the Scissor Man, this much *we* now know by heart. Fortunately for us—or unfortunately, depending on how dark the night—Hopkins only tells the truth: goodness comes at a fathomless cost. As much as we might wish otherwise, as with any aspect of our human experience, it takes more than it gives. Goodness isn't good. But, again, what is the alternative? Terrible as it must be, then, goodness *is* better. And Brian Hopkins's stories have it in abundance.

John Puerto Wiske
Brooklyn, NY
July 2021

A WRITER, A READER, A FRIEND AND THE PASSING OF TIME

BY MARK LANCASTER

I first encountered the writing of Brian A. Hopkins (known to his friends as "bah") in 1999, when his story "Five Days in April" was published in an online magazine called *ChiZine*. The story would go on to win a Bram Stoker Award for Best Long Fiction, the first of four such awards he has won. It's based on the 1995 bombing of the Alfred P. Murrah Federal Building in Oklahoma City. I found myself deeply moved by his sensitive examination of the depths of pain that such awful tragedies produce. I struck up an email correspondence with him to tell him how the story affected me, and as time went by came to consider him a dear friend, as well as favorite author. Now, over two decades later, we're still close and follow each other on Facebook, where he entertains friends and fans with some of the most lively and entertaining content you're likely to find anywhere on social media.

Bah has written some of the most emotionally searing stories ever to have been burned into my psyche. There's the aforementioned Stoker winner, of course. Then there's a story of family dynamics set in the future called "Parental Consent," which even after 20 years, when I started describing it to my wife the other day, I found myself getting choked up at the memory of the places the story took me. Or there's a lesson bah taught me about grief, in "Black Rider," that the pain felt from losing a loved one to the Grim Reaper is part of having loved that person. As he wrote, "To have [the pain] taken away... it would be like [you] never loved at all... Loss is life, as irrevocable as it is unavoidable... we must face [our losses] and learn from them if we are to flourish as loving human beings."

There is no length of fiction at which one might say bah is at his best – he is equally brilliant whether writing a six-page short story, a hundred-page novella, or a couple-hundred-page novel.

His novel, *The Licking Valley Coon Hunters Club,* is a private eye thriller like no other, a grand entertainment, with suspense and violence, characters fully fleshed out who you come to really care for, and thought-provoking prose, giving one pause at times to just sit and think. You don't find that in most P.I. stories.

No author can get my tear ducts working so well as bah. A good example is his novella, *El Dia de los Muertos,* which explores loss, grief, and terror in ways that are uniquely his, the raw and real sense of the fragile humanity of a grieving father and the supernatural path he takes to try to right the wrongness of his loss. I find that I strain to express how the grim beauty of bah's words moves me on an aesthetic level, even while they draw me into a pit of unthinkable horror.

Another novella, *La Belle Epoque,* may well be the most accomplished piece of writing he's yet published. Mainly set in the titular time period, painstakingly researched as usual so that one knows one is happily digesting history lessons and technical knowledge of various sorts while reading an absorbing story told with such aplomb, such mastery of plot, setting, action, and character, that the temptation to set the book aside to look things up on Wikipedia and learn even more is tempered by the need to keep turning the pages of this fascinating and emotionally involving tale.

I mention above that bah excels at six-page stories as well as longer forms. The story I had in mind is "Eleven Minutes in September." I'm hard pressed to say what my favorite bah-story is, but this one is what I'd call his most transcendent, the one that gives me a rocket powered feeling of life bursting into something that might come after life. Based, for the discerning reader, upon what it might have been like to be a passenger on one of the planes that took down the World Trade Center on 9/11/2001, it takes what could have been a nightmare of fear and panic, and instead presents a transportive experience of the disintegration of the material self and moving on to a higher ethereal plane. It's absolutely one of the most thrilling and exhilarating pieces of fiction I've ever read.

Would you like to go on an endless emotional and intellectual journey? Read Brian A. Hopkins, follow him on Facebook, and you just might make a new friend!

Mark Lancaster
Baltimore MD
July, 2021

ABOUT THE AUTHOR

Brian A. Hopkins is the author of more than a hundred stories most often pigeon-holed into the horror genre. His response to such classification is boisterous raspberries. You'll find no cheesy vampires or zombies here. He's won four Bram Stoker Awards and been a finalist for the Nebula, the Ted Sturgeon Award, and the International Horror Guild Award. He lives in the woods just east of Oklahoma City with a pack of wild dogs, ravenous chickens, and one saint of a woman. Recently retired from a career in software engineering, he should have more time for writing, but grandkids keep him pretty busy. You can find him on Facebook (https://www.facebook.com/bahopkins3/), where he tends to be fairly entertaining.

BIBLIOGRAPHY

Something Haunts Us All (1995)
Cold at Heart (1997)
Flesh Wounds (1999)
The Licking Valley Coon Hunters Club (2000)
Wrinkles at Twilight (2000)
These I Know By Heart (2001)
Salt Water Tears (2001)
El Dia De Los Muertos (2002)
Lipstick, Lies, and Lady Luck (2004)
Phoenix (2013)
Roads End & Other Fantasies (2021)

ABOUT THE ARTIST

Nuha Notion is a digital artist from Bangladesh. An architect by degree and a self-taught artist, she began creating in earnest during 2020's quarantine. One of the works produced in that period is "Scarecrow," which graces the cover of this book. Nuha is inspired by elements of nature, like sunsets, the moon, and sky, infused with human emotions and thoughts she expresses through her art, using strong colors and silhouettes. You can learn more about her by visiting:

https://linktr.ee/Nuhanotion

CROSSROAD
PRESS

Lightning Source UK Ltd.
Milton Keynes UK
UKHW010633100822
407113UK00001B/397